Love & OTHER Tropes

KAYLA MCGRATH

CONTENT WARNINGS

This book includes content that may be disturbing to some readers, discretion is advised. Content includes sexually explicit scenes, mention of residential schools, generational trauma, and parental neglect, disordered eating, allusions to eating disorders, body dysmorphia, and off page verbal abuse from a parent—body shaming.

For all those who adore a green flag, dog dad.

116

CHAPTER ONE
Illiana

Illiana was willowy grace and lithe muscles. Her face was serene and her blonde hair was pulled back tight in a bun, not a wisp out of place. She was careful with her plié—softly swooping her arms in the sun-dappled studio. The red brick, gleaming cherry floor, and walls upon walls of mirrors was the epitome of stereotype. It was in one of these many mirrors that Illiana watched her once flawless form buckle beneath her weight, her surgically repaired foot crippling her poise—and soul.

She caught herself on the bar at her side before she could crash to the wooden planks. And although physically she remained upright, emotionally she was in a million shattered pieces on that floor.

The pain was real, but it wasn't new. Two metal plates, six titanium screws, an ugly scar and you had a triple fusion. It was the name of the surgery that saved her foot and ended her career.

"You held on much longer this time, Ana," Mina, her physiotherapist and best friend, reassured her gently. "Maybe next week we can try out the pointe shoes."

Illiana ducked her head, staring down at her slipper clad feet, the edge of a glaring white scar creeping out from the right one. She knew it was futile to even try—the bones of her foot were *fused* for fuck's sake—but she didn't know how to be anything other than what she was told she would be—great. It didn't matter that the arch of her foot couldn't curve like it used to. It didn't matter that she'd lost a large percentage of mobility in her ankle. It didn't matter that standing on her toes was like shoving iron pokers in her bones. All that mattered was that she defied the doctors and their odds and returned to her world.

"You're being generous," Illiana admonished, unwrapping her ribbons and yanking off her yellowing slippers. These had lasted her the longest in her life—four months—and they showed little sign of requiring replacement. "I can't plié for shit and you know it. Besides, I'm still missing muscle-tone in this leg. I'm sure once it's up to par again things will be different." It's what she had to say, even if it wasn't the truth.

Mina crossed the room and Illiana watched her reflection approach, her spandex-clad legs flexing as she sat next to her, crossing her umber arms over her knees. The sunlight caught gold specks in Mina's hazel eyes and slanted across her face, casting her high cheekbones and full lips in an unfairly glowing light. She looked like a goddess, meanwhile, Illiana looked like a failure.

"It's been a year, hon," Mina whispered, the solemn words echoing vacantly in the empty studio.

Illiana tightened her jaw, staring hard at the spacers between her toes and the cotton covering them.

"I know, how could I forget?" Hot tears burned in her eyes, and Illiana refused to let them fall. "Why do you think I've been pushing myself so hard these last few weeks? I need to see progress, I can't stay—" she swallowed past the lump in her throat. "I just need to keep at it. Mind over matter, you know?"

"I know," Mina answered softly. "It's just…I don't mean to push, but maybe it'll be a good idea to get out of the city. Before, you know, the anniversary. Without the constant reminders."

"What do you mean? Like I should go on a weekend getaway? A spa trip? Camping? None of those seem particularly appealing considering I have no one to go with. And I'm not discounting you, I just know you're going to the west coast this summer."

"Well, see that's exactly what I was thinking. What if you joined me? You haven't been to BC since Christmastime our first year of college and instead of doing your sessions remotely, I can continue doing them in person. It's beautiful and maybe it can help you find some peace, or clarity, or solace, or whatever the hell you want to call it."

Illiana's mouth popped open. A summer vacation. With her best friend. In their twenties. Nothing could have prepared her for the serotonin and dopamine rush she was experiencing at the prospect. She thought that opportunity had passed her by in the final summer of high school, the definitive line that demarcated adolescence and adulthood. The wonder of a summer, unhindered by work, and a relationship that had turned to complacency. Was it possible Illiana could do this and get out of the ditch her life had turned into?

"But where would I stay?" Illiana had savings and a comfortable sum in her bank account, but her finances were being sparingly fed by Disability Insurance every two weeks but it was a laughable amount. She couldn't afford to fund a hotel room for the entire summer. Maybe if her settlement came in, but she wasn't holding her breath on that one.

"With me, of course! The pool house has plenty of room and my aunt has been harassing me for months to bring someone home with me. I'm sure she meant a new boyfriend and not my best friend, but you know she loves you."

Illiana hesitated, removing all her shoe prep and slipping on fresh cotton socks. "I really don't want to impose. Maybe I should just stay here and practice."

Mina grasped Illiana's hand, squeezing. "Please? I want you to come with me." A devilish smile spread across Mina's face. "If not for you, then for me! This way Aunt Lacey can harp on you for being single, too. I can't handle her reminiscing about Marcus anymore, it was five years ago and she had no idea how bad in bed he was. Please, Ana, I need you."

Mina wasn't single but things with David were so new they were hardly out of infancy. Much too soon to bring home, especially across the country.

"I bet that's something Marcus never heard."

Mina snorted with laughter but doubled down. "Come on, it'll be fun! And maybe you can forget about that douchebag, and find someone new." Mina gasped. "Ana, imagine having a whirlwind summer romance!" Mina fell to the floor in a dramatic swoon. "I'm picturing you being swept off your feet by some country boy. No, definitely a brooding hipster in an eclectic coffee shop. Ooh, actually—"

"Okay, okay, I get the picture." And she did. She hadn't wanted to imagine it, but what if she did? What if she saw herself sparking up a summer fling? Starry nights around the campfire, beaches with golden sand, barbecues on a sprawling green lawn, all of it accompanied by a handsome, nameless someone that gave her butterflies and made her heart race. Just like in the movies. Could she do it? Was she ready? It had been almost a year since Adrian left her.

"So, will you come with me?" Mina prodded eagerly.

Illiana inhaled slowly and then exhaled. "Yeah, I'll come."

Mina squealed with delight and threw her arms around Illiana's shoulders, rocking her nearly to the floor.

"We leave Friday," Mina announced. "I can't wait! This will be the best trip ever."

The pavement was baking beneath the hot Toronto sun. Despite the fact that the heatwave was only just beginning, people were already cranky in the evening light—wiping sweaty brows and fanning shirts. Illiana herself was uncomfortable in the heat as well, but she was good at hiding her discomfort after most of her life was spent on a stage. Ballet was where beauty demanded pain and serenity was granted on blistered toes. Her black bodysuit was tucked into a pair of grey sweat-shorts while white tennis shoes replaced the slippers that now resided in her dusty rose gym bag.

Her apartment was only six blocks from the studio her and Mina practiced at so she walked there three days a week, rain or shine—and in Canada that weather could depend on the hour. Popping in her AirPods to drown out the drone of traffic, buskers, and people yelling into their phones, Illiana began the trek home.

She limped ever so slightly while shards of pain radiated through her foot and up her leg. She'd really overworked herself today. Maybe she should have listened to Mina when she suggested water aerobics that afternoon, but Illiana was determined.

Mina called it stubborn.

Skyscrapers towered above her while the male singer crooned in her ears about being good to you. The landmark of the city, the CN tower, was crowned by wispy clouds far on the horizon. Illiana took a swig of water from her white insulated water bottle as she waited for the streetlight to change. It was moments like this, in the hustle and bustle of the city that she could pretend like she belonged. That she was just like the business man behind her, or the Cottage Core girl to her right. When she was among the people of the world's most diverse city, she didn't feel like her parents had disowned her or her boyfriend had dumped her for her understudy.

The light changed and WALK appeared above her head. With the suited man and the girl in a mushroom patterned dress with her, she smiled mildly to the music's vocals and crossed. She ignored the coffee shop the girl slipped into, suffocating the craving for a chocolate croissant, and she gritted her teeth when the man entered the hole in the wall Italian restaurant, her stomach rumbling for seafood fettuccine. She'd already gained six pounds since this time last year; she couldn't afford any more. The music switched over to Harry Styles and she quickened her pace with thoughts of roasted vegetables and lemon salmon to distract her.

As her building came into view, a brick and glass façade, the first beads of uncomfortable sweat were slipping down her spine. When she input her code, she was greeted with a rush of AC upon entry. The walls were cream and the floors an inoffensive shade of gray, the faux wood doing nothing for the arbitrary canvases of landscapes shot in black and white. She debated the stairs but the splints in her foot begged for the elevator. So, she rode the six floors up to her apartment quashing the regret.

The door pinged and she fished her keys out, a second Harry Styles song cresting the first chorus as she unlocked her door. As she removed her earbuds and was welcomed to an empty home, the magic of the city drained away.

When Adrian had left her a year ago, he hadn't just broken up with her, he had *abandoned* her. She was in the hospital being told that her dream of becoming a prima ballerina was as crushed as her foot. Upon hearing her career was over, Adrian promptly left, skating out with the poise only a ballerino could summon. Illiana thought he just needed time to digest the news, not an excuse to replace her with her own understudy. Within hours Adrian had packed his things from their shared apartment and moved in with Violet, taking the cat with him.

To add insult to injury, her parents—a set of two who hated each other and should never had been married in the first place—were devastated to hear about the accident. Not because their only daughter had gotten hurt and had to undergo surgery, but because their prized star that they had sunk thousands into was a now damaged thing and they weren't getting their money's worth. No celebrity and no accolades. Just burdened with a depressed child they had no interest in supporting beyond a guilt that lent them to pay the exorbitant rent on her one bedroom apartment in the heart of downtown Toronto.

So, in one fell swoop she was single, unofficially orphaned, and utterly alone. Mina became her emergency contact after dozens of phone calls from the hospital staff to Adrian and her parents went unanswered. The only response she got from Adrian was a voicemail ending their relationship and a text from her mother offering kind, hollow words and the promise to pay for whatever therapy she needed and that was all.

Illiana sighed as she dropped her bag and keys by the island counter and made her sad dinner of leftover fish and vegetables. After she finished the necessary meal satisfying the hunger and none of the craving, she headed for the bathroom for a cool shower. She placed her phone on the sink, prepared to hit her shower playlist but picked it up again.

I'm a glutton for punishment, aren't I? She thought as she stared at her lock screen, a non-descript floral thing she used to replace what was a photo of her and Adrian. Summoning her courage, she entered in her passcode and then texted her mom.

Hey mom I just wanted to let you know I'm heading to BC on Friday with Mina for the summer. I'll be back some time in September, I just wanted to let you know in case you decided to visit and I wasn't home.

She paused before adding more, glancing in the mirror at her tired blue eyes and the purple rings below them.

I've been practicing a lot and I think I'm making progress.

Illiana exhaled sharply, not knowing what else to type. She ended the message with an XO and sent it, then turned on her playlist and set down the phone.

In the shower Illiana washed away the days fatigue and wear, refreshing herself with new purpose and optimism. After, dressed in a set of blue bamboo pajamas she checked her phone. No message. She brushed her teeth. No message. She French braided her hair in two. No message. She sighed and climbed into bed, putting on Bridgerton for the third rewatch and envied the smoldering glances Anthony kept passing Kate.

No message.

CHAPTER TWO
Emmett

Located in Rose Point was a bar where Emmett and his buddies met at least once a week. Sometimes it was Tuesdays, sometimes it was Fridays. This was a Tuesday. It was dated and kitschy, stuck solidly in the 80s with wood paneling, sticky linoleum floors, and vinyl records hung from multi-colored Christmas lights. On the scratched and dented walls were old movie posters—a couple of which were signed by the actors—and none of the seating matched.

A beautiful redhead perched on a golden oak stool, and Emmett lounged in a red pleather booth with Graham, Nate, Kieran, Chase, and Jace, friends he'd made when he'd briefly enrolled in UVIC—University of Victoria—before transferring to BCIT—British Columbia Institute of Technology. For some reason, they stubbornly maintained a friendship nearly ten years later. Save for Jace, who was Chase's younger brother and attended only when he could manage an invite to the other's chagrin.

The redhead on the stool watched Emmett as he slowly took a swig of his cold beer, her eyes heavy lidded and liquid with attraction. She was in a short white dress that showed curves and a tattoo of a fox tracing her thigh. Emmett offered her a slight curl of his lips and returned his attention to his buddies.

"How is it that you're pulling in bitches and you haven't even said a word, while we beg after your scraps?" Jace complained. "Save some ass for the rest of us. Not everyone wants your sloppy seconds."

Emmett prickled at the whining and derision, but leaned back and leveled a look at the blond man before him. "Well, to start off with, I don't call women 'bitches', especially ones I might be interested in. And second, you make it sound like a woman having sex equates a lack of value—damaged, if you will—meanwhile…" he pointed with his beer, "you seem to think you're better for pursuing the same thing and somehow, you're not ruined by that very encounter? Maybe if you respected them, they might consider you." Emmett's eyes flickered to the redhead and a tall brunette nearby. "Women aren't dumb and they can see through your bullshit before you even know it's shit." His tangent, he was aware, was slightly exaggerated, but he wanted Jace to feel like the insufferable misogynist he was.

Jace, was like a bad caricature in a movie purely there as a plot device to either make the main character look better or to be some obstacle in the story. Emmett couldn't stand him.

Jace scoffed. "Cool it on the feminist act, man. You're making me look bad over here."

"It's not an act and you're doing that all yourself."

Jace muttered under his breath, something that sounded suspiciously like *fuck you* and swept from the booth, over to the brunette that had begun to eye Emmett. The brunette seemed less than thrilled at the blond man's approach. He rolled his eyes at

Jace's blatant disregard and self-righteousness. His self-awareness left much to be desired, as well.

"Man, I know he's your brother but he's a fucking prick," Nate told Chase in frustration. He wasn't wrong, it was a wonder how the two even shared genetics as they were so vastly different in nearly every way.

"Tell me about it," Chase huffed as he sipped his whiskey on the rocks. "I've been trying to educate him about toxic masculinity, and I swear it goes in one ear and out the other. Apparently accepting advice on how men should behave from his gay brother is pushing it too far. Notwithstanding the fact that I'm a goddamn psychologist."

"You can't choose family," Nate sighed.

"No, you cannot." Chase stopped, surveying Nate over the rims of his wire framed glasses, his blue eyes full of intelligence. "Speaking of family. Isn't your cousin coming to visit soon?"

"Yeah," Nate confirmed. "Mina will be here Friday night and she's bringing Illiana."

Emmett straightened. He'd heard stories of Illiana. She was an allegedly stunning dancer who'd charmed the entire friend group the month after he'd left to BCIT, leaving Nate fawning after her until Mina yelled at him to stay the hell away from her best friend. Ten years later and apparently, he still held a torch for her. Emmett found himself wondering what it was about the girl who he'd missed like two ships passing in the night. He'd never met her but something about the idea of her had him shifting his weight.

"Are you going to pant after her like last time?" Graham teased, cackling as he tossed back his draft beer.

"Oh, piss off," Nate blustered. "I did not *pant* after her, I just thought she was pretty and sweet."

"Right, because those are definitely the words you used to describe—"

Emmett raised a dark brow as Nate elbowed Graham.

"Shut up and drink your damn beer."

"Is she with anyone?" Graham inquired as he followed instruction.

Graham was dark haired and blue eyed. The kind of guy that spelled out Tall, Dark, and Handsome like a neon sign. He was the kind of guy women were innately drawn to, but unfortunately, he struggled to commit; waiting for The One to appear.

Emmett humored Graham's belief in soulmates, but he'd lost faith in the idea many years ago. He loved the idea, he just didn't think it was feasible.

Nate quirked a brow at Graham. "What are you thinking? You going to put the moves on her?"

All of them were painfully single aside from Chase who was in a long-term, loving, and committed relationship and would continue to be so long as the Earth continued spinning. The only difference between most of his friends and Emmett was that *his* was by choice. His last relationship had ended almost six months ago, and it was a blow he wouldn't soon forget. How could he have been with someone so long and not realized how wrong they were for each other?

"Well, I'm not going to rule it out." It was a hollow tease from Graham, but Emmett wasn't sure Nate realized it.

"I see. And what about you?" Nate's voice turned accusatory, and Emmett realized it was directed at him. He turned and met Nate's gold-green eyes. "Are you interested in Illiana, too?"

"How would I know? I've never met her." Emmett side-eyed Kieran who'd been suspiciously quiet throughout the night, but he decided not to draw him into Nate's evidently possessive questioning.

Nate gave a start at this and with a non-verbal conferring with Graham and Chase, they seemed to realize that Emmett was right and Illiana was little more than a phantasm to him.

Emmett sighed and rubbed the dark stubble on his jaw. "Look, as much as I enjoy seeing you guys fight like schoolboys, talking about Illiana like this feels wrong."

No, wrong wasn't the right word. It felt *dirty*. It felt like they were objectifying her, making her a goal, something to be won like a trophy. "I don't want Jace thinking he's finally corrupted you guys."

Emmett enjoyed women as much as the next guy however, he knew they were more than the physical parts offered to him—parts which he very much enjoyed, as well—but he wasn't shy in making clear when he was only interested in something physical. And he was just as transparent when he was searching for more. Sex required clarity and a mutual understanding. So did entering into a relationship. Emmett always wanted that line clear.

Graham and Nate made muffled and shameful apologies and quickly changed topics. Emmett checked his phone and saw the late hour. He sighed before draining his beer, got up, rifled through his pockets for a twenty, and clapped his friends on the shoulders.

"I hate to have to do this, but I need to get home to the dogs and get up early, so I'm out of here. Have a good night, you guys." Tossing the twenty down, he started making his way out, nodding at the disappointed redhead and offering Jace an obligatory salute while he continued to bore the pretty brunette.

Exiting the bar into a wash of cool night air with the song of frogs and crickets in the distance, Emmett tied his dark, shoulder-length hair back and dug for his keys. As he approached his SUV, he checked the cameras on his house via his phone and discovered both his dogs sleeping soundly on the couch. He smiled and climbed in.

It was after ten when he pulled into the driveway of his house, located on a quiet street in Rose Point, a small town just outside the hub of Victoria. It was a semi-modern, four bed, two bath house, with a fenced yard. It was the symbolic equivalent to the perfect white-picket fence life, only his fence was stained cedar with horizontal black slats. The house too was done up in shades of cedar and white with just enough charcoal to break up the scheme. Not to mention, the house was devoid of the wife and children that would fulfill the white-picket prophecy.

He thought he was close to that life once before, but he'd been proven very wrong.

The curtains twitched as his dogs awoke and heard his approach. They nosed the drapes apart, and Emmett was greeted with the wrinkled face of his English Bulldog, Gimli, and the lolling tongue of his chocolate lab, Leia. In unison, the two dogs wiggled their bodies and wagged their tails—in Gimli's case, rear—faster as Emmett unlocked the door and was jubilantly greeted by nails on the hardwood and excited panting—and slobber.

He crouched down to his dogs, giving them kisses and pats. "Do you think you need a mama? Is dad enough for you guys?"

After taking the dogs out to do their business and making sure they didn't tear out the peonies in the backyard, Emmett ushered them inside where they had a last drink of water and a bite of food before they took off down the hall and up the stairs to the bedroom. Emmett went around locking all the doors and turning off the lights before activating his security system. He finally followed his dogs lead to climb into bed where both dogs were already sprawled in their respective spots—Gimli at the foot, and Leia with her head just below the pillows.

As Emmett stripped down to his boxers and got into bed, he smiled to himself but he couldn't quite place if it was contented or solemn. He didn't dare admit it to anyone, but he was beginning to feel very lonely, and that lack of contentment was a void that the love he had for his dogs couldn't quite fill.

CHAPTER THREE
Illiana

Illiana awoke in her bed, alone, Netflix title cards scrolling across the screen as her alarm blared. She flopped her hands at her sides on her white duvet and turned off her phone alarm. Device in hand, she checked her notifications.

One new message.

From her mother.

All traces of fatigue gone, she hurriedly opened the text, surprising herself with the excitement that burbled forward. Upon reading it she immediately deflated.

OK

Not even "okay" or "OK *heart emoji*", just those two plain letters that felt like a slap to the face. Her mother didn't even make it a secret that she didn't try. That she didn't give a single damn about what happened to her daughter now that her promise as principal dancer—or dancer in general—was over.

Meredith Hastings was a right piece of work.

Illiana fought back tears as she discarded her phone somewhere amongst the downy bedding, staring at her flat white ceiling, seeing nothing while her eyes burned. Gritting her teeth, she laid there until she could summon the courage to start her day, but that willpower was so far out of reach, miles beyond the ecru walls of her bedroom. She let her mind wander, to wonder why the accident had to happen to her, why it caused everything in her life to fall apart. She was so close to the top, months away from touching the very peak…and in the blink of an eye it was all yanked out from under her. As if she were a rock climber and her carabiner snapped, sending her into free fall.

Pulling herself into a sitting position, Illiana leaned over to her side table and grabbed the butter yellow notebook nestled inside. As she began writing a To-Do List, she was suddenly all too aware of the fact that her leaving for the summer mattered to only one person—her landlord. She had to let him know—simply for safety purposes like ensuring there were no leaks or electrical failures during her absence. Even then, she didn't need to worry about remembering to pay the rent she wasn't using because her mother deposited the $2,700 automatically the account, and that money was automatically transferred to her landlord on the first of every month.

Her pen hovered over her list, there were only seven points. God, how different it was now. A year ago she had been overwhelmed with her daily routine, the demand of every moment of her life. Now…

Call landlord.
Buy plane ticket—get info from Mina.
Do yoga and/or stretches.
Drink green tea.
Eat.
Get sugared.
Finish laundry.

Pack.

Illiana stared at the last word: pack. She was really going to go. To head across Canada with her best friend.

Finally, adequately awake and motivated, Illiana leaped from bed and began enacting her list.

It was 11:00 a.m. when her list was completed. It was 11:05 a.m. when she took a paperback romance novel to her small balcony. It was 5:00 p.m. when she finished it. At 5:05 p.m. she was making chicken stir-fry, putting on a playlist that was belting out Taylor Swift. It was 7:00 p.m. when her dishes were clean and she'd finished in the shower. It was 7:05 p.m. when she climbed into bed and put on the last two episodes of Bridgerton's second season. She was asleep by 9:00 p.m..

No one but Mina had contacted her the entire day. No ballet friends, no university friends, no parents, and certainly no ex-boyfriends.

The flight was in the morning, and Illiana boarded without a hitch. She had a window seat in a row to herself, and there was no child kicking the back of her seat. Due to Mina's intense fear of flying, Illiana's best friend was taking an Ambien-induced nap next to her. Illiana couldn't help but snap a photo, because even with her jaw slack, pink neck pillow on her shoulders, and a magenta sleep mask over her eyes, Mina was pretty—the girl didn't even snore. It was during this time Illiana took this opportunity to read yet another romance novel—a contemporary summer romance—hoping to set the tone of her trip.

When Illiana was healing in hospital and at home, her mobility was seriously impeded by her casted foot, and there was only so much TV a girl could handle. So, for the first time in her life, Illiana had been bed and couch-ridden and discovered her love of steamy romance. She'd begun with classic bodice rippers that displayed covers of men without their shirts, or windswept embraces bathed in wanton yearning, but slowly discovered the modern illustrated covers that hid their not-so-innocent content. It was these that she then began taking with her out to appointments and to coffee shops—no one was to know the cartoonesque cover beheld multiple spicy love scenes. Within the year she'd burned through the entire Bridgerton series—prequels, spin-offs and all—then graduated from there.

She read for the entire flight, only stopping for an Instagram break when she checked the time. Toronto to Vancouver was a 5 hour flight, and they touched down only 12 minutes after that mark. Taking a flight directly to the island would have been more than triple the price, so they elected for the longer travel and took the ferry. By mid-afternoon Illiana and Mina were taking a car to the ferry—after grabbing much needed coffee after Mina's Ambien had well-disappeared from her system—and after two and a half hours they'd left the mainland and had touched down on Vancouver Island. In their rented car taken from Victoria, Mina took no mercy on the roads, speeding appropriately— didn't everyone drive 10 or 15 over?—and had shaved off half the drive from Victoria to Rose Point.

They had talked, speaking of excitement, Mina giving her the rundown on recent happenings in the family—updates on her cousins, how Sasha was engaged, how Jade was pregnant with her second, and how Nate just bought a house. But it was when it got to why Mina brought her to the west coast, why Illiana was reading summer romance, that butterflies began rioting in her stomach.

"Do you remember when you came to the island with me all those years ago?" Mina had begun, turning the music volume down on the 80s rock station—a genre Mina loved despite not being born until the following decade.

"How could I forget? You got blackout drunk off Smirnoff Ice and ended up crying about shelter dogs before Nate's friend—Graham, was it? —had to put you to bed."

Mina huffed. "That's the one incident you had to remember?"

"Oh, no there are many more, like when you—"

"Okay, anyway!" Mina interrupted. "I was going to say that Nate and all his friends are still—well, I guess I should say, currently—single. So, in that same breath, I ask if you end up falling in love in love, running off, and marrying one of those boys to have lots of sex and babies with, please don't forget about me."

Illiana laughed—a very not cute, snorting sound. "Do you really think a man has the ability to make me completely uproot my life and dump you?"

Mina smiled sadly and Illiana's brows furrowed. "That's just it, hon." Her eyes flickered to Illiana. "Your life *has* been uprooted, but nothing has motivated you to leave. What if this is it?"

Illiana's heart broke. Not only from the fact that Mina was right, but at the fact that Mina knew coming out here could possibly cause her best friend to move across the country without her. The thought was ludicrous though, she'd never lived anywhere else. Toronto was home. Even so, she realized what a good friend she had with Mina—how selfless—that she was willing to subject herself to this hurt if it meant Illiana's happiness. Hot tears burned in her eyes and she had trouble swallowing past the lump in her throat.

She knew what it was like to be left behind.

"No matter what happens, you'll always be my best friend."

Mina also had tears in her eyes. "I love you, bitch."

"I love you, too."

By the time they'd returned to less heavy subject matter—mostly Mina talking about the beauty of the island; the lakes, the mountains, the waterfalls—they'd spent the entire day traveling, finally arriving at her extended family's lake house in the evening. It was a gorgeous two story house done up in shades of white and robin's egg blue, the front door was a slightly darker shade and the door knocker was a silver rabbit. It was a traditional home with modern elements—like the glass railings and large windows that let in the unobstructed view of the glittering lake. The lamp-post spotted drive was curved and bordered by azaleas and hydrangeas, bursts of fuchsia and periwinkle among the verdant green, while birch trees with their ash and char bark were scattered throughout garden beds.

Mina parked their rental behind a 1970s vintage Beetle and popped the trunk. Together, the two of them hauled their bags and suitcases up the drive, tugging them along the stairs before the door.

Before they even got a chance to use the knocker, the door was flung open and Mina's aunt stood there with arms outstretched. She was tall and statuesque, her frame very similar to Mina's in that the both also had wide hips that Illiana envied and small chests. They looked more like mother and daughter versus aunt and niece, due to the fact that Lacey and Mina's mother, Laura, were twins. And to the best of Illiana's knowledge, the twins remained as close as possible, even to this day.

"Mina! Illiana!" Lacey exclaimed, gathering both the girls in a hug without hesitation.

Lacey was one of the few people who'd always pronounced Illiana's name properly with the "on" sound, rather than the "an" sound. Illiana did respond to both, but she preferred the actual pronunciation.

"Girls, I'm so glad you could make it!"

Illiana's heart simultaneously warmed and cracked when Lacey's wisteria-scented hug wrapped around her. She couldn't remember the last time she'd been held and, *damn,* she missed it. She hadn't realized how touch-starved she was until that moment.

"Hi, Auntie," Mina said, her voice muffled.

"Hi, Lacey. Thanks for having me."

Lacey pulled back just far enough to see the girls, her hazel eyes that matched Mina's, roved her niece, and then skipped over to Illiana. Illiana smiled when Lacey's full lips began to turn up, making her dark skin utterly shine.

"Lord, you girls get more radiant every day." She paused to grin. "Now, let's get you inside. You must be hungry and exhausted. I'll get the menfolk to get your things." Over her shoulder, Lacey called for Nate and Walter.

Lacey and her husband Walter lived in the lake house year-round, but in the summer, family flocked to the grand home and stayed anywhere from three days to three months—anything less was considered rude. Illiana knew that Nate no longer lived there, but as evidenced by the young man running out in mismatched shoes, he was currently visiting.

Nate, wearing one Croc and one flip-flop, grabbed Mina's bag, fondly hip-bumping his cousin as they walked up the driveway. He startled when he caught sight of Illiana, those hazel eyes that most of Mina's family seemed to possess widening. He was a handsome man; brown skin courtesy of his mother's complexion, dark hair he kept buzzed short, and wide, high cheekbones that lent a nearly model-quality to him.

Illiana waved with just her fingers; she was too tired to try much more. Travel always drained her and that was all she'd done that day.

"Hi, Illiana. It's been too long," Nate said, warmth sweetening his deep voice. He, like so many others, mispronounced her name, but she didn't mind. "It's really good to see you."

"It has been so long. Can you believe it?" she returned.

"Ten years later and you're even more beautiful than I remember."

Illiana blushed prettily—she hoped—and was saved from answering more than "thanks", when Walter came out and removed Illiana's bags from the trunk of their rental. Before Nate could say anything further, Walt's deep rumble of a voice welcomed Illiana, and she followed him inside. He led them through the house, passing open French doors, onto the wooden deck, across the concrete pavers of the patio, and into the pool house which was actually as big as her apartment back home.

It was two rooms—a living space and a bathroom. An island divided the sage kitchen with hand-painted tiles from the couches arranged in a neat L. The aforementioned sofas were pastel pink with a navy blanket tossed over the back of each— one plain, the other patterned with seashells—and lemon-yellow throw pillows tucked into corners. Plants dotted the place in funky pots and children's artwork over the years were proudly framed on the walls. Illiana figured they received their place of fame and pride without having to be an 'eyesore' from the main house. At the furthest end of the pool house were two beds, separated by a dark blue side table, the frames of the beds plain white with curved headboards. Both beds were dressed in dandelion yellow with ecru crocheted pillows and hand knitted blankets.

In a word, it was perfect.

It was a colorful, yet tasteful space, taking in even more from the bowing bookshelf to the chalk painted desk and the yellow velvet armchair wedged into a corner.

"If you girls need anything, don't hesitate to ask," Walter started as he deposited the bags with Nate in tow. "We did a grocery shop earlier today so the fridge and cupboards are loaded, but please let us know if you need anything special. We won't be harassing you much today because I know you had a long day of travel. Get some sleep because in the morning all bets are off." Walt's grin was infectious, wide, white, and warm and despite Illiana's exhaustion, she grinned back.

The moment Walter and Nate exited the pool house, Illiana was on the brink of crashing. Packed in her bag, on top of everything was a bamboo pajama set, which she pulled out before stumbling to the bathroom. She managed to shower away the grime of travel, change, and then immediately fell face first onto her bed.

"You want any?" Mina asked as she held out a slice of pizza from a box that—presumably—her family had brought in.

Illiana's stomach rumbled. "No thanks, I'm not hungry."

"Ana, the last thing you ate was a sandwich on the ferry and that was hours ago."

It was true, but Illiana had already filled her bread and carb quota by that alone; therefore, she elected to opt out of another meal so she wouldn't feel guilt.

"I'm just too tired, I'm fine." She paused, still face down. "Honestly."

"You know I know you're lying."

"And you know I would be spending the next day regretting eating a single slice."

"Ana," Mina said firmly. Illiana raised her head and saw her best friend's concerned face. "Have you addressed this in therapy?"

Illiana held her gaze, jaw tight. "It's come up."

"And?"

"And nothing. I'm not ready to deal with it. It's one thing for the accident to take away my career and dreams. It's another to let it take the fantasy of the appearance away. It would kill me to look in the mirror and see myself not looking like a ballerina anymore, especially since I'll probably never perform again."

Tears burned in her eyes. "I'm not ready to let it go, yet. I know it's not healthy and I know it's a problem, but I can't. It's one of the last things I have control over."

"Ana…" Mina's eyes were sad, the delicious-looking, greasy pizza limp in her hand.

"It's okay, really."

Mina let it go—for now. Illiana knew it would be another argument later. But tonight, she crawled beneath the covers and fell asleep to the soft sounds of her best friend moving around the pool house.

CHAPTER FOUR
Emmett

"I'm telling you man. This girl is something else."

Nate had been expounding on Illiana's virtues for the past twenty minutes while Emmett labored over a seized engine bolt. Illiana though, he hadn't even met her and the vision that Nate was painting had her depicted as more stunning than Aphrodite herself.

"She has these big blue eyes, and long blonde hair, and like…I don't want to sound crude but she has the most perfect ass."

Emmett stopped, leaning on the grille of the 1972 Z28 Camaro he was trying to fix, while wiping his hands on an old rag. He knew there was likely grease stains all over his face and namely across the bridge of his nose, so it definitely detracted from the serious face he pinned Nate with. "You're starting to sound like Jace."

"Aw, man," Nate groaned, rocking back on the stool he was perched on. "Don't say shit like that. That's just low."

Emmett shrugged. "I'm calling it as I see it."

Nate rolled his eyes. "You'll understand when you see her, I swear. There's just something about her that, I don't know, you just want to *exist* around her and you want her to notice you. You can't forget her."

"And it's not just you?"

"Nah man, it's anyone."

"All right, then introduce us."

"What?" Nate asked, seeming boggled.

Emmett shrugged again, wiping his fingers some more on the rag. "Introduce us so that I get what you mean, and stop thinking you're some obsessed stalker or turning into Chase's brother."

"I can't just—you—I…" Nate became truly lost for words and had to inhale sharply to compose himself. "I don't know if that's a good idea."

Confusion struck Emmett like a bowling ball. "Okay, then don't, but don't blame me when I don't understand why you're drooling and lovesick over this girl."

"I'm not lovesick!"

"Okay, so what are you?" Emmett asked, picking up a can and spraying it on the bolt. "Are you going to ask her out?"

"I don't know if she's interested in me."

"Well, have you asked? That tends to help answer the question."

"Look, man I don't have this weird exotic charm you do—"

"I'm literally half Indigenous."

"And part Chinese!" Nate added, pointing determinedly. "And whatever it is about your pretty face and nice hair, and whatever else you have going; women seem drawn to you without you even trying."

Emmett watched him carefully. "Did you just call me pretty?"

"Shut the fuck up," Nate groaned a reply. "How you've ever managed to hold down a long-term relationship is beyond me."

"Hey," Emmett rebuffed, the comment actually striking a nerve.

Nate seemed to immediately recognize his faux pas and was chagrined, cringing into himself. "Sorry, that was uncalled for. I should've known. Delilah is still raw, I guess?"

He'd been single for six months which was nearly half the time he and Delilah had been together, but the abruptness of the relationship ending left him still seeking closure. In his head he'd built up this fantasy idea of starting a life with her, really settling down, but upon meeting certain members of his family some of her ideals were made known—quite frankly, too—and that vision disintegrated. So, even though he hadn't been ready to try again, he didn't mind casual encounters to fill the void every now and then. It just wasn't as regular as the guys had made it out to be.

But his feelings on the matter were beginning to change.

"It's okay. I'm pretty over it," Emmett assured him. "Besides, it's not like she cheated. We just have very different plans and views on life."

Nate began fiddling with a nut and bolt, screwing and unscrewing it, and Emmett picked up on his energy. He was nervous. Emmett stopped and put everything down, folding his arms over his chest and raised a brow.

"What's really going on, babe? You usually don't skip work to hang out with me," Emmett questioned pointedly. "Not that you aren't welcome here, but something's up."

Their friend group had always used *babe* as often as *man* or *bro*, the nickname having no sexual connotation to them. They were all comfortable in their sexualities, and those that played for the same team or both, knew that such flirting, jokes, and nick-names were purely platonic.

Nate chortled, the sound dry and sarcastic. "Do you know that we've been graduated for ten years now?"

Emmett did a quick calculation. "Yeah, that sounds about right."

"Right, ten years and I have nothing to show for it."

Emmett's brows drew together. "What are you taking about? You own a house—in this economy, I may add—and you have a really good paying job."

"Yeah, but do you know what my parents had by this time? All that plus a marriage and kids."

"So, you're telling me you want to start a family?"

"I—shit," Nate was flustered and blood rushed to his face in clear embarrassment. "Yeah, I do. I've been thinking more and more, but with all the dates I've been on, I can't imagine myself doing the whole forever thing with any of them."

"But you're hoping Illiana is different?" Emmett hedged a guess.

That red on Nate's face intensified. "Maybe? I mean, I think I can see that future with her, but what if I'm just projecting what I think I know about a person on someone I think is attrac-tive?"

"That's…that's deep, Nate," Emmett said, running a hand through his black hair. "I didn't know you felt like this."

"I usually try to keep it to myself, but I don't know, it's been getting to me lately. Since we went to James's wedding last month. I'm just realizing how far away I am from all of that." He sighed. "It sucks."

"Hey," Emmett began, clapping his friend on the shoul-der comfortingly. "I'm not going to lie—I feel the same way. You don't think I want that whole wife and two-point-five kids with the dog life? I do, it's just…how do I get there and how do I know it's the right person? For a while I thought it might be Delilah, but obviously I was wrong."

"Well, you have two dogs already, you're a third of the way there."

"You failed math, didn't you?"

"Sure did."

"Yeah, your fractions are way off, man."

Nate laughed, a comfortingly booming sound. It was a genuine laugh, and Emmett was suddenly glad he was able to cheer up his friend, even if it was at mathematical intelligences expense. For a moment it was Emmett and Nate, two friends in such a similar boat, rowing beside each other for the same destination wondering which of them would find it first. It wasn't a race, it was just a matter of chance, luck, and fortune guiding the timeframe of their futures.

"What do you say I head out early?" Emmett asked Nate.

Emmett owned his own auto mechanic shop, Raven Point Automotive, which he'd built from the ground up after plugging away years at a shady shop that cut corners and slapped quick fixes together.

"We can grab a beer and a burger, what do you say?"

Nate shrugged. "Yeah, that sounds good. Wanna meet there? Blue's?"

"You know it. Be there in 20."

CHAPTER FIVE

Illiana sat at a small square table nursing her second gin and tonic alone. Mina and Illiana had just finished dinner when Mina's doctor boyfriend, David, called for their nightly FaceTime. He was going in to do a surgery, so instead of their late-night conversation during his break, they were having it in the early hours of the evening. They were still in the honeymoon stage of the relationship, so the phone calls and FaceTimes were demanded.

David was an all right enough guy, but Illiana hadn't met him enough times to form a proper opinion of the man. Though some narcissistic qualities had started to gleam through. It was because of this impromptu call that Mina was on the phone in their rental car, and Illiana was alone in a bar.

Illiana and Mina had spent the entirety of their day exploring the wonders of Victoria, hitting up three different book stores—an Indigo, an indie, and a used—and now the back seat of their rental car was littered with Illiana's romances and Mina's fantasy selections. Interspersed throughout their bookish jaunts were stops in little hole in the wall cafes and pauses in boutiques. For the most part Illiana kept her spending related to books as she was hesitant to buy any clothes that currently fit her—for reasons she was not ready to admit, though they were similar to why she was drinking gin when she really wanted white wine.

Fiddling with the straw of her drink, Illiana checked her phone. Mina still hadn't messaged her that she was done. She sighed and looked up at the signed movie posters—was that Harrison Ford's signature on *The Empire Strikes Back?* –and busied herself imagining what all the spills and stains that covered the floor were. All the while it was taking everything in her not to pick up the brand-new paperback beside her. She'd gotten into the habit of carrying a book with her everywhere—protected inside a book sleeve—because public transport was never on time and she wanted to be on her phone less. For many reasons. Illiana fingered the orange cover, debating on cracking that green spine.

"I guarantee you the guys in that book are far more interesting than anyone you might meet here."

Illiana looked up to the voice and found herself looking into angled, warm brown eyes. Ones that had a starburst of amber catching the light, and a straight, white smile. The man who'd approached her had wavy black hair and suntanned olive skin. Truthfully, he was *very* handsome and his lips were *very* full. Illiana's heart fluttered.

"Are you included in that assessment?" She inquired as she unconsciously covered her drink, straw between her fingers.

"Definitely. I'd say I'm the best friend character that doesn't get his own book until the third spin-off. Or the hookup before the endgame love interest arrives."

Illiana's heart fluttered at this man's awareness of the genre. She smiled brightly, leaning forward, while he read her cue and tipped his head toward her—a similarly warm smile on his lips.

"That might be the better book though. Many people wait for that best friend story with bated breath, begging the author via DM to show him some love."

"True, but then you have to consider I might be the obligatory hookup in the flashbacks that pales in comparison to the awe of the real love interest."

"Well-versed in the structure of the romance genre? What might you know about these sorts of books?" Illiana countered flirtatiously.

The man leaned against the far end of the table, resting his forearms close enough to touch, but far enough to give her space. He had a beer bottle cradled in his hands, label unpicked. As his muscles flexed, Illiana noticed a sleeve of native art tattooed up his arm. She could make out a bear, a wolf, a raven, and a hummingbird and she followed its course up, drawn to the sight of his chest straining against the white T-shirt he wore. Her face reddened in both embarrassment and arousal.

"I know that the women in them are strong and driven just as often as they're clumsy and quirky or even lost and full of heart. That the men are either respectful or entirely the opposite depending on which sub-genre you're into. But no matter which, he is *always* obsessed with the main character, even if he doesn't want to be."

"Mm," Illiana hummed and leaned forward, blue eyes sparkling with attraction. "Are you secretly a romance author?" she whispered.

The man laughed and it was a growling, rumbling sound that had Illiana's toes curling in her sandals.

"A friend of mine is. Apparently, a man's perspective is helpful for the characters to feel natural."

"And do they?"

"I don't know. Do you think I'm a typical man?" His voice held notes of flirtation, his fingers were swirling on the tabletop and she noticed they were scarred, some long healed and some still healing.

A man that works with his hands.

"Maybe in some ways," she demurred, taking a sip of her gin and tonic, watching his eyes stray to her lips. "You seem to be a hot-blooded man, but you're talking to me in a *bar* about romance novels. I'd say you're a little outside of the scope of typical."

The man placed his left hand over his heart—no evidence of a ring. "That is the greatest compliment I could've ever been paid."

"Good, because I charge a fortune for them."

He laughed. "How can I pay you?"

She considered for a moment, weighing her thoughts. She did come to the island to meet someone, did she not? Surely this was the universe pointing her in the right direction. She just hadn't expected it to be in Rose Point. She figured it would be during one of the jaunts to Victoria. She hesitated a moment longer before reciting her phone number. "For e-transfer purposes obviously. And of course, more fantastic conversation regarding romance tropes and cliches."

"But of course, I would never consider crossing that line. Leave romance strictly to the books." His fingers were playing with his phone's edges. "May I text you now? Just to make sure you get your money. I'd hate to walk out on a bill."

"Acceptable request."

"Great." He tapped away and then suddenly Illiana's phone lit up with a message from an unknown number and two emojis—a stack of books and a heart. She quickly added his contact name as Secret Romance Author.

"Received." She waggled the illuminated phone for emphasis, showing him the name.

He laughed and then showed hers—Book Bar Girl.

She beamed. But surely, she'd given her name? She thought back—she must've—and was pulled from her thoughts by her phone chirping.

Mina texted her that David's FaceTime call was over and they could leave. "Sorry to do this to you, but I've got to go. It was lovely chatting with you." Illiana got up, tucking the tempting book back into its protective sleeve and hoisting her bag over her shoulder. "I anxiously await payment."

He dug around his pocket and produced a twenty-dollar bill. "Do you take cash?"

"Oh!" Illiana blushed. "You didn't actually have to. It was a joke."

He gave her a disarming grin and placed it on the table between them. "I know, but I wanted to." He began backing away toward his own seat again. "Coffee next time?"

Illiana's heart felt like it was going to beat out of her chest, her blood was rushing and her lungs couldn't bring in enough oxygen. Was her fantasy coming to fruition? Could this heart-wrenchingly attractive man desire her in such a way?

"Sure." She grinned then headed towards the exit. "And I want the name of this romance author friend—who I'm not completely convinced isn't you."

He laughed. "I appreciate the faith, but I think you'd be sorely disappointed if you read anything by me."

"I'll have to read your work sometime then."

"Be ready for my elementary school dinosaur war story."

"Sounds life changing, bring it to coffee."

"It's a date," he said.

"Yes, it is," she confirmed.

She left the money on the table wondering if she also left his name behind.

CHAPTER SIX

Emmett

Emmett couldn't beat the smile off his face as he stared off in thought. He couldn't believe his luck. A beautiful girl with wit and charm gave him her number.

Something about her dazzling summer sky eyes and soft, golden blonde hair had him utterly entranced. She didn't know it yet, but she had him wrapped around her little finger. How simply talking and flirting with her was able to banish all the complicated feelings with Delilah. It was remarkable. He was even able to bring up her writing career without a twinge of pain. When he spoke about the romance books he'd read for his ex, he felt no awkwardness.

Speaking to this girl felt as natural and uninhibited as breathing.

On his phone, he pulled up Delilah's Instagram—something he hadn't done in at least three months—and website link, attaching both to a message. He hadn't even processed the fact that he didn't check Delilah's recent posts until after the message had been swept away. How had things altered so quickly? Just a couple hours ago he was speaking to Nate, the jab about his ex striking a nerve enough to bother, but now he was sending a beautiful stranger her information and links to buy any of her various books?

Delilah was a prolific writer; she'd always dabbled in it throughout the years but nothing concrete. It wasn't until Covid lockdown and she was stuck in her apartment that the dabble became a hobby, that then became a career. In 2020, she had self-published four smutty contemporary romances and she'd kept a quarterly schedule with such success she was able to quit her job in finance quite happily. Emmett had always admired this self-made quality and even though he'd begun dating her after her success had already taken off, he could still see the disbelief on her face every time she got those royalty statements. As if she couldn't believe her life or her luck.

It was with a shock that Emmett realized he was over Delilah just like that. Just like Romeo had disregarded Rosaline at the sight of Juliet.

Emmett's stomach dropped at the insinuations of such a comparison.

He refused to be star-crossed with the girl he'd felt such an instant connection with.

He was not Romeo, nor was she Juliet.

"Aw, man no. I thought we talked about the Instagram stalking?"

Emmett jumped at the sound of Nate's voice, surprised to realize that he had been so far in his own head that he hadn't noticed his friend arrive at their table. Nor the fact that his phone was still open to Delilah's author page.

"I hate to be a cliché, but this is *really* not what it looks like," Emmett responded, his voice sounding guilty even to him. "I met someone."

"And you had to moon over your ex because…?" Nate trailed off as a server arrived—Gina, who knew them as regulars—and dropped off their usual beers.

Emmett snatched up the darker of the two bottles, taking a swig. "I wasn't mooning. I was sending her Delilah's information."

"I fail to see how that is better."

"She reads romance. We were flirting and joking around and I told her my friend writes it."

"Your *friend*…" Nate drew the word out slowly. "You met a girl, hit it off, and immediately sent her in the direction of your ex. Your ex, which I may add has you and your…*skills*…to thank in her dedications."

Emmett paled, pulled the beer away from his mouth. "No one reads the dedications."

"I do," Nate countered.

"You don't read," Emmett argued.

"True," Nate agreed, taking a drink of his beer, "but when I do, I always read the dedications."

"Do you think she'll notice?" Emmett asked tentatively.

"I don't know. Did you introduce yourself as Emmett *The-Guy-Who-Really-Knows-How-To-Fuck-A-Lady-Against-The-Wall* King?"

"Jesus!" Emmett hissed, glancing around. "Do you think everyone in the bar heard you?"

"Maybe. I could say it louder next time?"

"Please don't. Besides that's not what it says. And it's not like I'm the only person to have ever done that—I didn't invent wall fucking. She's also not the first woman I—look, I'm just going to stop there, none of that is the point."

"I paraphrased, and I'm sure she wrote more for you."

She did. She'd dedicated one other book to him, but Emmett wasn't about to enlighten Nate to this fact. He wondered idly if she'd changed the dedications on some new editions or not.

There was a pause in their conversing while another round of drinks came and they ordered food. They quickly decided to share an appetizer before their entrees.

"So, this girl you just met, what's her name?" Nate asked once they got their second beers.

Emmett came up blank. Utterly, empty sheet of printer paper blank. "What?"

"Her name?" Nate pressed, arching a dark brow. "Generally people have at least two? Sometimes up to four? Anything more than that is obnoxious."

"I don't know. I don't remember if she said it."

"So, she left this massive impression on you, yet you don't recall her name or if she even gave it to you? Did you suddenly develop a goldfish memory?"

"She gave me her number," Emmett said defensively.

"Okay, great, ask her for her name."

"I can't just do that! What if she did introduce herself and me forgetting her name makes it seem like I didn't care?"

"And if she didn't give it, you're going to be going days without knowing it, texting a beautiful nameless stranger, hoping she slips up."

Emmett paused. "Yeah, actually probably."

"Oh my God," Nate groaned, looking skyward. "You're being foolish. No, actually, you're being an idiot."

"Okay, now I'm offended."

"Good, stop acting like a dumbass."

Just then Emmett's phone lit up, an incoming text from the mystery girl.

*Followed her and ordered the first book in the Daydream Lovers series and her three most popular. I'll keep you posted on the hints that reveal it's actually you, be ready for a red string masterpiece. *winky face**

She followed this up with the iconic meme of Charlie Day with a red string board from *It's Always Sunny in Philadelphia.* So, in addition to the banter, she had a good sense of humor.

Emmett checked Delilah's bestsellers list, just to ensure that the ones with dedications to him weren't among the books at the top. His stomach sank when he realized one was and it was her second best. The other one was her fourth.

Shit.

I maintain my stance but I'm curious about your detective skills, he sent back.

He stared for a while, trying to banish the anxiety from showing on his face. His jaw worked while he compartmentalized everything, Nate was oblivious, having taken up his own phone. Emmett took the reprieve gratefully. It was a few minutes longer before his breathing evened and his heart slowed.

Emmett pocketed his phone and took a swill of beer, savoring the cold before steeling his eyes on Nate. "So," he began, pursing his lips, "you want to talk anymore about earlier?"

Nate shrugged and shifted uncomfortably before he took a swig of his own beer, clearly stalling. His short nails worried at the label—a nervous habit that Emmett had recognized since college. "I just feel…stagnant."

"How so?"

"I just feel like I've been doing the same routine for so long. I have a Monday to Friday, 9 to 5. Beers with the guys on Tuesdays and Fridays, I workout Mondays, Wednesdays, and Saturdays. I do the same thing over and over and it's a cycle that never ends."

"Nate," Emmett said slowly. "I don't think a relationship is going to solve whatever you're feeling right now."

"No, not in the way you're thinking, but I'm tired of the monotony of being alone. With someone else around, the routine would never be the same. And thinking about coming home to a house that isn't empty? And maybe she decorated it to her tastes a little? Made it a *home*, instead of a place I live. *That,* I wouldn't mind."

Their nachos arrived just then and they dug in. With their mouths full, Emmett was able to ponder his thoughts without interruption.

Emmett could relate Nate's pains. He felt similarly, but rather than an entirely empty home, Emmett had his dogs to keep him company. They were no replacement for human affection, but without them Emmett would be lost.

He didn't want to admit it, but Nate's worries were encroaching upon Emmett's. And although he was usually comfortable speaking about his emotions, something in him didn't want to dredge up these particular ones.

He didn't grow up with stable male figures, what with his grandfather being a survivor of a residential school, and his father being a product of a parent raised under terms of dehumanizing abuse. His grandfather turned to drink and sex workers to forget, but sometimes before the alcohol took him, he remembered and he told Emmett. Those truths haunted him and left him hollow and angry. His father, not knowing a life without neglect and alcoholism fell into addiction and broken romances himself. He'd had several girlfriends, each varying degrees of just as messed up as he was, but it was his mother and his sister's mother that combined forces and raised the two kids together in an unorthodox unit.

Of course, in time they fell in love and were married to this day, but his father was an in and out of their life character. It was a sad trickle-down effect and unfortunately his dad got stuck in the cycle. Emmett was committed to breaking it.

He did have his mothers to thank for examples of healthy pairings though.

Emmett swallowed his mouthful of nachos, the plate decimated by their appetites, before he wiped his hands.

"So, why don't you ask Illiana out? What's the worst she says? No?" Emmett pushed.

"Not just that. It would make everything this summer awkward if she turned me down."

"Then either play it lightly, tell her it's an idea and it could be fun, or lay it out and tell her you're infatuated with her."

Nate mulled this over, twisting his lips in thought. "Maybe you're right. But maybe infatuated is the wrong word."

Emmett caught sight of their server and delight suffused him.

"Of course, I am. Now stop moping and eat your burger," Emmett said just as their food arrived.

CHAPTER SEVEN

Illiana

"*Irregardless* is *not* a word!" Mina shouted across the Scrabble board, red wine sloshing precariously in her glass.

"Is too!" Nate argued back, his beer safely on the table. "Look it up!"

"I will!" Mina riposted, pulling out her phone and tapping away, the ancient dictionary sitting battered and dusty by Lacey and Walt who were playing in tandem.

Illiana wondered if Mina was right, and she felt bad that Nate wouldn't be getting that triple word score that "*irregardless*" would have offered him. How it had started out as regard and transformed from there was a feat only the Ellis family could complete.

Illiana took a sip of her mojito and moved around a couple of her Scrabble tiles, anxious for her turn. She looked up and saw the exact moment that Mina realized she was wrong.

"Does Merriam-Webster beg to differ?" Nate taunted, a winning grin taking over his handsome face.

"Shut up," Mina grumbled, tossing her phone to the table.

"Well, *irregardless* of that, I'd like my forty-two points, please."

"You can have this," Mina retorted, flicking a cashew at her cousin. He caught it in his mouth, grinning before crushing it between his teeth.

Lacey—the only one they could trust not to cheat—tallied her son's recent points. He was in the lead with 248 while Walt and Lacey were bringing up the rear with 113. It was Illiana's turn next and she debated placement and then dropped her tiles above *irregardless.*

"*Queens?*" Mina approved, bumping hips and sipping her wine, a light glaze in her best friend's eye. She dipped her hand into the faux velvet pouch to replace her letters, smiling a half happy, partly forlorn smile.

Illiana wasn't used to family board games, and she certainly wasn't used to family *actually* following through on rain checks. When Walt informed them that he had to run into work for an emergency and had to postpone the activities he had planned for the day, Illiana was under the impression they'd just be cancelled. Despite the original plan's rescheduling, Walt still wanted to make up for the lost time so a night of drinks and games was suggested. Illiana and Mina had come home from dinner, finding Walt in the kitchen slicing up limes and listening to Rihanna, and the feeling of seeing such an odd display of domestication had Illiana excusing herself to the bathroom to fend off tears.

Her parents were never at the counter slicing fruit and listening to modern—or even semi-modern—music. Hell, her parents were never home. Illiana was raised by nannies, housekeepers, and tutors, her parents barely paying attention to her unless it came to her recitals or the amount of food she put in her mouth. They'd even gone as far as alienating her from her extended family—though her cousin, Leo, tried to maintain an open line of communication around his traveling adventures.

This scene would've never been something Illiana could have experienced with her parents, and she resented them for it.

For not caring.

This is what she should have had.

"Illiana you're now in second place, sixteen points behind Nate," Lacey announced as Walt shuffled their tiles.

Nate flashed her a warm smile. "Think you've got this, ballerina?"

Illiana hid the jab of pain the nickname elicited behind a swallow of her mojito. "It's possible. I do read a lot."

"Mina mentioned that actually. It's a new hobby for you? What are you currently reading?" Nate inquired genially.

Illiana was not about to tell him she was trying out the summer romance book she'd read on her flight or the equally dirty Delilah Rose books she ordered just hours ago, so instead she fibbed a little. "I just got into *People We Meet on Vacation,* actually."

"I don't read much, but that's cool. Is it like a love story?"

Illiana struggled not to blush. "Yes, I think so."

"Ahh, definitely not the book for me then, but I hope you end up liking it. I'm more into thrillers if I do pick up a book."

Illiana could understand the intrigue that a thriller held, but the world was already so messed up and dark, she didn't need to slip into a book to have more of it thrown into her face and glamorized. She read romance for comfort and escapism. Romance held the promise that everything was going to be all right in the end. Thrillers never offered that same vow.

"Your loss," Mina tossed at her cousin. "A lot of these books can teach you how to pleasure the ladies."

Illiana's face flared scarlet and Nate shifted uncomfortably. Walt and Lacey were in the own little world, but ordinarily

Illiana wouldn't dream up having conversations bordering on sexual topics with parents in the room. Evidently, Mina had no such qualms.

"I don't need any help there. I'm doing just fine thank you," Nate muttered.

"Are you?" Mina challenged. "Are you still single? Why haven't you introduced me to your girlfriend yet?"

"You are the last person I'd introduce my girlfriend to."

"Oh, so you do have one?" Mina arched a brow.

Nate's face went hot. "No," his eyes flickered to Illiana. "Not yet."

Awareness fluttered in Illiana's belly at the look, and she wasn't sure if it was flattered or worried. She contemplated it for a moment, but a flash of disappointment went through her at the lack of a draw.

Nate was incredibly handsome, but Illiana didn't feel that spark, not like she did with the guy at the bar. It was possible in time for it to grow, but did she want to force it, and potentially have a letdown? And again, she couldn't stop thinking about Romance Book Guy, he had utterly enthralled her—despite not even knowing his name.

"Well get on it," Mina commanded breaking Illiana out of her reverie.

"Maybe I will!" Nate huffed, stuffing a handful of M&Ms in his mouth.

"*Waffle!*" Walt announced with glee.

Illiana narrowed her eyes in confusion but then she realized that he had placed the word *waffle* on the board, intersecting with Illiana's *queens*.

A few more rounds commenced before Nate was crowned the winner, Illiana following in second with Mina behind her, and Lacey and Walt taking up the rear. The Scrabble was put away and Cards Against Humanity produced. Illiana had never played it before, nor had she seen the cards and she was aghast at the sayings.

"*'Daniel Radcliffe's delicious asshole'*? Is this actually in the game?" Illiana asked horrified.

Mina cackled. "That's literally my favorite card."

"You're not serious."

"Oh, deadly so," Mina said devilishly.

As more drinks were consumed the ludicrous answers became funnier and funnier. Illiana laughed perhaps the hardest because she'd never had the chance to do so before.

Family game nights were something she wished she'd never grown up without.

The outrage when answers weren't picked, the dismay when it was found out who played which card, the playful tossing of cashews and M&Ms.

It was bliss. After a hesitant start Illiana became the one with the raunchiest of answers, and soon she was winning nearly every round.

Eventually, Walt and Lacey retired to bed, leaving Illiana, Mina, and Nate to their drunken devices. So, in proper drunk fashion, they decided to go for a walk.

They filled metal travel cups with their drinks of choice and set out into the night. The air was heavy, the warmth from the day's heat still clung to it, and frogs and crickets croaked and chirped in the distance. Streetlights illuminated their path as Nate walked in the center of the group, all their arms looped together in a sort of chain.

Mina sucked the straw of her mug, staining it light pink with her wine. They were not drunk enough to be stumbling; however, they were drunk enough to take a tipsy walk in a lovely neighborhood.

Nate was warm against Illiana's side and despite the fact that she had a tall, hot-blood and flesh man beside her, she couldn't stop her thoughts from wandering to Secret Romance

Author, which she was changing to Romance Book Bar Guy— RBBG for short. She pulled out her phone and entered in the initials for his contact name. She added an H for good measure; she needed it explicitly clear that the man was hot.

"Who're you texting?" Nate asked, a funny lilt to his voice.

"No one," Illiana replied playfully. "Why would I be texting anyone when I am among such good company?" Although Illiana wanted to text HRBBG, she thought it would be in poor taste to drunk text a guy she was very interested in so early.

"I'm flattered," Nate said, guiding the girls through the neighborhood, nodding to a man walking his dog.

"You should be, it's a great compliment."

Nate laughed heartily and then faded into silence. They continued walking, Mina humming happily. Illiana thought it was a Creed song but she couldn't be certain. The balmy air was nice on her face and the warmth from Nate's body helped stave off any chill. What was it with men always running a thousand degrees warmer than women?

"What do you think people see when they look at us?" Illiana asked suddenly.

"Um, they probably see a guy walking with two girls," Nate responded. "Why?"

Illiana shrugged and took a sip of her mojito. "I'm always curious about impressions and reactions. Mina always gives me shit for watching reaction videos, but I can't help it—it's my guilty pleasure."

Nate cracked a shy smile. "I'm not going to lie; I watch those too. And gaming Let's Plays."

"See!" Illiana crowed at Mina. "It's not just me!"

Mina turned, broken from her musical—and disjointed— humming. "I definitely wasn't paying attention but if you two have something in common then it's definitely terrible." Illiana huffed and Mina's face changed, a touch of panic. "Speaking of terrible; I'm the worst, but we need to turn around. I have to pee. Like soon."

Illiana threw back her head and laughed and soon Nate swept them around, the trio returning to the house.

When Nate escorted them to the pool house, they bid him good night and Illiana helped Mina to the bathroom. She peed with the door open and kept a steady stream of conversation with her best friend as Illiana pulled out a cotton shorts pajama set, pink with flamingos on them.

"I'm just saying," Mina said, continuing her rambling from before. "You could do much worse than Nate."

"Are you really trying to set me up with your cousin right now?" Illiana asked dubiously as she shimmied out of her jeans. She pulled on the shorts, folding the jeans and setting them on the armchair.

"Maybe," Mina said after a pause. "It's not like you've met any other prospects, right?"

Her question was punctuated by the sound of the toilet flushing and the sink turning on.

"Actually…"

Illiana sensed rather than heard Mina freeze. She looked up and found her friend's hazel eyes on her.

"Oh, nuh uh, spill. You don't get to start like that and then pretend it didn't happen."

Mina finished washing her hands and returned to the living area, pants discarded in the bathroom while she continued stripping off the rest of her clothes. She pulled on an oversized gray shirt and sat cross-legged on the opposite bed. Illiana knew Mina didn't sleep in actual pajamas, preferring underwear and old tees. After several years of sleepovers, a girl who was obsessed with pajama sets began to notice when someone else was decidedly not.

Illiana finished buttoning her pajama top and brought her bag of skincare to the bathroom. She began with her routine, washing her face and applying the first step.

"When you were on FaceTime with David a guy came up to me at the bar." Her eyes flickered nervously to her best friend. "He was so hot, Mina. Like…he was built, but not like, cut. And he had that whole tall, dark, and handsome thing going on."

"That does sound hot."

"Right?" Illiana exclaimed, applying night cream to her face. "And get this, we were talking about *romance books*. Apparently, his friend is a writer."

"Just a friend?"

Illiana paused. "I didn't see a ring."

"That's promising."

"Yeah, so anyway," Illiana continued. "We exchanged numbers and before we said bye we agreed to coffee. But we haven't set a date."

Just then, Illiana's phone chirped.

"Would you mind checking that for me?" Illiana called into the living area.

"It's a text from HRBBG. What the hell is a HRBBG?"

"Hot-Romance-Book-Bar-Guy," Illiana told her.

Illiana dropped her cream and rushed to the room, scooping up her phone from Mina's outstretched fingers. She opened the message, grinning.

I know it's the middle of the night and it's probably very uncool for me to be texting you right now (I swear I'm not looking for a hookup) but I can't stop thinking about you. Are you free tomorrow for that coffee?

Illiana released a happy squeal and showed the message to Mina, she watched Mina's eyes scan the text and whistle in appreciation.

"No dick pic and no midnight 'wanna meet up?', that man deserves bonus points."

Illiana scoffed. "I swear the bar for men is on the floor."

"No hon, the bar is definitely in hell. Either you found a unicorn, or he's waiting before dropping the nice guy act."

"So cynical!" Illiana admonished. "What if I did find myself a golden retriever man?"

"Then I expect a wedding invite next year."

"Mina!" Illiana said aghast.

Did Mina really think Illiana was ready for that level of commitment? Illiana thought that she was coming here for a summer fling and then returning to her life in Toronto. Did Mina really expect her to stay on the west coast? Her life was in Ontario. *Mina* was in Ontario. She couldn't just abandon her best friend in the city.

"I'm just saying, don't let him get away if he's a good one."

Illiana bit her lip and fought off a smile while she typed. Before she could overthink it, she hit send.

How does 11 sound?

And I can't stop thinking about you either.

CHAPTER EIGHT

Emmett

Emmett was lying in bed, one hand on Gimli, his bare foot strok-ing Leia, who was snoring at the end of the bed, when his phone went off. He nearly shot forward to grab it, having set it face down beside him, ignoring the urge to constantly check for a re-sponse. Gimli let out a nervous bark at his sudden movement, and Emmett immediately soothed him.

He read the messages and he swore his smile just became permanent. His fingers rushed over the touchscreen as he re-sponded.

Perfect, don't forget your red string, he typed.

As long as you don't forget that childhood dinosaur fic, she replied with a silly, tongue out emoji.

I don't think the world would be the same if that came to light, he responded.

This is why I need to see it. I need something revelational in my life. There was a pause before she sent another message. *Btw, "Never You" is set in Victoria, the first pin is in the board and I am currently unwinding my string.*

Let me know when you get to the first kiss scene and maybe you can try for yourself and compare.

It was a few seconds of silence while Emmett watched those three moving dots tease him from across the screen. Maybe he'd been too forward. They'd just met and already he was talking about kissing. He was familiar with hookups but he was clear when it was just that.

This was not that.

He was never like this with other women he wanted to date. Normally he kept a respectful boundary, waiting out any romantic or dirty talk after several dates, and definitely after the woman initiated it, but the desire that swept through him at the prospect of this nameless beauty was absolute.

His phone dinged.

For research, of course.

But of course, he sent back, *I would not presume otherwise. But don't you know? This is how all the romance books go. They pretend it's fake when they're both too stubborn to admit it's real.*

Don't worry, I'm definitely not too stubborn to admit it.

I need proof: how do I know you're real? he wrote.

A picture arrived in their messaging thread, a dim photo of the beautiful woman from the bar, face freshly washed, hair tied in two braids, and the shoulders of pink flamingo pajamas peeking over the edge of a yellow blanket. She was throwing up a peace sign and smiling, the tip of her tongue sticking out.

He wanted to taste it.

He analyzed the picture over and over, finding new pieces of her to fall into. Her eyes were so breathtakingly blue, they reminded him of cloudless summer skies. And her lips were so lusciously pink, her Cupid's bow well defined. All Emmett could do was think about kissing that mouth, feeling it on his neck, on his chest, that tongue hot on his abs…he stopped himself before he let his thoughts go further.

Proof, she sent.

Ensuring any arousal was firmly put away, Emmett took a picture of himself. He was shirtless, but his gray duvet was pulled over himself, revealing the cut of his collarbones and the muscular shape of the top of his pecs. Further, his tattoo sleeve stretched down his arm, extending onto his chest. His arm was around Gimli, his wrinkled face pressed into Emmett's ribs.

In case you had any doubts, he replied, sending his own photo.

Oh. My. God. You have a bed frame and a dog? I don't think you can actually be real after all.

He snapped a second photo. *I actually have two,* he corrected, sending off the photo of Leia. His chocolate lab was still contentedly snoring.

Feet pics too? Man, I hit the jackpot with you. A second message rolled in. *Just for absolute transparency, I do not have a thing for feet. It was a joke.*

Well, I do have beautiful feet, he replied.

I'll leave that assessment for the feet experts, maybe they'll apprentice you. A pause. *On that note, I'm going to go to sleep before I dig myself a deeper hole,* she sent. *See you tomorrow.*

Goodnight, he sent.

Goodnight, she replied. A kiss emoji followed.

Emmett couldn't stop smiling and rereading their texts over and over, stopping every time to stare at her picture, noticing her long lashes, a silver necklace resting on her collarbones, the strands of hair she missed in her braids. He even stopped and analyzed the kiss emoji she'd left.

Overcome with anticipation, Emmett rolled out of bed and walked over to his closet clad only in checkered pajama pants. He surveyed his clothing options, staring at the few dress shirts he owned—was a button up too formal for coffee? His options were a blue, small floral print with short sleeves, an orange pattern that was akin-to-but-not-officially-floral, also short sleeved, or white and salmon—or coral, Emmett could never tell them apart—stripes, this one full length but he could roll them up as needed. He stared at his three options, the longer he looked the less likely it was that any of them would be a good choice. Should he just wear a tee shirt? Would that send the wrong message? Maybe choosing pants first would help.

Emmett wandered over to his dresser, nervous energy coursing through him. He only owned three types of pants—shorts and sweatpants not included—and they were jeans, black trousers, and khakis. He knew he was being stupid, but he was genuinely stressing about the impression he was going to leave on this girl. He thought about texting his boys group chat—Beer Boys—but elected not to. For some reason he wanted to keep this mostly to himself, at least for a little while.

A sigh escaped him and he made his choice before he could overthink it, tossing the shirt and pants onto the gray armchair in the corner of his room.

At 10:30 Emmett had secured the perfect table on the café's patio. It was half in the shade and half in the sun and luckily the day had not yet risen to sweltering degrees. He was nursing a vanilla latte—his taste in coffee was something he would not defend; he felt no need to drink motor oil to prove his masculinity—while he waited for his date to arrive.

His date.

The concept was near jarring in its singularity. He'd had dates in the sense of hookups, but his last real date was with Delilah. Had it really been so long ago?

He picked imaginary lint off of his charcoal gray pants and readjusted his sunglasses. Anything to keep his hands busy and nervous energy at bay. His eyes watched the patrons come and go, some setting up shop with laptops and creative beverages of choice, others immersing themselves in conversation with friends over baked goods. He saw more than one person pushing a stroller or chasing a tot and he had to glance away and into his coffee.

He'd elected to have the date in the city, rather than in Rose Point. There was little that happened in a small town that didn't end up as local gossip within hours, and he wanted just a little privacy. It was often noted when people from Victoria came into town for the day, visiting the farmers markets and such, but not so much vice versa. It was too populous, too busy for anyone to care, and he assumed she couldn't be from town as he'd never seen her before. Victoria was more convenient.

At 10:50 he caught sight of her through the large café windows.

She was dressed in light jeans that clung to her legs and a striped button down with the top three buttons undone. Her blonde hair was pulled up in an elaborate, messy bun that seemed effortless, but he knew was artfully curated. A pair of tortoiseshell sunglasses covered her blue eyes, but they could not hide the charming smile he knew touched those same eyes. She was just as he remembered her; average height and slender with a grace that seemed perfected like an art form. Beside her was a girl also wearing sunglasses, her hair covered in a protective style with a silk wrap, and clad in a breezy set of loungewear in sage green.

Emmett was staring. He knew, but he couldn't help himself. When she glanced over and caught sight of him, he grinned and gave a small wave. A faint blush touched her cheeks, and she waved back. Her friend noticed and glanced at the movement, giving her a playful shove that he received as approval.

He hoped.

The two girls ordered and patiently waited in line, but Emmett noticed the anxious energy radiating from the blonde. He was nervous too. Glancing down at the white wrought iron table before him, he stared through the gaps in the metal and to the concrete patio below, trying to reel in his emotions.

Finally, they got their drinks and lingered in the doorway to the open patio. His mystery girl halted her friend and ushered her back inside.

"I'll be fine out here, trust me. You can see him, and I'm sharing my location with you," she said fairly quietly while waving her phone for emphasis.

"If you're sure," her friend replied warily. She rubbed her brow and winced as the glare of the sun caught her eye.

"I am. Look, you're far too hungover to be out and about right now, let alone in direct sunlight. Go. Find a dark corner." Her voice was soft but her tone firm. She wasn't to be argued with, but she was also appreciative.

"If you need me, Ana…"

There it was. Ana. Her name. It was sweet. Fitting. He'd heard the name often enough at his brother's house, as *Frozen* was his niece's current obsession, and the name was held by one of the two sisters.

"I know—you'll be there."

"Right. Okay, best of luck."

Ana's friend wandered back into the shop with some sort of frappe clutched in her hand and her forehead in the other. He did not envy her situation, he strived very hard to avoid hangovers like the plague.

As Ana approached Emmett stood. He pulled out the opposite chair and urged her towards it. She smiled and the warmth in it made his heart beat unevenly.

"Thanks," she said sweetly. "That's your second point today towards earning the title as endgame love interest."

Emmett took his seat once again and cocked his brow, pleasantly surprised where she was directing conversation. "What was my first?"

"The shirt. Blue floral says you're secure in your masculinity and that you have no qualms wearing flowers outside of Hawaiian shirts."

"Perceptive, aren't you? You'd be right, but honestly it was between this and pink stripes."

Ana pursed her lips. "I'm glad you went for the floral. Stripes would have been too serendipitous. We can't be matching already. Maybe after our tenth-year wedding anniversary."

"Of course. But in true romance book fashion we'd be engaged by the end of summer, and married by Christmas, so we would have to put a rush on the matching outfits. Maybe after the fifth anniversary." Emmett considered. "Though, I won't propose till next year at the earliest because that trope screams Hallmark."

Ana fake sighed. "And here I was dreaming of finding the perfect engagement ring in a Christmas ornament. How you shatter my dreams."

"Christmas proposals are overrated."

"Overrated or popular?" Ana countered.

"The 'only one bed' trope is popular and, while often expected, will never die. Christmas proposals meanwhile, are predictable in the worst of ways and are an easy way to opt out of gift giving."

"All right, I can get behind that," Ana agreed while taking a sip of her matcha. "I see your tropes and raise you another. Second chance lovers or enemies to lovers?"

Emmett plucked off his glasses and looked at Ana dubiously. "This one is no contest, I'm sure you know."

Ana shrugged with a coy smile. "Humor me. I'm open to being surprised."

For a while there Emmett would have said the former. The pining over Delilah's lost love was embarrassing and upsetting, and for a time he debated if he could compromise for her. But it was Kieran who'd knocked sense into him, telling him that it was not a comprisable thing and resentment would grow between them. Emmett had been forced to admit his friend was right.

"Enemies to lovers."

"Agreed. But are we talking 'we're meant to kill each other' or like academic rivals?"

"Touché. Depends on the mood and sub-genre."

"Doubly agreed."

The conversation continued like that for a while, comparing and debating tropes and sharing smiles and laughs. Emmett really felt himself compelled by Ana, she was so charming and bright, and just so easy to talk to. He could see her seamlessly inserting herself into his life, his home, his everything. It was their first date and he was already smitten. How?

"How did you get into romance books anyway?" she asked after an active debate on romance series: interconnected stand-alones with different couples or following the same couple.

Emmett smirked, a crooked little thing. "You're probably thinking it started with my friend, but that was just the resurgence."

"The friend who is really you," Ana teased.

He laughed. "The one who you *think* I am, sure. It actually started with my moms. They had these old Harlequin romance novels in boxes all over the house. Classic bodice rippers, cowboys, Fabio and all. They couldn't keep up with how many books I'd burn through in a week—financially and just finding time to take me to the library—so I'd go hunting in the house and read whatever I could get my hands on. There was some nature nonfiction—edible foraging, wildlife in the area, stuff like that—but that didn't last. The romance books did though."

"And you were the ripe young age of…?"

"Eleven," he admitted, cracking a smile.

"Your poor mothers. A sex fiend so young!"

"I kept it to the books for a while, not to worry." He sipped his latte. "What about you? What started your indoctrination into the genre?"

Ana ducked her head shyly and delicately lifted her paper cup to her mouth. "I got hurt last summer." She seemed to hesitate, and Emmett could tell that whatever hurt her was something she didn't want to talk about. He decided he wouldn't pry.

She swallowed and then continued. "So, I couldn't walk around for a while, and I got into the show, *Bridgerton*. From there I got the books and then the train kind of derailed. I think I own more unread books than read ones at this point though."

"You'll learn that's quite normal," he joked.

Ana lifted a brow. "I'm imagining a room in your house is floor to ceiling bookshelves full of erotica."

"I'll keep the truth to myself for now, but maybe I'll show you sometime."

"I'd like that," she replied brazenly.

They kept up effortless conversation and soon enough they were lifting empty cups to their mouths, both of them clearly not wanting the date to end. Emmett was utterly captivated by her presence and the thought of her leaving caused something inside him to rebel.

"I'm having a really good time here. Any chance you want to continue this date elsewhere? I go to this hole in the wall bookshop that I think you'll love. Then lunch?"

Ana beamed. "That sounds great. Give me one second." She pulled out her phone and presumably texted her friend to reassure her of the day's new plans. The text must have gone over well because Emmett watched Ana's friend get up and leave, waving to them casually.

He gave Ana's friend a head start before they also departed, Emmett gesturing and Ana following. Disposing of their cups, they exited the patio and set foot on the sidewalk. They walked the short distance together, hands brushing but not holding. There was a palpable tension there, an energy that begged him to reach out and twine his fingers with hers, pressing their palms together. But he did not. Instead, he let that electricity build, relishing the desire that burned beneath his skin.

When they arrived inside the bookshop Ana gasped. It was a small, boutique-style shop. Elegant plate glass windows in white frames, pale pink walls and faux flowers in a multitude of pastels. The shelves were floor to ceiling in weathered ivory, the same shade as the floorboards. Upon display tables were stacks of books decorated with peonies and carnations while pale, glittery butterflies marked corners and walls. And even more of those butterflies made up a fluttering chandelier. Ornate, silver-framed mirrors hung about the store and armchairs and poufs nestled in books and alcoves, urging patrons to rest and flip through pages.

A sign above the checkout desk proclaimed it Sugar & Spice Books.

"This is Victoria's best hidden gem," Emmett revealed in a low voice with all the grandeur it deserved. "A bookstore dedicated to all varieties of the romance genre."

Ana had a hand cupped over her mouth. "There's no way this is real." She whirled on him. "There's no way *you're* real."

"Oh, but I am," Emmett chuckled. "And I would love it if you did me the very real pleasure of choosing my next book."

"Really?" she said in a breathy voice. Stunned.

"Really, really. And I would appreciate it if you placed in me your trust to decide *your* next book."

Ana bit her lip. "Deal."

As they pursued the shelves, he watched Ana weave through the aisles, gently fingering spines and caressing pages. She evoked a peaceful air of genteel and poise. How was a human so elegant while just browsing through books? She made it seem so simple, but she moved with such sinuous detail. As if conscious of every one of her body's movements. Of the tensing and releasing of muscles. Aware of how everything within her connected in her being. He was utterly enchanted.

Ana pulled a book from the shelf and held it quite decidedly as she read the back cover. She smiled and then pressed it to her chest. "This one," she announced. "This one is yours."

Emmett stole a glance at the mint green cover. "Is that a Christmas book?" The title didn't seem to betray a Yuletide theme but other hints were present.

She shrugged a dainty shoulder. "You got me in the mood earlier, what can I say?"

"Fair play," he conceded.

Since it was his turn, he looked over the shelves while keeping Ana in his vision. He kept reminders of *Bridgerton* being her introduction to romance in his mind as he scanned the options. It was when he saw a light blue cover that he knew he hit the mark. After pulling it out and reading the summary, he grinned at his success.

"This is perfect." He proudly displayed his find to his date. "*Bridgerton* with magic and enemies to lovers. It's perfect."

Ana grinned and averted her eyes. "Yes, it is."

Emmett plucked his book from Ana's arms and brought the two books to the counter where one of the regular workers, Olivia, was behind the register.

"Emmett!" Olivia greeted warmly. "Did you find everything all right?"

"More than all right."

They made casual small talk while she scanned their items and then Emmett produced his card and tapped it to pay. The books went in a white paper bag with the shop's logo stamped on it and then Emmett and Ana were on their way.

"Hungry?" he asked.

"Starving," she replied.

Luckily the sushi spot he had in mind was also within walking distance and in moments they were seated with menus before them. They stuck to water to drink and when it came time to order Emmett noticed she ordered very little that wasn't vegetables and virtually no rice. He said nothing when she refused his offer of tempura, but he noticed how her eyes betrayed her hunger. He made sure she knew the offer was open. Eventually, she did cave to her body's wants and she stole a piece of deep-fried sweet potato.

They lingered over their food, talking of basic get-to-you-knows such as "favorite movies" and "what do you do for work" and the like. Emmett noticed she held back though. Not that she was secretive, but more like she wasn't telling the entire truth. He believed her when she said she was between jobs, but he sensed there was more to it.

"And what are you looking for?" he asked. "Romantically."

"Oh, big questions now." She laughed, covering her mouth. "I'm not sure. I'm dating, but not seeking if that makes sense."

"Are you opposed to more?"

"I'm not sure where I'm planning to put down roots," she deflected.

He hoped she would elect for close by.

When lunch was over, Emmett paid and the two of them walked closely. They were heading back the way of the café when Emmett stopped them.

"Can I take you somewhere special?"

Ana looked at him and considered, a slow smile bloomed across her face. "Sure."

Emmett's own grin responded in kind as he led Ana to his black SUV, telling her to feel free to send pictures of the license plate and vehicle itself to her friend, and opened the passenger's side door for her. She gave him a look, and in her eyes, he read something along the lines of *and they say chivalry is dead.*

He got in on the driver's side and started the engine. Within moments he was merging into traffic, and he was easing them along the roads, familiar with Victoria's far too many one-way streets and deceptive traffic lights. It wasn't a far drive, but the day's heat was at its peak, the sun just past its zenith, so he was immensely grateful for the A/C blasting them.

When he pulled into the lot Ana made a sound of delight. "I've been meaning to come here!"

"Then I'm glad I get to be the one to take you."

Emmett paid their fee to get into Butchart Gardens and let Ana lead the way. Within the gardens, famous to Victoria, were several different areas such as the Rose and Japanese. Somehow though, Ana was heading straight for a place in Emmett's heart. He didn't say anything but it felt as if a tether was connecting him to the place and she was following it with a hand on its rope.

Sensing his emotions, or falling to her own wants, Ana reached out and took his hand. He enfolded her tiny hand in his, dwarfed by the contrast in size and color and texture. Her skin was pale with the slight glow of summer, while his was perpetually bronzed from his heritage. Small knicks and scars peppered his fingers and knuckles, hers scar and blemish-free. She was also soft where he was rough and callused.

But somehow, they fit.

"So, tell me more about your moms," Ana began, walking the path. "They must have been pretty remarkable people if they managed to raise a man who reads romance *and* works hard with his hands."

"They are," he admitted. "For it to make sense it's a bit of a long story."

"I have the time."

They headed towards a glassed-in building, and Emmett could see the lights flashing already. It reminded him of childhood and special moments.

His lips quirked in a sad sort of smile. "My dad…he's complicated. He's been in and out of my life, off and on employed, and constantly bouncing from woman to woman. His dad, my grandfather, was in a residential school and experienced just…untold abuse. I don't know the extent, but I know enough. Because of what he endured he couldn't cope so he turned to booze and other…things.

"Because of that he didn't know how to treat a child and in turn, hurt and neglected my dad. That cycle, my dad repeated. Alcohol and poor choices. Some of those choices were falling into all different women." He glanced at Ana, and her eyes were urging him to continue, rubbing small circles with her thumb against his hand.

"My mom and him weren't together very long when she discovered she was pregnant with me. She knew she wasn't going to let the same things that shaped my father shape me. So, she left.

"Later that year he got another woman pregnant and my mom found out about her. They decided to…*team up*, for lack of a better word. And raise their kids together. Eventually, they had me and my sister, and as you can tell as time went on, they fell in love with each other."

Ana exhaled slowly. "What a tragic life, but what a beautiful result. I'm sorry."

Emmett met her cerulean eyes. "I'm not. I think it's the greatest gift to have been given to see your parents fall in love." He bit his lip and looked away. "I know we're an unorthodox unit and most people would gag at the idea of seeing their parents give affection, but I count myself as one of the lucky ones."

"You are," she told him. "My parents are completely toxic for each other and should've never set foot in the same room, let alone have had a kid together. It didn't give the best parameters or standards for relationships either."

"You have a bad ex?" he inquired.

She sighed. "The Ex Talk already? It's our first date."

He shrugged. "Only if you want."

She shook her head as if clearing it. "Let's just say he was more infatuated with the *idea* of me than the actual me, so when it came down to real life, he ran. And replaced me." There was a bitterness in her voice that instantly piqued Emmett's attention.

"Does that happen a lot?"

She turned, a question on her face.

"People wanting you based on the illusion of you? Of what they think you are or should be?"

They paused in front of the carousel, lacquered animals rotating and sliding up and down their spiraled, gold poles. Pink roses framed the top of the ride and mirrors reflected facets of them as music tinkled about the space.

Surprise lit her face and her delicate mouth dropped open, her Cupid's bow rounding until her lips formed a perfect O. She blinked; her brows arched high before she composed herself somewhat.

"You see a lot, don't you?" she asked.

"I see you."

Ana's breath caught. Surprise and pleasure warred in her gaze. She took him in, and he watched as her eyes traced the planes of his face and lingered on his mouth. He didn't know if she had done it consciously, but her small pink tongue darted out to wet her lower lip while she stared at his lips.

He had a strong reaction to it.

"Tell me what you're thinking," he whispered, still holding her hand.

Her breathing was slightly shallow and she paused. "I'm thinking that I'd really like to kiss you, but it's probably too soon."

"Mm, it probably is," he agreed, his eyes trained on her mouth. "But the thing is we don't have to play by any rules or tropes. We can do whatever we want."

"A novel concept," she breathed.

He quirked a smile. "It is, isn't it?"

And then he leaned down.

CHAPTER NINE
Illiana

Emmett's hand flattened against her waist, the other cupping her chin. He tilted her face towards his while he dipped down and his eyelashes fluttered against his cheekbones. Illiana's breath skated across his mouth when her lips parted. Immediately, her eyes shuttered in anticipation as their lips met.

His mouth slanted over hers carefully with expert pressure. As his lips moved against hers, she reached up to press her palms against his chest where his heart thundered. She smiled at the sensation of his kiss as she delicately slipped her tongue against his lower lip. He met hers with his own, his tongue gentle and slow, probing.

Emmett was such an excellent kisser.

She was so thrilled to finally know his name. She was certain he hadn't given it before so she was eternally thankful to the bookstore worker that had greeted him by name.

Emmett.

It was perfect. It was warm and unique, and she liked it more than she thought she should.

The kiss continued, languorous and sweet. His hands moved subtly against her, his fingers smoothing delicately on her jaw, spreading against her waist. Illiana felt butterflies tumble in her center as Emmett tilted her head back ever so, smiling against her mouth as he pulled her lower lip between his teeth. She gasped at the sensation, surprised at how much she liked it. She'd never been kissed like *that* before.

Emmett drew back and Illiana saw a glimpse of pure male satisfaction in his eyes. He was a gentleman, yes, but she could tell he knew when he'd struck a distinctly pleasant nerve in the opposite sex.

"I feel like I've monopolized you today. Should I get you back safely?" Emmett inquired softly.

Illiana was mildly dazed from that intoxicating kiss—was this what the *Bridgerton* ladies felt like? —and she figured it would be best if they called this date to its conclusion. She felt such a visceral connection to Emmett that she didn't trust herself not to spend the entire day with him—and more.

And she didn't know if she was quite ready for that yet despite specifically seeking a fling.

She felt nervous about admitting it, which was why she hadn't answered him properly when he'd asked what she was looking for at lunch, but she knew it would come.

Because she very much wanted him.

It had been nearly a year since she'd had sex and even longer than that since she'd had *good* sex. And she could tell that from their connection alone, the sex *would* be good. Mind-altering. Life-changing.

She nodded once she had compartmentalized her thoughts. "Yeah, that's probably a good idea."

They left the garden together in comfortable silence and when they got back to the vehicle, Illiana asked if he could take her back to the coffee shop they'd met at. Mina was coming to pick her up there so it was more convenient than making him drive all the way out to the Ellis property.

When they arrived at the coffee shop, Illiana lingered in Emmett's SUV, fingers playing with his over the center console.

"Have we struck any tropes?" Emmett asked.

Illiana raised a brow. "I thought we weren't playing by those rules."

"We're not, but I'm curious."

"Hmm," Illiana paused. "Well, we're certainly not enemies to lovers or second chance love. I don't think grumpy and sunshine fits the bill either."

"So, no. Not yet at least."

Illiana quirked a smile. "Not yet."

"I'd like another chance to try though."

"Oh?"

"Go out with me again tomorrow."

Illiana's heart raced in her chest, thundering an explosive rhythm. "Okay," she whispered, sliding her fingers along his. Feeling the calluses.

"Okay," he echoed. "I'll text you some ideas and times."

"That sounds like a date to me."

Just then, Mina pulled up in their rental vehicle and Illiana sighed. Disentangling their hands, Illiana looked into Emmett's eyes.

"I'm really glad you asked me out today. Thank you for everything."

Quickly, she darted forward to give him a peck on the cheek but Emmett was faster and cupped her jaw. He slowed her advance and gently brought his lips to her, kissing her with talented pleasure. He drew the kiss out long, sensually drawing her lower lip into his mouth. He broke the kiss and stared at her with heated eyes.

"I'm really glad you said yes, Ana." He smiled softly and she beamed at him as he brushed a wisp of hair from her face. "I'll see you tomorrow."

"Yes, tomorrow."

And with that she stepped out of Emmett's SUV and into the hot June afternoon. It was seconds when she was in hers and Mina's rental that her best friend stared her down.

"Hon, tell me I did not just see you make out with that gorgeous man," Mina said, stunned.

"It was just a kiss; we weren't making out." Illiana looked over her shoulder to see Emmett watching her leave, the most dazzling smile on his face.

"Semantics. It looked like *some* kiss, though." Mina side-eyed her as she pulled out of the parking spot.

"It sure was."

"Spill!"

So, Illiana did. She filled the drive with regaling tales of Emmett's chivalry and banter, his emotional depth, and his delightful kissing skills.

"I can't believe you," Mina says, shaking her head at the road. "Here a couple days and you're already finding a hookup! I told you a summer fling is just what you needed!"

Illiana was saved from answering by Emmett's incoming text.

Farmers market tomorrow? 11?

Illiana smiled and typed up a reply. *Sounds wonderful.*

"We're going out again tomorrow."

Mina's stunned green eyes were pulled from the road— thankfully they were at a red light. "He asked you again? *Already?*"

"He actually asked me out again *while* on the date. We're just confirming plans."

"Fuck me, girl." Mina blew out a breath. "You've got him hooked."

The conversation pivoted from Emmett and Illiana to Mina's cousin's antics. Family was going to start to pull in this week from all over the country for the upcoming holiday and the notorious Ellis family pool party. This was the first year Mina's parents wouldn't be making it due to a research trip they were taking in Peru. Though, while hearing about the party was exciting in and of itself, Illiana found herself more grateful for the fact that Mina didn't notice—or mention—her lack of response towards a fling.

A summer fling is what she had come here for, but after meeting Emmett, just a fling didn't seem like enough. And that intensity scared her. More than the prospect that Mina had brought up back in Toronto. That nothing was keeping her there anymore. And now there might be something drawing her here. Or rather *someone*. But she didn't want to scare him off.

She realized also, with a start, that Emmett didn't know she was just supposed to be here for the summer. *Just* the summer. Because she hadn't expected *him*.

But she was getting ahead of herself. Everyone always left her, why would Emmett be any different?

She shoved the thought away.

The drive continued with more gushing about Emmett's dreaminess—from the bookshop to the kiss—and soon enough the girls were pulling into the lake house's drive, laughing. Illiana had to shush Mina as the other girl began to make a crude allusion that had Illiana blushing furiously.

Inside, they were greeted by happily wine drunk members of Mina's extended family. Lacey and Walter were breaking out what looked to be the fifth bottle of Prosecco split between five of them. Evidently, the older adults were smarter about the indulging than Mina had been. Immediately, they were urged to join. Mina refused. Illiana accepted a single glass.

As she neared the dregs of her wine, Illiana's phone went off with a text.

You have unmatched taste.

Attached was a picture of Emmett, fingers between the pages of the book she picked out in a way that shouldn't have been sexual, but felt extremely so. The wine enhanced her blush. She put the phone down before she could make some ill-advised quip about other tastes.

Butterflies danced in her belly as she waited outside the farmer's market. Illiana was dressed for the sunny day in a white linen dress and floppy sun hat. On anxious feet, she wore caramel leather sandals that covered the worst of her ballerina battle wounds.

Dancers like her were not known for their pretty feet.

Mina had dropped her off only minutes before Emmett texted that he was just parking. Illiana fidgeted with her bracelet, twisting the silver circlet about her wrist.

It was seconds later when Illiana caught sight of Emmett, her gaze zeroing in on him like a magnet. Attracted and unable to pull away. Her heart leapt into her throat, thrumming there, while those dancing butterflies suddenly learned acrobatics.

He approached her, his gait sure and effortless. He wore a white button down with several of the top buttons undone and the sleeves rolled to three quarters. It was virtually the sluttiest and hottest thing a man could wear, and it had all of Illiana's blood going. She suddenly felt those butterflies lower in her body, fluttering as she watched his powerful thighs move in his fitted black pants.

Yes.

Extremely slutty.

The only thing that would have put her over the edge would have been if he'd decided to wear one of those regency era blouses, soaking wet, sticking to his—

She stopped herself from daydreaming when Emmett arrived before her, an endearing white smile spread across his face. Just for her.

"Hello, stranger," he said warmly, running a tanned hand through his loose black waves. "How was the rest of your night?"

He knew exactly what her night was like. He'd been texting her into the wee hours of the morning. They'd bantered back and forth, Emmett sending pictures of his dogs and Illiana cooing over them, her teasing him about secretly being an author. She knew he wasn't, but it was fun to play.

"It was scintillating," she replied with a soft smile. "I was talking to a man."

Emmett reached for her, tugging her by the hand against his chest. He smelled divine, like the lightest touch of woodsy cologne and musk. She wanted nothing more than to bury her nose against his neck and stay there. He brushed a lock of her blonde hair behind her ear, lightly cupping the side of her face.

"A man, you say?" he responded teasingly. "He must be quite the conversationalist to receive such glowing praise. *Scintillating.*"

"Mm," she demurred. "You'd hate him. He's in touch with his emotions, enjoys romances books, has these adorable dogs, and smells wonderful."

"Does he? Goodness, he sounds like a catch. How concerned should I be about my competition?"

"Oh, very. He's also quite the kisser."

"Care to compare?" His mouth graced over hers and she allowed the slightest pressure.

"Oh, he's incomparable." Illiana leaned forward, a delightfully coy smile on her mouth. "But a lady never kisses and tells."

Emmett tilted his head closer to hers, his breath ghosting over her lips. "Tease."

With that, he pulled away and intertwined their fingers. "Are you ready to go in?"

Illiana and Emmett perused the stalls, hand in hand. White tents stretched overhead, blocking out the worst of the sun. Illiana found herself drawn to the homemade syrups and instantly plucked up a bottle of blackberry. She exchanged money with the vendor, and they popped over to the next shop.

Together, the two of them brushed their non-holding hands over hand carved bookmarks of thinnest cedar. Emmett got himself a star patterned one and purchased a hollow floral one for Illiana.

"You didn't have to do that," she protested weakly.

"I know, but I wanted to."

They continued through the throng of people, music played by a live band filtered about the air, and the scent of deep-fried mini donuts saturated Illiana's mind. Against her better—which was actually an unhealthy—judgement, she dragged Emmett over to the mini donuts.

"One order, please!" Illiana said to the food truck worker.

Within seconds, a hot, oily bag of cinnamon sugar goodness was foisted into Illiana's hands. She inhaled the scent deeply before plucking out the fried dough and taking the most delicate of nibbles.

It was divine.

Illiana decided not to think too much on the calorie, fat, carbohydrate, or sugar content, but rather on the delightful taste exploding across her tongue. She bit down on a moan as she took another bite and suddenly realized she felt Emmett's eyes on her.

Self-consciously, she glanced up at him and found his warm brown eyes locked on her lips. He held his body in a tight position, his muscles rigid, arms tense at his sides.

"What?" she asked after swallowing a mouthful of donut.

A muscle feathered in his jaw and he rolled his lips between his teeth. "That sou—" he began before pivoting. "You have sugar on your lip."

"Oh!" Illiana blushed, going to move to brush the evidence of her indulgence away.

"Let me," Emmett said, and suddenly his thumb was on the luscious swell of her lower lip.

She felt the pad of his thumb, slightly roughened, on her mouth, caressing away the fine granules. Even after she felt all the evidence disappear, he continued the slow, sultry slide of his thumb. Illiana's mouth popped open and she could see the thought in his eyes as clearly as it crossed her mind. She wanted to wrap her tongue around that digit, to slip it into her mouth, and let him imagine that sensation on other areas of his anatomy.

But before she could act on the impulse, he was pulling away. To her shock, he licked the sugar from his finger. Watching her. Her heart thundered.

"D—do you want one?" she asked to distract her horny thoughts, extending the white paper bag to Emmett.

His lips twisted into a smile. "Sure." He plucked up a mini donut and the two of them continued their stroll through the market.

"I have to tell you something," Illiana blurted.

"You're married," Emmett guessed, deadpan.

"No, no of course not."

"Then whatever it is will be fine with me."

Illiana fought a smile at the comfort and ease he placed her in. Instead, she drew in a breath. "I'm only here for vacation, but there's a chance I could stay."

Emmett halted them in their tracks and he searched her face. She saw earnestness in his features, and she wondered what he saw in hers.

"I just wanted it to be clear," she continued. "I didn't want to start whatever this is with a time limit hanging over our heads."

"You said there's a chance you'll stay?"

"There's a chance, yes."

"Then let's not worry about it right now. If it's not a sure thing either way. Let's enjoy whatever this is we have and decide when it's time."

"You're wonderful," she said softly, not fighting the grin this time.

"I try." Emmett continued walking and then tossed her a teasing look.

"What you do you want it to be?"

"Let's go at your pace for now."

"So, can we call this a fling?"

"We can call this a fling, or we can leave it unlabeled until we're ready."

"Sounds perfect to me."

"So, since that hiccup is out of the way, we should get the rest of the big questions answered. Don't want to fall into the tragic miscommunication or missed-important-discussion tropes."

"Wouldn't that be the worst?"

"The absolute worst." Emmett tapped his chin in a reenactment of thinking. "Do you want kids?"

"Wow, jumping to the heaviest one first, huh?"

Emmett shrugged. "I feel like that stance isn't something people should compromise on."

"That's fair." Illiana drew a breath and considered, walking up to a booth selling hand-made grow-with-me pants for babies and toddlers. Her eyes were drawn to a pair patterned with bumblebees and she touched the bee she had tattooed on her chest fondly, smiling. "Yeah, I do think I want them one day. For so long, I didn't think it was going to be possible with my career—" she cut herself off, turning from the baby clothes. "Probably one or two."

Emmett nodded, thankfully not asking her to expand on the comment about her career. "I feel the same. Kids are a huge commitment, but it's something I've been feeling more strongly about lately."

"Noted. Do you want to get married?"

"Absolutely."

It went on like that, life events and political views, gender roles and social views, both of them sharing similar sentiments and when they differed, they were minor things. It was her opinion that these conversations were important to have early on, especially to save any heartache later on. Eventually, it devolved into simpler preferences like sweet or savory and cat-person or dog-person.

"Well, considering I have two dogs, it would be an insult to them to say I prefer otherwise," Emmett joked as they neared the end of the market, having picked up a few more items during their discussions.

"I used to have a cat," Illiana answered haltingly, "until my ex took him. But even then, I'm still more of a dog-person. I love having dogs around."

"Would you want to meet mine?"

"Sure, when?"

"Right now?"

Illiana cocked a brow and laughed. "This is the way you get me to come to your house and into your bed?"

Emmett flushed furiously with mortification. "That wasn't my intention."

Illiana continued giggling. "It's okay. I'd love to meet your dogs. Let's go."

They left the market together and Illiana shot off a text to Mina letting her know she was going over to Emmett's place. Mina's response consisted of several emojis including an eggplant, side eye, a drooling face, some finger movements, and a pink heart.

Fuck off, she wrote back jokingly.

Make sure he wraps it! Mina texted back with a kiss emoji.

Illiana rolled her eyes as she climbed into Emmett's SUV, delightful butterflies circling her belly. She didn't know for certain what the evening's plans were; however, she did want to experience a summer fling and it seemed she was perfectly on track.

How had she gotten so lucky as to have stumbled upon this man she connected so well with? She gravitated to him; he consumed her. Her thoughts were saturated with him.

When Emmett got in the driver's seat, Illiana immediately sensed the virtual vibration of his frame, the way excitement flared beneath his skin. Her eyes followed the strong line of his arm, tracing the black ink that covered it, all the way to his fingers and the way he gripped the wheel. She could see him carefully curving around, flexing, and Illiana had the startling thought that for a mechanic, he had beautiful hands.

Not beauty in the traditional sense, but in the way a ballerina was—through hard work and beneath cuts and blisters. His fingers were long and graceful, but covered in signs of manual labor all over them.

"Do you want to send your friend my address?" he asked her as he shoulder-checked before making a turn. He rattled off the numbers and street name in Rose Point.

She thought she should be surprised that he lived in the same small town as the Ellis family, but truthfully, she didn't know how common it was coming from a big city.

"Either this is a romance book and you're being the dreamy, considerate love interest, or a thriller and you're the charismatic villain who's taking me to get tied up in your basement."

Emmett laughed. "I prefer the first option." He cast her a sidelong look that had heat flooding through her blood. "And if we discuss tying up, it won't be in the basement."

That heat turned into an open flame as everything in her became absolutely ablaze and awash with desire. Illiana ducked her head as she sent Mina the address, staring at her phone and willing the arousal to vacate her bloodstream.

She tucked the phone beneath her thigh and shook her hair out. The blonde strands tickled her neck and she was acutely aware of the leather seat beneath her bare legs—the way it stuck to her.

Mere minutes later and they were pulling up to a house of white, with cedar accents and black trim. It was gorgeous.

She stared at the fence and the metal detailing of the same Indigenous art that wound up Emmett's arm. As soon as they pulled in the drive, she saw two snouts nose apart the curtains, a sliver of fawn wrinkles and a taller one with brown fur apparent. Illiana scrubbed her hands on her white sundress, trying to vanish the perspiration on her palms as Emmett shut off the engine. She took a deep breath as they got out.

Casting her a shy smile, Emmett led Illiana up the pathway to the front door, sorting through his keys. With his other, he held it out extended. She blushed with several mixed emotions and took it. Her heart felt like it was about to beat out of her chest; her skin was heated—both from the sun bearing down and the thrill of what was to come within this house.

Suddenly, realizing she'd been lost in her own thoughts, she heard the exuberant sounds of claws on hardwood and excited panting. Emmett was softly greeting his dogs who were turning themselves in circles for his affections. He scrubbed a hand through their shiny coats as they continued their wiggling.

Illiana crouched down and immediately the short and pudgy bulldog caught sight of her and barrelled over. She caught him softly with an oath of surprise, but he weighted more than she anticipated and she lost her balance toppling onto her bottom, dog following.

"Gimli!" Emmett exclaimed, aghast.

Emmett rushed over and prodded Gimli away before taking Illiana's forearm and assisting her to her feet. Due to her operated-on foot, she over-compensated and ended up stumbling into Emmett. He caught her yet again, arms going around her. She could feel the heat of his chest beneath her hands, the hammering of his heart that matched the tempo of her own. She glanced up through her eyelashes, meeting his dark eyes. Her mouth gently popped open and the heat in them—the lust in them.

"Your dog must have been hired," she quipped softly.

"Whoever they are, I should pay them more." His fingers tightened on her waist.

"Is this the part where your other dog bumps into us and pushes us even closer?"

"Leia would never. She's a princess and chores are beneath her."

Something struck Illiana with astounding clarity at the word *princess,* and delight swept through her. "Gimli and Leia…You're a closet nerd."

One of Emmett's hands coasted up her back and tangled with the hair at the nape of her neck. "Oh, there's no closet, sweetheart. I wear my nerdiness with pride."

Illiana tossed her head back and laughed, utterly melting into this man—*this man!* "*Star Wars!*"

"Don't forget *The Lord of the Rings.*"

"You can't be real—who is the woman who wrote you?"

"I *was* raised by two women and a sister, likely that explains it."

"Partially. But I have to confess—I've never seen any of the movies; I just know the Pop Culture references."

Emmett feigned shock. "We're going to remedy that today, Ana. And of course, we'll put the movies on, but under the guise of watching the show, we'll just get closer…" he tugged her firmly against his body. "And closer…" Another tug and she was fully flush against him, even feeling a thrilling *something* beginning to press against her. "Until we throw away all the pretenses and I have you in my lap."

"I thought you didn't bring me here for that?" she chided.

"I didn't. I'm just following the course we're on."

"I thought we didn't have to fall into the tropes."

Emmett shrugged. "I might press them when they're to my advantage."

She shook her head, biting her lip. "I can't fault that logic."

"I am still a man," he whispered heatedly, pressing his mouth to her jaw. "And you, sweetheart, are a dream." His mouth coasted across her skin, nipping at the hinge of her jaw.

A slight sound escaped her, and she responded breathily. "Then don't let me be the one to stop the plans."

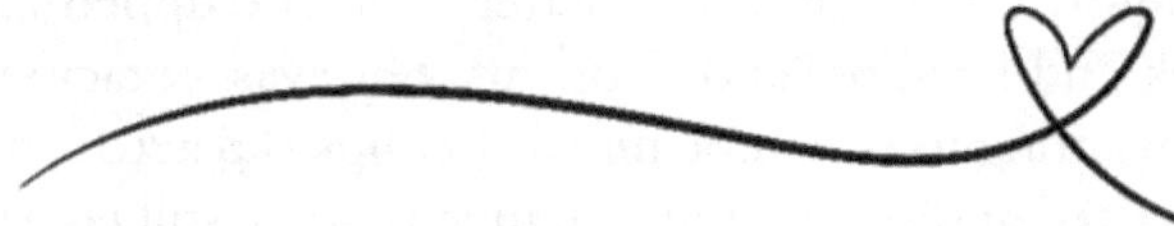

As predicted, the movies were queued up, put on, and immediately disregarded. The prequels were playing, but Illiana was toying with Emmett's hand. Soon, those small ministrations changed and her fingers were skirting up his forearm, over the bold ink. Emmett's hand meanwhile, was tracing the linen edge of her dress, fingertips brushing her thighs in a way that had her clenching and wanting to part them wide. He kept up that slow decadent back and forth—like petting; smooth strokes.

Illiana knew where this night was destined to end—she'd already decided a while ago, as early as the morning when she'd put on matching underwear. It was a summer fling. It was what she'd come here for.

Gimli and Leia slept soundly on the opposite end of the couch, perhaps sensing where this was going and wanted no part of it.

The movie droned on in the background, but it was all a buzz. Illiana was electrified as she shifted closer. Emmett did the same. Her fingers were now gliding over his biceps, tracing over his shirt. His were sliding just beneath her dress.

She had zero intentions of letting him stop.

Over the span of the next few breaths those gentle touches turned more insistent and his fingertips turned gripping. Illiana shifted, seeking friction, her own fingers grabbing. Desire swept through her before she mentally said "fuck it" and she swung her leg over and straddled Emmett.

His hands immediately locked on her hips, rocking her against his lap. Illiana's fingers found the nape of his neck, tangling in the loose strands that escaped from his topknot. Her white dress was hitched up, his hands grazing the pink lace of her thong.

Before she could think better of it, she tipped Emmett's head back and her lips landed on his. She was voracious in her appetite, wanting to consume him as her lips slid across his. Their mouths parted and their tongues danced—they still tasted of cinnamon sugar from the donuts. A soft sound slipped from her throat and Emmett chased it, seeking more as a delectable groan escaped him. She pressed her passion into him and as she broke for breath, Emmett seemed addicted to her and his mouth coasted down her jaw, her throat, his hot mouth leaving sensual heat in its wake.

One of his hands went up her waist and cupped her breast over her dress. She felt her nipples harden to points beneath his attention and all she wanted was his mouth on them, his hands kneading her.

"More," she rasped as she grinded on him.

Emmett's hand slipped from her hip and dipped his fingers into the waistband of her panties below her belly button, a breath away from where she was so desperate for him. She could feel wetness on the lace, frustrating her. She was utterly *aching* for his fingers inside her.

"How much more?" he finally responded.

"I don't know."

He froze.

"No," she whined, seeking him. "Don't stop."

"I just need your boundaries, Ana."

Her nickname on his tongue had her licking her lips. "Besides this just being physical, I don't know what they are."

One of his brows rose. "You're not a v—"

"No," she cut him off. "No, it's just all been very…vanilla."

Emmett's hand cupped her jaw. "Vanilla isn't always a bad thing."

"I want more, though," she admitted. "And I want—I want to come."

"Did your previous partners never get you there?"

"Some. But not many. Definitely not my most recent ex."

Emmett worked his jaw, a muscle feathering there. He met her eyes and matched her heat. "What do you want, sweetheart?"

"I want to take this upstairs."

He kissed her and smiled against her mouth. "Say less."

In one fluid motion, Emmett stood and wrapped Illiana's legs around his waist. She let out a surprised yelp as he palmed her bare ass, free, courtesy of the thong. He carried her away from the couch—away from the movie—and effortlessly took them both to the staircase. Without sight—his face buried at the crook of her neck—he managed to navigate the stairs with ease, and Illiana's heart hammered in response.

This was happening. They were doing this. God, it had been so long since she'd had sex, and even longer since a man gave her a climax. She had no reservations that Emmett could get the job done—he read romance books for fuck's sake.

He walked down a hallway and at the end he pushed open a door. Cool air rushed against her skin from an air conditioning unit, and she shivered for more than one reason. Depositing her on the bed, she bounced against the gray coverlet and leaned back on her hands, knees bent. Emmett watched her, eyes devouring, and with boldness, she parted her thighs.

Emmett looked like a man in pain. He took an involuntary step toward her and she could only imagine what he saw. Her long slender legs, firm thighs, pastel pink lace, and arousal that was surely coloring her underwear. As he approached the end of the bed, his eyes flickered and he caught sight of her foot. She flinched as his eyes locked on the scars, a question in them.

"It was broken, so I had surgery. I don't want to talk much more about it."

"All right," he whispered. Then resumed his visual devouring.

Soon, that visual turned physical and Emmett's hands found her ankles, cuffing them. He traced his hands up her calves, beneath her knees. Then his lips followed. A soft gasp left Illiana's throat and then her head flopped back against the bed, the scent of clean laundry and Emmett's amber woods scent enveloping her.

"Is this good?" he whispered against her skin, his hands on her thighs, his lips at the underside of her knee.

"Definitely good."

"Tell me if I do anything you don't like."

"Noted," she gasped as his hands found her underwear, fingertips dipping beneath the lace and to her bare pussy.

Before she'd left Toronto, she'd gotten sugared and removed virtually every bit of hair from her body. Her preference typically was hairless, but she'd gotten *everything* done in anticipation for *this*.

He hooked a single digit against the crotch of her underwear and tugged it aside, baring her for his eyes only. She bit her lip and stared up at the lazily spinning ceiling fan, begging for his next touch.

Emmett's nose coursed up the inside of her thigh and she let them drop open even further. His breath brushed against the most intimate part of her and she whimpered, rolling her hips.

"Still okay?"

"Yes. Please," she begged.

The next second, his tongue slid against the seam of her and she gasped.

"Fuck, sweetheart. You taste so good."

She was melting. Utterly fucking melting beneath Emmett.

Tugging the material aside further, his mouth returned to her and he laved up her center before swirling his tongue against her clit. She thought she would perish on the spot from the divine torment. He flicked his tongue against that bundle of nerves and she couldn't help it when her hand shot to his head, fisting in his hair and urging him against her. He understood and acquiesced to her demands and then pulled her clit into his mouth and *sucked*.

She was going to reach nirvana.

He neatly tugged her panties fully to the side and then shoved her dress up around her waist. Emmett's palm flattened on her stomach, holding her down as his other hand found her entrance. A finger slipped inside and then he curled it.

An orgasm immediately started building.

She'd never had a man find that spot on her. Her previous partners—few as they'd been—had simply pumped a finger inside her as if they were trying to press some mysterious button within her. But *Emmett*—he knew what to do.

Illiana began bucking against his touch, seeking more, chasing that building release. She felt it coiling low in her belly as Emmett's mouth alternated between flicking and sucking. It was so good and pressure was building.

Suddenly, a flood of wetness gushed out of her and she immediately tried to clamp her legs closed in shock and withdrew her hand from his head.

Emmett pulled away from her, his lips wet from his pleasuring of her while his finger still pumped and curled inside her. Liquid lust burned in his eyes.

"I didn't know you were a squirter, Ana."

"A wh—? I didn't know."

A satisfied smirk crossed his mouth. "Happy to have treated you to this experience then. It's very hot, Ana."

"Your bed—" she protested.

"Will be fine. I'll deal with it when I'm finished with you."

And then he returned to his efforts.

Illiana crossed an arm over her eyes while her other hand once again tangled in his dark waves, pushing him against her pussy as she begged for release. It was mere breaths later and she felt the orgasm right on the edge, taking her to the precipice.

"Oh, Emmett. Oh, I'm going to come."

He sucked her clit hard into his mouth, and she shattered.

Illiana came with a breathy cry, hips undulating against Emmett as she rode the waves. The climax was intense, sublime, and incandescent. When she came down from the high, her chest was heaving with the breaths she drew, legs wobbly from the intensity.

Emmett crawled up the bed and she realized he was still fully dressed. Then with a start she realized that she *also* was still fully dressed. He hovered over her and Illiana's heart raced.

"Is that enough, or would you like more?" he murmured, dipping to her throat and kissing the crook of her neck. Her eyes rolled back in her head and electricity shot straight down to her clit, already eager for another orgasm.

"More. So much more."

"Then allow me to oblige."

Emmett pulled Illiana to sit and helped tug her dress off. It came over her head and they tossed it aside, and as soon as it was gone, her hands went to his shirt and yanked it from his body. Her hands eagerly touched his chest, over the tattoo of some kanji over his heart, down the center of him and over his muscled abdomen. His muscles weren't aggressively defined, but they were strong and he was built. Her fingers traced down, tucking down into his belt. She worked it free, and then she went for the button.

"You're a very attractive man, Emmett," Illiana whispered as she popped it free and went for his zipper.

"The greatest compliment from a virtual goddess."

Illiana positively glowed from his awe.

As she was slipping his pants down his hips, he halted her with a hand.

"Are condoms okay?"

"They're great," she returned.

He allowed her to continue and helped her free him from his pants. Now, they kneeled together, his black boxer-briefs betraying his very potent, very hard arousal. Illiana reached out and palmed him, skimming down his contained erection. He was heavy and thick without being terrifyingly so. He hissed pleasure in response and she giggled as she repeated the action.

"Fuck, Ana. You're going to make me come just like this."

Taking pity on him, she pushed the shorts down, only to free him and immediately take his shaft in hand, pumping him from base to tip. He groaned and sagged against her, his brow at her neck, hands twisting in her panties.

"These need to come off," he said with clenched teeth as she pumped him again.

"Then what are you waiting for? Permission? You have it."

Emmett pushed her down and faster than she could blink, he was dragging that soaked lace off of her. He flung them to the floor and gazed at her.

"You're so beautiful. But fuck is this pussy pretty. I can't wait to ruin you for anyone else."

Illiana thought she was turned on before, but that possessiveness…arousal surged through her blood and her skin heated. She needed him—now.

Together, Illiana removed his briefs while his deft fingers worked the fastenings from her bra, casting them both aside. Emmett moved her up the bed and notched himself between her legs, his pelvis flush against hers, the short hair on his legs tickling.

"If I do anything that you don't like, or hurts you, please let me know."

"I'm not as fragile as I look," she responded, blue eyes darkening with wanton yearning. "I like to be handled a bit roughly. Do you understand what I mean?"

"Loud and clear."

"Good."

Emmett lunged for her, mouth crashing against hers. Their tongues slipped against each other and she could taste herself on him, and it made her core clench. Too soon, his mouth slipped from hers and trailed down her, this time nipping as he went, on her collarbones, down her breast, before he found one of her nipples and dragged it between his teeth.

Illiana thrust her hips upward, legs bracketing him as he flicked his tongue against that hard tip and wrapped his lips around it. His hand slid up to the other and he rubbed the neglected nipple between his thumb and forefinger, squeezing. She bit her lip and reached down for his cock, pumping him. He thrust into her hand and she could feel him throb from her.

"Condom?" she asked, as if it was a magic trigger word.

It acted as such and Emmett reached over her to the nightstand, opened a drawer and reached in. The crackle of the packaging met her ears as he tore it open and smoothly rolled it down his perfect length. As if testing her, he slid two fingers within her center and curved them once to find her dripping wet and ready. She bucked and mewled, loving his invasion. In one smooth motion, he hitched her knee up high on his side and lined himself up with her entrance before sinking into her.

Illiana moaned and tossed her head back as Emmett began to thrust into her, every pump seating him a little further inside her. Her pussy kept taking him, and he kept filling her. She was spread before him as he kneeled above, eyes glassy with desire. His one hand cupped her ass, holding it to keep her leg at his side, while the other reached for her breast, thumbing the nipple. Her gasp of pleasure ignited something within him and he increased his pace as he sank to the hilt. Illiana could do nothing but grab at the sheets and twist them in her fingers, as Emmett delivered undiluted bliss to her.

He was so thick and filled her so well, hitting that divine spot within her. She chased his thrusts to create their symphony, the rhythm a learned song as they fucked. Emmett hiked her leg higher to his shoulder, spreading her wide, that newly freed hand going to her clit and rubbing small, firm circles there. She shuddered and more wetness covered them, the pressure ratcheting up.

"My girl," Emmett practically purred. "Tell me—are you mine?"

"All yours—fuck," Illiana groaned as he changed the tempo just so that new arousal surged.

"Good girl."

Her building orgasm crested and blasted through her without warning. She didn't have a breath to do anything but rasp his name as the climax roared down her spine, fireworks igniting behind her eyes, her mind blanking—seeing, thinking, smelling, sensing nothing but Emmett and the feel of his skin, the scent of amber woods, the way his cock slid in and out of her with rolling thrusts. It was all him. Him and her. She'd never felt this connection with anyone.

Illiana shuddered as she came down from the high, clit over sensitized from Emmett's attentions. He shifted the hand that was playing with those nerves to the smooth expanse of her skin, skimming over her ribs, the soft underside of her breasts. Wrapping an arm around her waist, he shifted her leg from his shoulder to his side and picked her up. And as if she weighed nothing, he held her to his front and continued driving in and out of her.

Her lust-addled eyes met his, her breasts crushed to his chest. As her mouth popped open in surprise, from everything about this lovemaking, Emmett leaned forward and captured her lips. The gentle, lingering kiss was such a juxtaposition from the possessive thrusts.

"*Ana*," he groaned as he came, lifting her and pushing her down his length with the last throes of his passion.

Illiana sank against him, he curved over her, still seated inside. Her breaths were wild, she'd never made love like that before. She'd never had anyone have her reach two climaxes in a session—one was enough of a rarity. But he knew if she needed more on her clit, where within her to press, she'd never known anyone to be so…*aware* of her needs.

"Is it presumptuous for me to request we keep doing this?" Emmett asked against her throat.

Illiana laughed. "I was hoping you'd ask that."

They continued the day like that, interspersed with efforts to watch the movies and breaks to eat. As well as a few message updates to let Mina know she hadn't been killed or kidnapped. Many emoji filled and lewd texts followed. Today Illiana allowed her to indulge in some of the foods she normally didn't allow herself—she justified that their very enthusiastic sex was enough to burn it off. It was the third round where Illiana was riding him, his hand fisted at the nape of her neck, laving her chest with hot kisses that a thought struck her.

She didn't want to let him go.

She didn't want this—whatever it was—to end.

She was in a word—many words—fucked.

Later, sated and tangled together naked in his bedding—that true to his word he'd laundered after the first round, as well as her underwear. AC drifted across them, the sun sinking below the horizon, as Emmett gazed down at her.

"Spend the night with me?"

Illiana smiled softly and brushed back a tendril of his hair—his topknot utterly destroyed—wrapping it around her finger. "Mm, really?"

"Please," he responded, kissing her fingers. "Stay with me."

"Well, how could I resist? Especially when there's a vicious rainstorm outside,"—she gestured to the clear sky beyond the window—"and—oh no—there's only one bed! The tension!"

Emmett chuckled and cradled her, rolling her beneath him. "Whatever will they do to keep warm? There's no wood for a fire. And oh my, their clothes are all wet, they're going to have to take them off to keep warm." He tugged her close. "Stave off the hypothermia, and all."

She touched his chest and felt lower. "Wow, you work fast. Our clothes have vanished."

"I'm a man of many talents."

"Mm, don't I know."

She traced his lips with a finger and he kissed them.

"Are you sure you're real?" she whispered. "You feel good to be true."

"I was thinking the same thing."

CHAPTER TEN

Emmett

He woke up next to a dream come true.

Beside him was an absolute goddess.

All he wanted to do was consume himself in her, devour her, taste her, lick her. Utterly have her

But alas, he could not because he had to work.

Emmett gazed down at Ana sleeping peacefully against his pillows—in his bed—golden hair in a sunshine spray on his pillows, gray blanket just barely covering her chest and those breasts he'd touched and kissed only hours ago.

Quietly, he slipped from the bed and padded over to his discarded sweatpants, pulling them on before shutting the door quietly behind him. He descended the stairs, the perfect afterglow in his wake, with the mind of keeping up with the most obvious cliché after a night rife with pleasure and fucking.

Jesus, he'd fucked Ana. Made love to her. And God, if it wasn't the best he'd ever had. Her sounds…

He had to readjust himself as he made his way into the kitchen.

There, he grabbed ingredients from the fridge and a bowl, whipping together the only recipe for pancakes he'd ever known. Carefully, he poured the batter onto the griddle and formed hearts—was it cute? Corny? Cringey? He didn't know, but he was doing it anyway.

Bacon went into the oven on a foil-lined sheet—he knew she wasn't a vegetarian, but she did seem to have some qualms with certain foods. He'd mentally catalogued it, sensing there were some reservations she had about her body's appearance.

He didn't presume to know, but she was beautiful—lithe and graceful, perhaps even on the lower side of slender. In a perfect world, she'd see herself as he saw her. He didn't care for what shape she was; he'd dated a variety of women with various different body types, and it had never mattered to him—scars or stretch marks; none of it.

As he was finishing up the pancakes, he heard the gentle pad of footsteps behind him and glanced back to find Ana standing there at the entrance to the kitchen, golden hair sex tousled and *fuck*—his white button down on her and completely open. He could see the small swells of her breasts between it and the flash of her sweet pink underwear.

It took everything in him not to pick her up and have her right there.

And then on the counter.

The thoughts raced through his mind, the fantasy vivid and visceral.

"Good morning, sweetheart."

"Morning," she replied shyly, ruffling her hair. She plucked at her—his—shirt. "I hope this is okay."

"It's more than okay," he told her, a hint of possessive desire in his tone.

She blushed. "I hoped so. It's a cliché, but it's a good one for a reason."

Emmett crossed the threshold and swept her up, kissing her with all the warmth and desire he could summon. Fuck, she tasted of strawberries and cream and sex. He wanted to bottle it up and have it every day.

"If we had time before work," he murmured against her lips. "I'd have you again right now."

She smiled back and kissed him. "Pity that you can't."

He tangled their tongues together once again, hands coasting down her spine, feeling every knob he'd memorized yesterday and last night. He tilted his head, deepening the kiss. He couldn't get enough—he was utterly addicted.

"I made you breakfast, but I have to work. Feel at home and let yourself out whenever, I can pay for a taxi, and text me when you're safe." He kissed her and paused. "Unless you'd like me to take you somewhere."

"No. I'd like to eat. I can get my friend to pick me up. I might steal a shower."

"Steal away."

"Great, I'm kind of fond of that rainfall head. You won't miss it when I take it with me, will you?"

He laughed. "It's yours."

"Perfect." She sealed the deal with a kiss.

When he left, he did so completely not wanting to. He had an angel in his house—a golden glowing goddess—and he wasn't there. It was a crime. It was *insanity*. Ana consumed his thoughts as he drove to work, mind trained on her when he should have been mentally ordering the day's schedule.

When he got to the shop, he couldn't focus and his employees noticed. More than one brow was raised at the obvious ease in his step. They'd made some assumptions—correct ones—and snickered. It was when Ana finally texted him that she was home safe that he relaxed. A photo—poorly edited—of his showerhead in her hand followed.

Thanks for the head.

He nearly choked on his laughter.

This girl was going to ruin him.

The next day Emmett had beer with the guys. He and Ana had been texting intermittently throughout the day before and of, back and forth jokes and deep conversations, the dialogue of which flowed seamlessly into each other. He was jittery, anxious, constantly checking his phone for an update from her.

At his usual table, Nate slid in next to him.

"You're perky, babe," Nate jostled him. "Have something to share with the class?"

Emmett grinned and flipped the phone face down. "I never kiss and tell."

"Oh bullshit. Fuckin' tell me. Who is she?"

He knew a dreamy look crossed his face from the way Nate groaned. "Oh man, you're fucked already."

"Certainly am," he said, innuendo on his tongue.

"You sly dog." He held up his beer in cheers. "So, it was the girl from the bar the other night?"

"It was."

"Hell yeah, man. I'm happy for you."

Emmett looked down shyly. "I'm happy for me too. She's just…incredible."

"You going to see her again?"

"I really hope so."

Nate cocked a brow, humor in his green eyes. "Is it serious?"

Emmett hesitated. That's one thing he and Ana hadn't discussed further. For now, they were calling it a fling, but he wanted to renegotiate it, though at the same time he didn't want to scare her off with this intensity and lose this wonderful thing between them after two dates.

The label wasn't adequate; he knew his feelings, and he knew for himself that he was smitten, so to Ana he was exclusive, whether or not she felt the same way and if she wanted to do as she pleased that was her prerogative.

"We haven't gotten that far yet. I think it is for me."

"Well, that's something then, isn't it? Have you found out her name? Or have you just been calling her pet names and hoping she slips up?"

Emmett brightened. "Ana. And there's nothing wrong with pet names."

"Mmhmm," Nate murmured against his beer. "Excuses."

"Oh, enough with excuses. How are things with Illiana?"

This time it was Nate's turn to brighten. "I think I'm going to ask her out tonight."

"Really? Hell yeah. What are you planning?"

"I…" Nate hesitated. "I don't actually know. What do you think?"

Emmett shrugged. "I'm not sure. Ice cream? The beach? A picnic? Depends if you're going out day or night. Or in or out."

Nate scrubbed his jaw, debating. "I guess I'll have to ask her and go from there."

Just then Kieran and Graham arrived, shoving shoulders playfully, drinks in hand.

"Seems like Emmett has found the one, boys!" Nate called out.

A set of cheers went up and Kieran looked on with a glimmer of—something—in his eyes. Like happiness and relief. It was subtle, but Emmett had known him long enough that he could see it. He mentally filed it away for later inquiry.

Emmett imagined that maybe he was feeling the same way as Nate had, feeling behind—because honestly, who wasn't feeling that way with the constantly stress from society? The push, the need, the demand to be more, to hustle, to have a side hustle. The obsession with productivity and furthering yourself all for the greed of money and wealth.

Emmett shook himself from the thoughts and returned to his friends.

"No Chase tonight?"

Graham shook his head. "Had some clients late, says he's sorry but will meet us next time."

"Well, at least that means Jace won't be joining—thank fuck," Kieran chimed in.

They all drank to that.

"Do you think he'll ever grow out of that shitty attitude of his?" Graham asked.

"There's hope—he's like twenty-one or twenty-two. Maybe a girl will come around and put him in his place," Kieran answered.

"Wouldn't that be a show?"

"I'd kill to be a fly on the wall when it happens."

"Em." Nate elbowed him. "Eyes on you at ten o'clock."

Emmett glanced over as directed and sure enough, there was a blonde eyeing him up—but not the blonde he wanted. His eyes met hers briefly and then her green gaze flickered to the rest of the men at the table, a suggestive question in them. Emmett turned away without indulging her interest.

"I don't think she means me specifically, Nate," Emmett said. "But even if she did, I wouldn't be interested."

"You're actually serious, aren't you?"

Emmett took a drink of his beer. "As a heart attack."

CHAPTER ELEVEN
Illiana

Illiana was sitting at the kitchen island of the Ellis's main house, flipping through the book Emmett got her, fingers skimming the pages with the memory of their touches. She was trying to read and ignore the demanding desire to check her phone. She was biding her time, waiting for Mina while she FaceTimed David just outside the glass doors overlooking the lake.

The sound of the front door opening caught her attention, and Illiana craned her neck to see Nate walking through the door. He gave her a beaming smile and crossed the threshold to her.

"Hey there," Nate said, leaning against the island next to her. "How's it going?"

She returned the pleasantries and tucked her phone into the book, serving as a bookmark and to hide the evidence of her messages. She wanted to keep Emmett a secret a little longer.

Nate poured himself some water and then returned to his post at the island. "Can I ask you a question?"

"Sure," Illiana said with surprise, turning her attention to him. Definitely not on her hidden phone. "What is it?"

"Would you be interested in going out sometime?"

A slight flare of panic rushed through her veins, but she quelled it and schooled her features so it didn't show. She wasn't in a relationship with Emmett, but she had the feeling dating someone else would be crossing a boundary—both hers and his.

"In what way? Like a date or as friends?"

Nate seemed to waver with her response. "Any way you want."

Illiana contemplated his offer, trying to navigate the waters of this friendship. Mixing things with her best friend's cousin was muddy, made muddier by whatever was between her and Emmett already—after only days. Nate was good looking but she didn't have that extra attraction for him.

He didn't give her that extra zing. Or butterflies, like she got with Emmett.

"Sure, we can hang out," she responded. "What were you thinking?"

"I have a half day at work tomorrow, want to get ice cream and go to the beach?"

"That sounds nice. Mina was actually going to meet me at the beach after she visited a high school friend if we all wanted to meet up instead?"

Nate seemed to hesitate, and Illiana sensed this wasn't the answer he wanted. She was pulled in multiple directions. She didn't see him that way, especially with her thoughts so consumed with someone else already. But she also didn't want to hurt his feelings, nor did she want to get his hopes up.

Fuck, this was getting messy.

"Sounds like a plan." He looked disappointed, but hid it well. "We'll go get ice cream together around noon and then the beach with Mina?"

"Yeah, that sounds good." Illiana hesitated, trying to make a balm on the hurt. "I'm looking forward to it."

The moment the words left her lips she immediately regretted it and cursed herself. Hope glowed in Nate's eyes.

"All right then." He patted the countertop and made to leave. "I'll talk to you later."

Nate left with a backwards glance, and Illiana looked down with a mix of flattery and shame.

Illiana was left with her thoughts and the memory of her recent conversation with Mina. The way she'd told her everything with Emmett, what he did to her, what he made her body discover it could do, what she even liked him doing. Mina was thrilled and demanded more detail. She was fanning herself and teasing, genuinely just encouraging her to pursue whatever it was and to have fun.

"I'm glad you're seeing someone. It's been too long since Adrian."

"Far too long," she'd confirmed. Adrian was the last person she'd been with sexually and he left little to be desired. "But we're more than making up for lost time, now."

Mina squealed and the two of them had descended into bouts of giggles and secrets.

Taking her from her memories, Mina stepped through the glass doors and Illiana opened her mouth to tell her about Nate's proposition before she froze, taking in her best friend's stunned features.

"What happened?" Illiana asked in concern, getting to her feet and rushing over.

"David was cheating on me."

"He what?"

"He flat out told me. Told me it had been going on for months and now with me away he realizes how much he just wants to be with her. He was…so aloof about it. Like he was just reading me a diagnosis. He didn't even feel bad."

"Oh, Mina. I'm so sorry." Illiana wrapped her arms around her best friend.

Mina shrugged. "I'm sad, but I'm not devastated. I didn't love him—we didn't know each other well enough for that—but shit, this kind of hurts." He blew out a breath. "Man, I'm bummed now."

"Do you want to do something? Get your mind off it?"

"Yeah, actually. Want to go out to Gloss?"

Illiana quirked a brow. "That pink club in Victoria?"

"Yeah, it could be fun."

"Okay, yeah. Why not?"

The two of them got ready in the pool house, Mina pulled on a gorgeous sage dress that clung to all her curves and dipped low between her breasts. She paired it with gold jewelry, an assortment of rings, necklace and hoops. Illiana, meanwhile, dressed in a slinky silver dress that swept down the length in holographic ripples, the back of which was completely open, the hem brushing the tops of her thighs. It was very short. Luckily, Emmett hadn't left any visible hickeys on her—to her intense surprise.

Both girls left their hair down and put on soft, dewy makeup. Touching up their nails before slipping on heels, they headed to their Uber.

Before they'd left, Illiana had insisted on drinking water because she was sure it would be quickly forgotten once they got to Gloss. However, she began to regret the hydration with the insistence in her bladder. As soon as they arrived, the hot pink lights of the club casted them in an effervescent glow, and they positively glittered. They were quickly ID'd, and let in, and Illiana immediately found the toilets.

They were surprisingly clean and the entire thing was bright, bubbly, pink.

As she was washing her hands she got a text. She dried her hands and grinned at the name.

Should I start this conversation with "what are you wearing?" or something more cliché?

Illiana smiled and then took a quick selfie, showing just the hint of the silver dress that she knew would make him wild. She bit her lip at the thought. She loved that power she held over him—already so soon. Though, if she were honest with herself, she knew he held a very similar sway over her.

Even though she felt so strongly, Illiana was conflicted. She couldn't just leave the province she grew up in for Emmett. What if this turned into something more and didn't work out and she was stuck here in an awkward limbo? It was the course all her other relationships had taken. No, the fling was fine.

Her phone vibrated.

I'm going to go with the classic cliché of: That dress looks amazing on you, but would look so much better on my floor.

You never know where the night will end, she replied. *Maybe you'll put it there.*

I will be awaiting your command. Say the word and I'm there.

Sorry, baby. She sent the term of endearment before she could second guess herself, then continued. *Girls night.* And added a kiss emoji to salve the wound.

She hesitated, lingering by the full-length mirror that was adorned with fake flowers of every riotous shade of pink before it faded to pastels and white.

Have fun. Be safe and let me know if you need anything. With a heart.

She tucked her phone away and exited the restroom and found Mina at the bar. There was a girl Illiana didn't recognize next to her, laughing, smiling, and throwing her arms around her. She approached, feet aching in her heels already, surgical site barking with pain.

Mina caught sight of her. "Ana!" she exclaimed happily. "Come here—this is one of my old friends from high school!"

Illiana sidled up to Mina as she took another shot. "Hi, I'm Illiana," she extended a hand out and the other girl took it.

She had long luxurious auburn red hair and pretty brown eyes, so light they were almost caramel. Her skin was a flawless shade of gold, as if she tanned entirely naked. She was more than pretty; she was stunning. Bronze makeup graced her features, giving her a beachy summery glow that was so complimentary to her soft features.

"Oh my gosh, you're so pretty! Jas has told me so much about you, but she didn't mention that you're fucking gorgeous."

Jas. Not Mina. Because Jas was her high school identifier until she decided she wanted to change it.

"Oh!" Illiana blushed. "Well, thank you, so are you. I, um, sorry I didn't catch your name."

Illiana was not going to live another introduction faux pas like with Emmett.

"Madeline!" she told her as the bartender slid a shot across the bar. She held it out. "Do you do shots?"

"Oh…oh, no I shouldn't."

"Okay! More for me then, girl!" Then she downed the liquor with a hiss and a shake of her head. "Ugh, I still hate tequila."

The bartender caught Illiana's eye. "Anything for you?"

Illiana debated quickly then caved to her wants. "Can I get a glass of Prosecco?"

"Coming right up."

Illiana's heart raced in her chest. She pushed down the regret and the thoughts of the scale and calorie counting and simply allowed herself to enjoy what she wanted. Her mother wasn't going to harp on her for the glass. She wasn't going to be told no one wants to see a pig dancing Swan Lake. Nor a whale performing The Nutcracker.

But hadn't she been indulging plenty?

She squandered that nefarious thought.

No, she was allowed to have small things. It was all about moderation.

The wine arrived and Illiana didn't allow herself any more questioning.

"So, the guy really just told you it was over? Like, just on a Facetime? Like it was nothing?"

"Yep," Mina confirmed, popping the P. "It sucks to be cheated on, but I wasn't that attached. Not yet at least."

"And what about Graham? Isn't he still single?"

Illiana quirked a brow. This implication was news.

Mina scoffed behind her cocktail. "Graham? As if! The guy loathes me and the feeling is mutual."

Madeline looked at her dubiously. "I find that hard to believe."

"Watch him interact with me once and you'll see it." A thought clearly struck her. "Oh, you'll see him at the Canada Day party—you have to come! Ana will be there, too!"

"Sure, why not? That way I can see for myself if you're blind as hell or this is all a misunderstanding."

"You're going to be disappointed, but okay." Mina took a sip of her drink. "I'll text you the details."

"Oh my God, speaking of disappointment! Did you hear Justin Grant and Lola Kennedy got engaged? They literally just broke up two marriages, and they're already heading to the altar! I mean, they haven't even signed the divorce papers yet."

Mina gasped. "No! Are you serious?"

"Totally! The affair was going on for like six months. And get this—Justin had a newborn at the time!"

"Trash. Utter trash."

"Right?"

Illiana nodded along with the conversation but suddenly felt very self conscious. Although Mina didn't mean it, Illiana felt cut off—cut out, like a third wheel. Awkwardly, she sipped her wine and tried to keep up; laughing when necessary, gaze cutting between the two of them trying to pay attention when she wasn't afforded any herself.

By the time Illiana finished her glass, Mina and Madeline were well into shots, and she was suddenly very grateful she'd convinced her best friend to hydrate beforehand because it was more than evident that no more was happening now.

"Look, Will Knowles is having a little get-together to-night—you two used to be close! Do you want to come?" Madeline flickered over to Illiana as if with a second thought. "You're welcome to join!"

Illiana felt that the invitation was genuine; however, there seemed like there was nothing Illiana wanted to do less.

"No, no I'm good. But you guys go, have fun! I'll catch an Uber."

Mina seemed to sober up momentarily. "I'll come home with you."

"No," Illiana insisted. "Go, have fun. You have your location shared?" Mina nodded and Illiana continued. "I'll keep an eye on you, just don't drive home. Stay there or catch a ride, all right?"

"What about you?"

Illiana waved her off. "I have someone I can call."

"You mean you have your man you can call." Mina waggled her eyebrows suggestively with her tongue out while her hips did a lewd shimmy.

"Oh, hush. But yes."

"I'll wait until he gets here then."

Illiana rolled her eyes but she was internally thankful. She texted Emmett asking him if he'd like to come pick her up and put that dress on the floor.

Be there in 20.

Illiana grinned and put her phone away. "He'll be here soon."

"So," Madeline inquired. "Who is this guy?"

"We didn't go to school with him, if that's what you're asking."

Madeline pouted. "Damn. I'm nosy. I wanted to know."

"Just know the man is—" Mina shook her head and bit her lip. "Very good looking."

"Oh, I *have* to see him."

"You two are worse than men."

Mina pretended to plunge a dagger into her heart. "A devastating blow."

Illiana simply stuck out her tongue.

A few minutes later her phone went off.

Here.

Illiana wrapped Mina in a hug and pecked her on the cheek. "He's here, please stay with Madeline, and if anything changes—*please* text me."

"I will," Mina said, returning the embrace and kiss. "Love you."

"Love you, too," she said untangling from her best friend. She turned to Madeline. "It was nice to meet you, take care of her."

"You've got it, girly. Go get some."

She smiled and rolled her eyes, cutting through the pink lights of the club.

"Practice safe sex!" Mina yelled across the space.

Illiana didn't turn around but held up her hand, phone still clutched in the other, and gifted her the middle finger.

Mina's cackling laugh followed her out.

The dense heat of the June night sunk into her as she stepped out of the club and onto the sidewalk, small groups vaping and mingling the required distance from the exits. In the small parking lot, Emmett's large SUV stood out in stark relief against a lamppost, illuminated to a blinding ebony shine. Emmett himself leaned against the hood, arms crossed over his broad chest, watching her with hunger. His white T-shirt showed off that body she so enjoyed touching, the one that had delivered her unimaginable pleasure.

"Hey there, stranger," she greeted coyly, walking across the lot to him.

"Hi, sweetheart," he returned, striding over to her and gathering her in his arms. He kissed her and groaned softly. "Like strawberries and wine; you're killing me."

"What?" she asked in surprise within his embrace.

"Your taste. Strawberries and wine tonight. I'm used to the strawberries and something sweeter—cream? Vanilla?"

"Oh!" Illiana blushed. She hadn't even mentioned her gravitation to strawberry scented and flavored products, he'd just noticed it.

"I have a confession," he whispered.

"Oh no, you're the one who's secretly married, right?"

He chuckled. "No, something worse."

"You wear speedos to the beach. Damn, I knew something had to go wrong."

"My dirtiest little secret." He laughed. "But no." His voice shifted. Turning growly, lusty. Illiana felt her knees weaken in response. He murmured against her ear. "I parked this far away so everyone could see you walk across that parking lot and watch your sweet little ass in that *fucking* dress, knowing you're coming home with me."

Arousal, pure and unadulterated, swept through her bloodstream, heating her. The inferno of desire flushed her cheeks, and she couldn't deny the effect his words had on her. He was always such a gentleman, but then this side came out and utterly ignited her.

"You're taking me home now, are you?" she teased.

"Mm, maybe not right away." He toyed with a lock of her hair. "Do you want to get some food first? Ice cream? A walk?"

Illiana glanced down at her shoes. "If we can walk somewhere, I'm going barefoot."

"I know just the place."

They got in the vehicle and before they took off, Emmett looked at the club with a critical eye. Or perhaps it was Illiana's expectations that had her thinking it was criticism.

"It's a lot of pink," she supplied.

"Maybe a bit much, but some is nice."

"You're a fan of pink?"

He shrugged. "Why not? It's soft, it's comforting."

"So, if I decorated your house—say with some pink rugs and throw pillows—you'd enjoy it?"

"Talking about moving in together already? I'm honored. I think we've moved up the story's timeline, are we at six months now?"

"At least," she joked back.

"I wouldn't mind it in the least. It could use some color."

Illiana mentally thought back to Emmett's house while he turned over the ignition and rolled out of the lot. He was right, his place was fairly colorless, not in a stark way, but in a way that was somewhat thoughtless for aesthetics. Dark grays, charcoals, deep browns, and the like. There was a bit of navy blue, but nothing so bold as a jewel tone—let alone a pastel.

With the windows down, Illiana's hair whipped around her, cooling the perspiration on her skin. The night around them was turning to that gorgeous orange-violet of summer sunsets, the kind that lingered onto the day's rays, begging you to stay out longer, pulling colorful excuses from the air. Fooling with its resistance to fade that it wasn't past ten at night.

A few minutes into the drive, they found themselves at an empty beach. Illiana looked at him drolly. The idea of sand in her underwear, grating against her ass and vagina was the most unappealing prospect; despite how hot it would be to fuck in semipublic. She knew it was romanticized in books and movies. What they didn't show was the probable UTI after the fun event.

"You and I both know this night is ending with sex, but I can't be tempted to screw you in the sand."

Emmett laughed. "I promise I won't attack you on the beach."

"I'm not worried about you; I'm worried about me."

"Can't restrain yourself?"

Illiana held his gaze heatedly. "When it comes to you? No."

Emmett inhaled sharply and after a moment he silently restarted the vehicle and pulled to the road in the direction of his house. Illiana laughed as he conspicuously shifted to alleviate certain…discomforts.

"I'll make you regret that laugh, sweetheart. When it's my turn to tease."

Illiana bit down on a whimper at how tempting that sounded.

Trying to calm her racing racy thoughts, she mentally scrolled through topics.

"Are you doing anything for Canada Day?"

Emmett gave her a sidelong smile, noting exactly what she was doing. "Yeah, I have this annual party I go to. You?"

"My friend invited me to her family's thing."

"Any chance you can sneak out to watch the fireworks with me?"

Illiana smirked. "Are you suggesting we crash each other's parties?"

"Or ditch them entirely."

"All for me?"

"All for you," he replied heatedly.

"I'll think about it."

They pulled in the driveway and Emmett didn't give her a chance to climb out herself before he was at her door and tugging her out. He wrapped her legs around his middle, his hands at her thighs, just beneath her ass.

"Emmett!" she called out in shock.

"Ana," he chimed back.

"I can walk!"

"And I can carry you. Besides, I know your feet hurt."

"You don't have to—"

"Then I'll use the excuse of selfishness. This is the fastest way to get you into my house and in my bed."

Illiana shut up after that.

Emmett, using fancy one-armed maneuvers, shut and opened all the necessary doors in addition to locking the ones that warranted it too. Not once did he set her down, managing it all as if she weighed nothing, as if she wasn't burdensome in the slightest. It was a new feeling for her, especially as she'd never been told she was particularly light—there were jabs her mother used to make, or Adrian during practice.

Before she knew it, the air was rushing up around her, and Emmett had tossed her on the bed. She bounced once and then caught herself, looking up at him from beneath heavy lids.

"Stay there," he commanded. "I just need to take the dogs out quickly."

"But what if I want to get started without you?" She began to drag a strap down her shoulder.

Emmett groaned. "I'll be quick."

"Better make it extra quick or I might decide to touch lower."

Emmett practically sprinted from the room, and it took everything in Illiana to keep from laughing.

In seemingly record time, Emmett returned, and when he did, he shut that door firmly behind him. There was a change in his eyes—something utterly feral, and she wanted it to devour her.

"Do you remember what I said about your tight little ass?" he purred.

A thrill shot through her. "A little."

"Has anyone ever touched you there?"

Illiana swore he could hear her heart hammering. "I—I, a little but I didn't like *how* he did it."

She put certain emphasis on the words, making sure he understood that she wasn't opposed to all of it, but some of the way it was done was not something she enjoyed.

"I'd like to try something as long as you're comfortable."

Illiana hesitated. "I'm interested in trying."

"Good. Keep that in mind because I hope you remember what I said about laughing as well."

That thrill shot straight to her clit this time. She did remember.

He started prowling towards her and a mixture of emotions struck her. A thin sound slipped from her.

"Wait," she managed. Emmett stopped completely, pulling back. She continued hastily. "I just meant that maybe I should shower first. I was just at Gloss, and I'm not confident in any bar's hygienic standards."

"I don't mind," he retorted softly, gaze traveling up her body and all the exposed skin, the silver dress.

"You don't?"

"I don't."

This gave her a bit of a start. Adrian would've never touched her after going out—even for as short a period of time it was. She'd been too caught up in Emmett the last time they'd been intimate, but after their date and the hours on her feet and walking around would also have had her ex demanding her to wash before he had sex with her. Emmett, evidently, was not like that.

"Well…" She gathered her confidence and let that wanton yearning surge through her—heating her blood, darkening her eyes. She parted her thighs. "I'm ready for you, then."

Emmett wrapped a hand around her ankle and tugged. He dragged her down the bed. She slid with an oath of surprise as he rose atop her. He notched himself between her legs, fitting his pelvis snugly against hers and gave one sensual roll of his hips. The hardness of his cock rubbed against her clit at a perfect angle. Her eyes rolled back.

To her intense surprise, Emmett's hand softly cuffed her throat and he tilted her jaw up to meet his kiss. His lips brushed against hers, decadently soft.

"Is this okay?" he murmured against her mouth.

"Yes," she breathed back, hands grabbing the sheets.

He answered with returning to the kiss, sliding his tongue against her lower lip before delving into her mouth, their tongues meeting and tasting. He matched his tongue's strokes with the rolls of his hips, causing a riot of sensations to consume Illiana. His free hand traveled low, pushing that short hem up her hips, fingers toying at the waistband of her panties. As he pushed against her again, he used his knee to push her leg higher, parting her wider as the next stroke of his tongue and hips went deeper.

A spark rushed through her and she wondered if she would come from this alone. She'd never understood the allure of dry grinding, but now she did—and there was nothing dry about her right now. She was so wet. Wound so tight. She felt like she would burst from the pressure if Emmett didn't get inside her soon.

"More," she begged, fingers scrabbling at his back, pulling his shirt free, and coaxing it over his shoulders.

Emmett broke the kiss long enough to free himself from the constraints of the fabric before being drawn back against her—like magnets. He tugged down the thin straps of her dress, the shimmering fabric catching holographic fractals of light across their skin. Urging it further down revealed her strapless black bra.

"Sorry, it isn't anything special," she joked.

His hands covered her breasts. "Everything about you is special."

The bra quickly disappeared and as a rush of cool air touched her skin, her nipples hardened to pink peaks. Emmett's mouth immediately found them, and she bucked against him, meeting a stroke from him again, the friction between their legs making her moan. He paid expert attention against her skin, pulling the nipple into his mouth and flicking with his tongue. Her hands thrust into his hair and tugged the thick roots in blinding pleasure.

"When are you going to be inside me, Emmett?"

"Do you want me inside you, Ana?"

"Yes."

"Do you remember what I said earlier."

"Which part?"

"Laughing."

She whined, knowing he was going for delayed gratification. "Please."

"Such a pretty word coming from those lips. Say it again."

"Please."

"And excellent manners."

With that, Emmett pulled away and flipped her over. She landed on her belly and before she could comprehend what he was doing, he helped her to get on all fours, hands coasting up her backside, cupping her cheeks and pushing the dress around her waist.

"Arch that back for me, sweetheart." And then he nipped her on the ass.

She startled but did as told; fingers flexing in the blankets.

"Good girl," he said, kissing the small hurt.

Before she could beg him for more, he was hooking his finger in the band of her panties and dragging them down her thighs, working them free from her knees. She bit her lip, knowing he could see everything from this angle and pushing down any insecurity. Adrian had hated this position for many reasons—ones she didn't want to think about.

"Fuck, Ana. Look at you. This pretty pussy. This sweet ass." His fingers kneaded her soft flesh. "Is it all mine?"

"Yes," she managed. "All yours."

His palm stroked up her back and through her hair. He twisted the long tresses in his hand and pulled her hair back—consciously grabbing the back of her hair, not the nape where the sting was far less pleasurable. He forced her to face him.

"You're in control here. Say the word and everything stops."

"You better not."

Emmett grinned, and with his opposite hand he slipped it between her legs and slid a finger in her core. He pumped it in and out, slickness coating the digit before his thumb found her clit and pressed on it. She gasped as he learned that firm slow circles had her gushing around his finger. She felt her inner muscles relax and clench around him, and then slowly he added a second finger.

Illiana groaned low at the filling pressure. She bit her lip, wriggling herself against him—seeking more, wanting more.

"Fuck me now."

Emmett didn't hesitate. He shucked off his pants and she heard the package tear as he opened the condom. He rolled it on his cock and then lined himself up at her entrance. She felt the blunt pressure of him begging for her and she rocked back, taking the head of him inside her. Emmett hissed, hands going to her hips—either to steady or to use as leverage—fingers still wet from the bliss he'd been wringing from her.

In a single stroke he entered her and she threw her head back at the stretching pleasure he sank into her. He began thrusting in and out, the angle utterly divine, hitting that spot and covering them in involuntary wetness.

"God, you squeeze so tight when that happens, sweetheart." It seemed like he said it through gritted teeth, as if he were trying to keep from coming.

The thought of that power she held nearly sent her over the edge.

One of Emmett's hands slid from her hip—the wet one—and she felt the tracks of her desire slicking against her skin with its wake. Slowly, he dragged it to the small of her back before he stroked down the seam of her backside while he fucked her.

She glanced back and saw him draw his thumb into his mouth, tasting her flavor and soaking it anew. Tentatively, as if allowing her plenty of time to stop him, he slid that newly wet digit down.

She did not stop him.

Pleasure began addling her brain as she felt it at the tight muscle of her ass, circling it and pressing softly. Not entering her, but massaging it.

Oh.

Oh

This was far different than what she was expecting.

She liked it.

She practically moaned like a porn star as she rocked into him, biting her hand as the pleasure spiraled in tightening circles. Her orgasm built fast and hard; she was rocketing to the precipice at record speed. She felt a wall inside, like it was all that was holding her from falling into heaven. She shattered through it as she came, Emmett still fucking and rubbing her.

Whether it was the sound or finally him losing control, he came with her. He groaned, a low, throaty, sexy sound.

Together, they collapsed once the waves left them, breathing heavy.

CHAPTER TWELVE
Emmett

"Is that a plan, then?"

"Is what a plan?" she asked him.

"Watching the fireworks together."

Ana giggled, tucking her chin down shyly. As if he hadn't just seen and touched *everything*.

And God, how good *everything* was.

"It's a date."

He realized as she bestowed him with a smile that he could already be falling in love with her.

He wasn't there yet, but he felt himself teetering on that precipice.

The realization hit him like a truck. Suddenly, the world was divided into two sections; before Ana, and after Ana. It crystalized so vividly that he had to blink away the burned impression on his psyche.

He didn't want to forget the messy blonde hair, the gentle curve of her shoulder, the flush of her skin, the glitter in her blue eyes. Or the fluid way she moved, with practiced grace that was so effortless, the way she parted and came for him. The way she smelled of strawberries and vanilla cream and white wine tonight. How she tasted fucking divine.

This wasn't casual.

This was it.

The thought struck him like Cupid's own arrow, and he needed a moment to compose himself.

He used the excuse of disposing of the condom to slip into the bathroom to pull his maelstrom of thoughts together. After getting rid of the protection and washing his hands, he stared at his reflection in the mirror. He still looked the same—same dark hair, half tied up still, waves hanging about his face, sleeve of tattoos on stark display, the one on his chest beating above the heart that Ana was stealing—but he felt entirely different.

When he reappeared, Ana was completely naked, the dress that had somehow survived their lovemaking no longer around her waist and now on the floor.

"I was supposed to be the one to put that there."

"You took too long," she teased.

"We could always go for a round two."

She laughed. "How about a shower first, and we can attempt the dress removal later. I'm sticky," she said the last part with a wrinkle of her nose—and fuck, how he wanted to kiss it.

Her *nose*. Her fucking nose he wanted to kiss. He had it so bad.

"Well, you need to return that showerhead you stole."

Ana's eyes darkened with promise. "I'm sure I can manage some shower head."

Emmett's cock immediately started stiffening. Her eyes flickered to it and she quirked an eyebrow. As she licked her lips, she slid from the bed and strut past him, dragging her nails across his chest, as she stepped into his ensuite bathroom.

He followed.

Ana was already in the shower, the heat cranked, steam rising in the room. Already, it smelled of heat and sex and strawberries and wine. Emmett joined her. The shower itself was very large with plenty of room, the rainfall head falling between them. There was a convenient ledge placed serendipitously, too.

Emmett let Ana go through the motions of washing herself, soaping up her hands and rubbing her breasts with sudsy strokes…he shut his eyes against the thoughts. As she washed the stickiness of her arousal from her skin, Emmett sank to his knees, and let the water course down Ana's body as he looked up at her. Prodding her foot to that ledge, he opened her wide and set his mouth against her core.

He sucked and licked at her clit, laving up the center of her. Her eyes rolled back as she tried to steady herself on the slick surface. He went deeper against her as she caught her bearings, her hand fusing in his hair.

"I thought it was your turn," she rasped.

"I just needed a taste."

She tugged him back by his hair and urged him to stand. As he did, she sank down, drawing her hands down his chest, his abdomen, before coming to her knees before him. He was hard again already and when she took his cock in hand, it took everything in him not to lose it. Ana wrapped her soft hand around the base of him and pumped him once. His hips bucked, and he groaned. On the second pump, she took his tip in her mouth and sucked. When she did it a third time, he saw stars. She began wrapping her lips around him, pulling him deeper into her mouth, moving her hand with the same rhythm. Her tongue stroked beneath the length of his shaft, flicking the head of him as she nearly pulled him out with a slight pop.

"Fuck, Ana."

She hummed happily and took him in her mouth again, bobbing her head up and down. He felt that he was going to come soon, he felt it building at the base of his spine. It was rushing up, the ecstasy right at the fringes of his reach.

"Sweetheart, I'm going to come. If you don't want it in your mouth, you need to stop."

She simply looked up at him, blue eyes devilish as she increased her efforts.

A stream of obscenities left his mouth as he spilled into hers. His climax took him as he thrust into her mouth, and he felt her swallow his release, swirling her tongue around him to take every drop.

Fuck, if that didn't make him want to come again.

They finished up the shower together, helping the other to wash, running hands through hair. There was no complaining when backs needed to be washed, especially as he took it as the perfect opportunity to massage her perfect little ass. When they got out, Emmett gave her one of his T-shirts to wear. She put it on and wore nothing else.

Lord, he was so hopeless for her.

"I know it's fast, but would you want to meet my moms?"

Ana turned to him, a question in her eyes. They were laying in his bed, attempting to watch Star Wars again, the dogs at the foot. They'd just recently ate something before settling in, Ana letting her friend know she was staying over, her friend confirming she was also safe. Her hand was on his chest, tracing the tattoo there as she contemplated.

"What would that mean to you?"

"What do you mean?"

"This…" She gestured between the two of them. "Meeting the family…it kind of goes beyond a summer thing."

He nodded. "Where this goes is up to you."

"Where would *you* like it to go?"

"Somewhere serious," he said honestly.

Ana looked down with a shy smile. "Do you think they'd like me?"

"They'd love you."

She bit her lip. "Okay, then. Let me think about it. When?"

Emmett deliberated. "Next week sometime?"

"I'll get back to you, but I might be able to make that work."

They repeated the same routine as last time. When they woke Emmett sneaked down the stairs and made breakfast, leaving it ready for Ana. He kissed her goodbye, told her to shower, eat, and lock up behind her.

As he left, he realized this was the life he was dreaming about, and he was hoping he'd never have to wake from it.

CHAPTER THIRTEEN
Illiana

Illiana was second-guessing her outfit choice. She didn't want Nate to get the wrong idea, but she still wanted to look nice. She was also mindful of the fact that after ice cream they were going to the lake, so she wanted something that she could easily use as a coverup over her bathing suit. In the end, she decided on a pastel blue sundress patterned with daisies, her flamingo pink bikini beneath it.

Mina had picked her up from Emmett's place in the morning, her best friend looking a little worse for wear, but nothing as bad as Scrabble night. It was the first time she'd seen Emmett's place, as Illiana had called for a taxi the last time she stayed over. She had cocked her brow at the house, impressed, and smirked at Illiana suggestively as she came out in her silver dress.

"Ana baby, I've never seen you do the Walk of Shame."

"Oh, shut up," Illiana threw back as she clicked on the seatbelt. "And don't you dare tell anyone back at the house. He lives in Rose Point; they're bound to know of him."

"Swear on my life that I won't not say something."

"That's a double negative."

"Is it?" she asked with faux innocence.

"Tell anyone about this, and I'll cut the pinky toe out of every pair of socks you own."

Mina gasped with feigned horror. "You heinous bitch."

Illiana smirked. "Keep your mouth shut and you can keep your piggies nice and warm *and* contained."

"Fine, fine!"

They drove home with Hozier playing between them, Mina regaling her with stories from the party—high school friends she hadn't seen in nearly a decade, and outlandish tales of drunken stupidity from some of the party goers. Illiana had listened and when it came time for her to share her night's antics she revealed small details—such as how Emmett had touched her and *where*.

Illiana shook her head from the morning's events as she waited in the main house at the kitchen island, her water bottle in front of her and decorated with strawberries. Nate was supposed to meet here while Mina visited a friend before they all went to the lake together. Unfortunately, though, Illiana glanced out the window and noted the weather looked rather overcast and the slight dreariness was not conducive to wanting to swim.

Exactly on time, Nate stepped through the door. He crossed the threshold, a smile on his face, and the scent of light cologne following him. Illiana returned the smile, and as handsome as Nate was, he had no effect on her heart. Not like Emmett.

"You look beautiful," he said, a hint of adoration in his voice.

Illiana blushed, mild discomfort on her skin. "Thank you," she responded, smoothing the skirt of her dress as she stood. "You've dressed up a bit yourself too."

Nate practically preened. He was dressed in a dark pair of trousers, a sage green button down with the top two buttons undone, a silver chain hanging around his neck, as well as a matching one around his wrist and an expensive-looking watch. Illiana realized with a surge of dismay that Nate had dressed for this as if it were a date. But no, that wasn't fair. Maybe he just dressed this way daily and she was thinking too highly of herself.

He thanked her.

"Ready to go?" he asked her, gesturing towards the front door.

"Ready!"

Illiana gathered her things and followed him out. He kept a small distance between them, enough that she could reach out if she wanted, but he wasn't making her do so. When they got into Nate's truck, he waited until she was buckled in before pulling out of the driveway. Once they were on the road, he looked at her, a smile on his full lips.

"How are things with your dancing?" Nate asked, then his eyes widened and he backpedaled a bit. "I mean, I know what happened—last year—but I just meant progress-wise. That is, if you want to talk about it."

Illiana flinched slightly but shrugged. "It's okay. I'm not where I wanted to be, but I'm still working at it. Mina has been really supportive. I don't know where I'd be without her."

"She's pretty great," Nate agreed. "You know, she's my favorite cousin, after all."

Illiana laughed. "I'm sure that's what you say to all your cousin's best friends."

He laughed in return. "Maybe I do."

Illiana pivoted topics. "So, what are you doing for work now?"

Conversation continued like that—easy, formulaic, the back and forth of work, friends, music, basic current events, his family. It was nice—pleasant, even—but it didn't thrill her. There was no spark when he regaled her with tales of his sailing ventures—which were interesting, but didn't give that extra…sparkle. He told her of his friends from university, glossing past names as if he'd forgotten she wouldn't know them.

She managed to open up a little about her friendship with Mina and how they'd met when Illiana needed someone to look at her knee after she hyperextended it during practice and one of her fellow dancers mentioned that her friend—who was picking her up that day—was studying to become a physiotherapist, and she could probably take a look at it. Mina did, and had advised her—under the direction that she was not certified—to rest it. They'd offered Illiana a ride home and from there they got chatting and she and Mina hit it off, exchanging numbers and social media by the end of the car ride.

When Nate pulled up in front of a small ice cream shop, Illiana came to the firm conclusion that there was never going to be anything romantic between her and Nate—even if Emmett wasn't in the picture. That extra chemistry just wasn't there. She liked him; he was nice, but that was all. She'd hoped they could be friends—at the very least friendly—while she stayed for the summer.

But what if she stayed?

What if she stayed for Emmett and left her old life behind? Emmett wanted her. Seriously. He wanted a serious thing with her. She hadn't been ready to accept it, nor acknowledge it last night, so she hadn't. Even so, the thought haunted her because she didn't know if any of this was even going to work.

She shook her head from the thoughts.

One day at a time.

"I don't mean to talk about Mina when she's not here," Illiana said as she shut the passenger's side door. "But she's pretty sad about the split with David. That is to say, she isn't broken up about it, but getting cheated on is a burn no matter how you feel about the person."

It was just so much worse when love was involved.

"No, you're right. I've been cheated on before and it sucks."

"Me too," she said with a tired sigh. "It really makes you question your self worth, let alone be around any sort of romance."

She was hoping he'd pick up on her hint. To have a gentler excuse for no flirting or dating-like talk because she was a coward. Luckily, it seemed that Nate was smart and picked up on her suggestion.

As they walked up to the order window of the small shop painted a vibrant turquoise, the sign above decorated with a chocolate fudge sundae with a cherry on top, Nate prodded her into a new line of conversation.

"Are you excited about the party this weekend?"

"Yeah, actually. Mina has been raving about it. I'm guessing this annual thing gets bigger every year?"

"Yup," he said. "We've always had a bunch of people come. Family, extended family, family friends, high school friends, dates, our individual friends, our parents' friend's—all that. It's a bit of a mix of everyone. My buddies from university will be there, and I know Mina has a few high school girlfriends coming. And then there's tons of games and food. Honestly, it's pretty fun—though I have to admit, the political tone of the last few years changed it a little and now a lot of people don't wear any specific color anymore."

It came to be their time to order and as they stepped up, Illiana unhesitatingly ordered strawberry ice cream. Nate picked maple walnut. They took their desserts and picked their way to one of the picnic tables. As they sat together, conversing about nothing of import, a voice caught Illiana's ears.

Illiana turned and there was Madeline, definitely not looking like she had been doing shots last night.

"Illiana! Hi!" Madeline walked over to her, a genuine smile on her face. "I just wanted to say I hope I didn't make you feel left out last night. You know, being sober and hindsight and all that, I realize that you might have felt awkward, and I just wanted to apologize if you felt that way. I was going to wait until the party to say something, but I saw you and I thought it was a sign."

Illiana was simultaneously grateful for Madeline's words and horrified at her presence. She did not want Madeline to bring up Emmett in front of Nate. She didn't want to break his heart right out in the open.

"Oh, I really appreciate that."

"It's no problem! But I don't blame you, especially when you had that man to get back to." She winked conspiratorially, and Illiana realized two things simultaneously.

One, she'd saved Illiana by not naming Emmett.

And two, she'd totally fucked Illiana by not naming Emmett because now Nate thought "that man" was him.

Illiana gave Madeline a tight smile. "How was Mina last night by the way? She told me she crashed at your place?"

"Yeah, we got some take out and then wasted time on our phones until we fell asleep."

Just then Nate's own phone chirruped. He checked it and immediately got up.

"Sorry to cut this short," Nate apologized. "But Mina finished up with her friend early and wants us to pick her up."

"Oh!" Illiana said, getting up, spoonful of strawberry ice cream in her mouth. She looked at Madeline apologetically. "So sorry, but it was nice chatting. I'll see you this weekend."

Madeline smiled. "Sounds good, see you later."

Madeline departed with a wave and then got into the lineup while Illiana and Nate made their way back to his truck, eating their ice cream in silence.

"Sorry that this part of our day got cut short."

Illiana waved it off. "It's okay, there will be other days."

"I really hope so. Just between this weather and all…I don't know."

"Are we talking about the weather now?" Illiana teased.

Nate shook his head ruefully as he began pulling out of the lot. "That's just pathetic, isn't it?"

"I can bring up some better conversation topics."

"Please do." There was a hint of playful desperation in his tone.

"Well, I could start by telling you the whole sad sob story of my career ending. But that feels a bit heavy. Maybe books?"

Nate glanced at her sidelong. "I'm realizing that the kind of books you're reading are definitely not the same as mine."

"Maybe not. Okay, so. Mina said you bought a house. Are you doing any decorating?" She was completely stealing ideas from her conversations with Emmett now. She forced herself not to mention the word pink.

"Doing some renovations right now actually."

"Oh?"

And finally, conversation shifted fully away from the weather as they finished their ice cream on the drive. Nate explained how he was taking out a couple walls and replacing all the windows. He'd already torn up the ancient, shag carpet and laid down laminate hardwood in its place. As the conversation continued, they found themselves at the restaurant where Mina stood outside, arms around herself.

Immediately she hopped in. "That breeze is really kicking up out there," Mina warned, pulling up the sleeves of her butter yellow knitted cardigan.

Illiana had to agree. The sky was gray, the clouds choked with the threat of rain, a chill breeze pulling off from the ocean. She stared at it dubiously, doubting that the lake would be in the cards for the day.

"Should we change plans?" Nate asked, a bit of disappointment in his tone.

"What did you have in mind?" Mina asked.

"A movie? A bar?"

"I mean," Illiana began to interject. "As long as it doesn't rain, we could still go and just stay on the sand. I'm sure it won't be busy that way."

The three of them glanced between each other and shrugged in agreement.

"Why not?" Nate said and continued on their drive. "It's just nice to spend time with you two."

Illiana tried to ignore the comment and not show a reaction to not give Nate false impressions, but at that exact moment Emmett texted her and she smiled as his name popped up on the screen. She caught Nate's rather pleased look and she cursed the timing.

She was going to have to talk to Mina about unwinding this mess.

Secretly, she checked the message and it was one line that had her biting her lip.

Thanks for the shower head.

Winky face.

And then a picture of his hand on that luxurious rainfall shower.

She tried to desperately rein in her laughter. She covered her mouth and looked out the window.

God, she had it bad.

Thanks for providing the opportunity to use it, she responded.

Sure enough, when they got to the lake, it was indeed sparsely populated. The three of them unraveled the beach blanket and sat upon it, plying the center of it with snacks and drinks as waves gently rippled across the surface of the lake. The water was a clear, sparkling blue, free of stirred sediment that a more popular day would have churned up. The space was wooded, ringed with trees on all sides, the beach sandy with pebbles strewn in. A mother and her two small children were nearby, splashing at the shore in bright pink and orange suits. On the opposite side were two college-aged guys tossing a volley-ball back and forth in the water, uncaring of the cooler temperature of the day.

It was a gorgeous place and Illiana's heart panged with how the beauty struck her. Even on a dreary day.

Meanwhile, Illiana felt a chill and unrolled her towel across her thighs. She was deeply regretting wearing a sundress at this point. She picked daintily at the vegetables she'd packed, gnawing on the celery while the taste of strawberry still lingered on her tongue.

As they settled in for the afternoon, Illiana couldn't help checking and rechecking her phone. Mina didn't say anything, but her raised brow said it all. The outing was nice, but Illiana's heart wasn't in it—though Nate was none the wiser—truthfully, all her thoughts were consumed with something else—*someone* else.

But even more so, the idea of *here* was catching.

There were people here who genuinely seemed to like her, and wanted to be around her. And the more she thought about it, the more she felt she could get used to Rose Point. Her parents weren't waiting for her back in Toronto—they didn't care. Even so, she had her hesitations, because what if Emmett decided to leave her just as Adrian had? Even if she wanted more with Emmett—which she felt was happening—she didn't know if she was brave enough to risk her heart.

It was a scary prospect.

Eventually, the chill won out and they packed up, returning to the Ellis house. Illiana could tell Nate was disappointed with the entire turn of events and while Illiana felt a twinge of guilt, she didn't share the same sentiment.

CHAPTER FOURTEEN
Emmett

It was Friday at Blue's, and Nate was gushing about Illiana again. They were seated at their regular booth, Emmett, Nate, Graham, Kieran, and Chase, nursing their respective drinks, leaning close together over the bustle of voices around them and more than one rowdy drunk.

"So, get this; her friend hinted that Illiana was wanting to get back to me last night. Now, I'm kicking myself for not staying over when I was helping clean the pool yesterday. But then today on our date, I said it was nice spending time together and she just got this huge smile on her face. She tried to hide it, even looking out the window, but I saw it." Nate was utterly beaming. "I think I might make a real move tomorrow night."

Emmett was thrilled for his friend that his longtime crush was finally coming to fruition. He considered perhaps he was extra happy for his friend as he, himself also had someone incredible in his life now; Ana, the fucking goddess his life now revolved around—okay, maybe that was a little much, but she was just everything he wanted in his life.

"I'm happy for you, babe," Emmett said, clapping Nate on the shoulder. He held his beer aloft to the boys. "To Nate—finally his longtime devotion is paying off."

"Shut the fuck up," Nate returned with a smile, shoving him but cheers-ing to himself with the rest of their friends.

"To Nate!" they chorused in unison.

The glass clinked together, and the five of them drank deeply. The ice-cold beer sliding down Emmett's throat was one of his favorite things after a long week of work, but he expected that the current projection of his life was going to change that very soon.

"I haven't been able to spend as much time with her as I wanted, though," Nate admitted. "She's been so busy helping prep the food and stuff the past two days with my cousin and mom."

"Getting along with her future mother-in-law, already?" Emmett chided, elbowing him.

Nate elbowed him back.

"So, do we need to bring anything to the party tomorrow?" Kieran asked.

Nate shook his head. "Nah, you ask that every year—which I appreciate—but no, unless you want a specific beer or other drink we don't have."

"Do you need any extra help setting up?" Graham offered.

Nate seemed to deliberate. "Maybe, but I'd have to check with my parents."

"I'm busy until eleven, but I should be completely free at noon to help."

"I can help first-thing," Emmett interjected.

"May as well. And if not, you can get a kickstart on drinking."

"What do you think this is?" Emmett said jokingly, waggling his bottle.

"You're going to have a bad time if you're drinking all through tonight and next."

"Trust me, I've had one bout of alcohol poisoning—I'm not itching for another."

"Is that the same time that Kieran fell asleep on your deck?" Graham asked.

Kieran shook his head, black hair swinging with it. "It's a nice deck."

"The kind of *deck* you *really* want to sit on."

"Who doesn't want a nice big *deck*? Best thing to wake up on."

The one letter shy of a different work entirely was not lost on them; neither was the innuendo.

Laughter chorused up around them.

"Yes, that was the alcohol poisoning night." Emmett had elected to drink the mystery beverage that they'll all poured a little something into on his kitchen island. When he'd been dared to, he hadn't backed down. It was awful. A medley of all different alcohol—Wisers being the worst—topped with grape juice. He was immediately sick.

"Are any of you bringing anyone?" Nate asked. "I know you're bringing your boyfriend, Chase." He turned to Emmett. "You bringing Ana?"

"Nah, she's got her own thing." He neglected to mention how they both planned to sneak away from their respective parties to watch the fireworks together. "Either of you?" He turned to Graham and Kieran.

"Just myself," Graham said, but there was a weight to his voice.

"I don't have anyone in my life," Kieran pointed between Emmett and Nate. "And don't you two start getting big heads. Up until last week you were both in the same single boat we were."

Nate innocently batted his lashes. "I'm still single for you."

"Not for long. Not from what you're staying about Illiana."

"That's the hope."

They, all thrilled for him, got another round of drinks.

The next morning Emmett woke up bright and early—much to his fatigue's despair as he'd stayed up to an ungodly hour texting Ana. He did a quick workout and then took his dogs for a walk before feeding both himself and his fur babies before loading them up and taking them to his mom's place for the day. Since he'd be gone all day and most of the night, it wasn't fair to abandon Leia and Gimli—especially when the fireworks went off. His moms were more than happy to pup-sit.

"You're uncharacteristically cheery," his mom said teasingly.

He'd inherited Ashley's brown eyes, softer and more amber brown than the extreme dark of his father's. The shape, however, was a mix of the two. His mom was half-Chinese, but due to her own mother having been adopted into a Caucasian family, she had almost no ties to that part of her heritage—much to her dismay. Although, she was beginning to look into a DNA kit to see if she had any blood relatives she could reach out to.

"Am I?" he said deflecting as he smooshed Gimli's face between his hands, kissing his nose.

"You are," his mom pushed. "Is it a girl?"

"Mom," he bemoaned.

"It is!" She turned to the kitchen. "Danika! He's seeing someone!"

"He's *what?*"

He groaned as his other mother crossed the threshold, a dish towel in hand. Her green eyes glittered with mischief.

"Well, what's her name? Who is she?"

"Ma!"

Danika—Ma—simply quirked a dark brow, waiting.

Emmett sighed. "Her name is Ana."

"Like from *Frozen?*"

Emmett stared skyward at the ceiling at the sound of his little sister's voice. "Yes, Sloane, like from *Frozen.*"

Sloane snickered. She was perched on the arm of the couch, long black hair twisted over her shoulder, a brow cocked in amusement. She'd been born with their father's night dark eyes and the two of them shared his complexion, but her features were a mix. She had the high cheekbones and proud mouth from him, but her jawline was the softer shape like that of Danika's. She'd also taken after her mother in stature and build, short and soft where their father was tall and wiry.

Emmett pinned his sister with a dark look.

Even though Sloane was his younger sister, she was only younger by four months due to his father's inability to forge lasting or committed relationships. This was further cemented by the fact that they also had an older half-brother that they didn't discover until they were seventeen. As adults they'd made the effort to make a relationship with their newly discovered sibling and while they loved Riley and there was a bond there, there was also a lack due to not having been raised together. His moms even tried their best to include him in their lives and traditions, but Riley was so used to just him and his mother for so long that it was difficult. Though, he was always kind and appreciative of the offers.

Riley had a family of his own though, two daughters and a lovely wife. He'd cut off all contact with their father years ago, vowing to never be like him and to never put his children through what he had. He was only three years older, but those three years felt like eons with how established and secure Riley was compared to Emmett.

"I'm actually wondering when I can bring her by for you all to meet her."

Three pairs of eyes zeroed in on him.

"How's Thursday? Dinner?" his mom asked. "Oh, and did you want to ask Nate to come? Has he met her yet?"

"Not yet, actually. But that's another thing—he's seeing someone, too."

"Oh!" Danika's eyes widened. "Tell him to bring her, too then! The girls can all have something to talk about. Maybe we should ask Riley and the girls too."

"As if you've always been the ones outnumbered."

"Oh hush."

Emmett grinned. "Love you, Ma." He kissed her cheek and then turned to his mom and did the same. "Love you, Mom. Thank you both for watching the dogs."

He kissed both his dogs goodbye and made the women promise to send him picture updates. They swore, and he made sure they all had everything they needed. On his way out the door he waved to Sloane. "Love you, loser."

"Yeah, love you, dork," Sloane tossed back.

He chuckled as he left and he was positively beaming as he got into his SUV, one step closer to Ana and fireworks tonight.

He had twelve cases of various beers, ciders, and coolers in the back of his vehicle. The glass tinkled together as Emmett cruised up the driveway of the Ellis lake house, all lush green lawn, birch trees, and that big blue house. The only vehicles in the drive this early was the vintage VW, Nate's truck, and a plain rental SUV. It was nearly eleven, and the sun was already shining down bright and hot. Emmett had dressed in a white button-down and jeans and had packed a duffel just in case it got too hot or elected to go swimming—every year was different.

Emmett was excited and nervous to meet Nate's mysterious Illiana. He'd heard so much about her, and he was curious who this woman was who'd captured his best friend's heart. She was this specter about his friend. He supposed he could have checked for her on social media, but he'd been so busy with Ana that the thought hadn't even crossed his mind—Illiana hadn't crossed his mind. Not when he had his sweet goddess.

As soon as he put the SUV in park, Nate bolted out, rushing to help. He climbed out and Nate immediately sidled up to him.

"Please be cool around her," Nate said, a thin thread of anxiety in his voice. "Just don't tell her how much I like her, or joke about it."

Emmett became serious. "I would never do that, Nate."

Nate exhaled sharply. "I know. I know. I'm sorry, I'm just...I'm freaking out." He scrubbed a hand through his short hair. "I'm worried that maybe I read things wrong after all."

"Why do you say that?" Emmett asked, furrowing his brow.

"She's just been so busy this morning—helping and all— and I haven't had a chance to talk with her—ask her about *us*, I mean."

The scent of sun and honeysuckle was thick in the air, fresh cut lawn and barbecue in the distance. Emmett drew in a breath of all those scents.

"Look," he said, wrapping an arm around Nate's shoulders. "You're an amazing guy and any girl would be lucky to have you, but if she's not interested, you can't force her. However, from everything you've told me, it seems like she is, so maybe just ask. Be straightforward with her. Tell her you like her. Fuck, even ask her out properly—because I'm guessing you didn't before."

"I offered it to be a date, but she opted for it to be just a hang out."

"Okay, well. Either take the hint, or ask in case she was too nervous to accept. Maybe even if she's into it, ask to kiss her if you're feeling bold. Just respect her decision if she tells you no."

"I'm not Jace."

"Thank fuck for that." He softly punched Nate's bicep. "So, are you going to help me with all this beer and shit, or not?"

"Yeah, yeah man, I'm helping."

"Oh, also my moms invited you for dinner on Thursday, they said you can bring Illiana—be there for six?"

"Yeah, that sounds great."

Together the two of them started carrying the alcohol in, walking up the paved drive. They ascended the stairs to the front door, carefully navigating them over the cases in their arms.

"And you're sure your new girlfriend can't make it?" Nate asked.

"First, she's not my girlfriend—not yet, at least. And second, no, I don't think so. She's staying with her friend and promised to go to their thing."

"Bummer."

"Yeah." Emmett shrugged. "But it is what it is."

They walked through the house and Nate called out to his mom. "Where do you want all the booze?"

"Just by the back door! They need to be loaded into the coolers."

The two men did as they were told. They set the cases down on the white marble floor of the kitchen, a compliment to the walls painted a soft, powdery blue. Just as Emmett scrubbed his hands down his jeans before fixing his topknot, he heard foot-steps enter the kitchen.

"Oh, Illiana, hi!" Nate started. "I wanted to introduce you to my best friend. This is Emmett King."

Emmett looked up with a smile just in time to see the shocked face of Ana.

Ana.

Illiana.

The smile dropped from his face instantly.

Not *Il-Li-An-Nah*, as Nate had been mispronouncing all this time, but *Il-Li-On-Nah*.

Illiana, the girl his best friend had been imagining himself in love with for nearly ten years.

Ana, the girl *he'd* been seeing and fucking.

Illiana, the girl his best friend thought was interested in him.

Ana, the girl *he'd* been falling for.

Jesus fucking Christ, he was so fucking fucked.

Emmett froze.

Illiana froze.

Her blue eyes were so wide, her perfect pink mouth was popped open—that mouth he'd kissed and fucked.

Fuck.

Her fair skin had that rosy flush that always burned on her cheeks from his presence—that blush usually had him hungry for her.

He swore that if he had been holding something he would have dropped it.

Was Ana—Illiana—actually interested in Nate? Or was Nate misconstruing and misunderstanding her? He did say that when he offered for their outing to be a date that she chose it to be a hang out with friends, so there was that. Was she just using him?

His stomach soured at the thought.

No, he didn't think it was like that. Sure, she'd mentioned she didn't know what she wanted, but this? Them? It went beyond a fling. This was the real deal and he was going to get to the bottom of it.

Horror churned through him as he stared down at this girl, his best friend, and the shit storm his life had just turned into. He felt the panic lace through his veins with its noxious substance, his head got light, his pulse roared in his ears.

"Hi," he said, his voice thin. "I've heard so much about you." Illiana's face fell, hurt crossing her eyes, and before she could respond, he turned to his friend who seemed too enamored with Ana—*fuck*—Illiana to notice his complete panicked spiral. "Nate, do you mind if I get some water before we grab the rest of those cases?"

Nate shook his head free of the fog from his girl—jealousy roared through Emmett. "Yeah man, you know where the glasses are."

And with that Nate turned on his heel and strode for the door.

Emmett went to the cupboard for a glass and immediately filled it, downing it in one gulp. Illiana sidled up to him with a quizzical expression on her face, her body language slightly guarded—as if afraid he'd discard her. Fuck.

"Do you want to tell me what all *that* was about?"

He gasped as he finished the water. "Your name is *Illiana. You're* Illiana."

She looked at him with a mix of excitement and confusion, stroking a hand down his arm. He jumped. An even more pained expression immediately crossed her face, and he cursed himself for it.

"Yeah, but Ana is a common nickname. It's pronounced with the '*on*' sound, but everyone always messes it up, so sometimes it's easier to go by Ana. I think it's a fifty-fifty split what people call me."

Emmett was fucking sweating bullets.

Oh man, oh man, he was so *fucked*.

He was the worst friend.

He scrubbed a hand down his face.

This was a nightmare.

A total and complete nightmare.

This would devastate Nate.

"My friends all know you. You're the one they talked about meeting that one time."

"They did?"

"Can you—" he started from beneath his hand. "Can you do me a favor? Can you…not tell Nate about us? Or that we know each other?"

Confusion and pain bled into every line of Illiana's features. She stepped back slowly, eyes watery, a tremble to her lip. All he wanted to do was kiss that shiver away.

"Why?" she asked softly.

Emmett cast a look over his shoulder and pulled at his hair. "I—I just don't think he'd be okay with it. Can you trust me?" He paused. "I'll let him know soon."

Suspicion was bright in her eyes, and Emmett knew she wasn't stupid. It was seconds, and she had already put the pieces together.

"He likes me."

Emmett sighed heavily, and nodded.

She looked away. "I figured as much. He asked me out, but I turned it into a friend's thing."

"He mentioned that."

Her gaze shot to him. She softened. "Just so you know, I don't have feelings for him. I'm not interested in him. Not like…" she trailed off and brushed her fingers across the back of his hand. "Not like I am in you."

His heart threatened to burst out of his chest. Threatened to fucking devastate him.

"But for full transparency, we did get ice cream together—just the two of us before meeting up with Mina."

That twinge of jealousy took over him like a wave. Emmett stiffened. He wanted to tuck Illiana beneath his arm and smuggle her out of there. Away from Nate's fantasies.

Jesus, he was worse than a caveman.

He managed to rein in his emotions and nodded.

"Just…pretend for a little. I'll tell him after the party. Okay?"

"Okay," she agreed, still trailing her fingers across his.

He grasped her fingers and gave her a quick squeeze. "I have to go help Nate."

With that he slipped away, his mind a maelstrom as he put all his own pieces together.

Illiana was only here for the summer, just like Ana had said her being here was temporary. Mina was her best friend and Nate's cousin—he should have recognized her. As Ana she'd told him she was between jobs, because he knew as Illiana she'd been in an accident that stole her ballerina career. A fucking ballerina. He should have known—she always moved with that beautiful dancer's grace. It was so obvious now. She even mentioned this very party. Jesus, Mina was probably outside the bar when he'd met Illiana, Nate only moments away. All four of them missing each other like ships passing in the night.

And the most convenient kicker—they'd both neglected to exchange names, so when Mina had called Illiana by her nickname, Ana, Emmett had just run with it as if that was the name Illiana herself had given him.

Holy fuck.

The thoughts rushed through his brain as he descended the steps to his SUV.

"You okay, babe?" Nate asked, arms loaded with more cases of glass bottles.

"Yep, I'm great. Can't wait to crack open one of these." He added a rueful smile.

"You and me both!" Nate paused. "By the way, are you totally sure your girl can't make it today? She'd probably fit right in with Illiana and the others. They all like books too."

The knife of guilt twisted in Emmett's stomach.

"Ah…things are kind of up in the air there."

"Oh?"

"Yeah, she—never mind. I don't want to bring down the mood."

"Awe, well I'm sorry. Whatever it is. You're a good guy, Em—don't forget it."

Emmett returned to his vehicle and stared down at the cardboard boxes praying he had the strength to pull off the act he needed to play.

CHAPTER FIFTEEN

"We have a problem," Illiana whispered in Mina's ear, grabbing her best friend by the bicep and dragging her into the hallway that led to the laundry room.

"What is it?" Mina hissed quietly.

Illiana looked over her shoulder, noting only Lacey and two of her friends in the kitchen, immersed in the charcuterie board they were beginning to assemble. She returned to Mina, holding her hazel gaze with her blue one. Mina was calm and concerned while Illiana was concerned and panicked.

"That guy that I've been hooking up with?"

Mina made an expression as she processed. "Yeah? Emmett, so—" her eyes flew wide. "Oh shit! It's Nate's Emmett!"

"*Yes*," she said with low lethal calm. "Apparently no one seemed to put it together. You'd think they would with a small town and all."

"Don't look at me, I've barely met him. I just know him mostly by name—well, I seem to have forgotten, but it makes sense now."

"Yes, it does, doesn't it?" she said sarcastically. "The problem now is that Emmett and I have been…"

"Fucking?"

"…fucking, but I think it's more than that. Or it could be. I don't know. But here's the worse part. Nate likes me. Like…*likes* me."

Mina's eyes grew wide. "Oh shit. Oh *shit*."

"Yeah, *oh shit*. Did Emmett break the '*bro code*' or something? What is he supposed to do?"

"Did he know who you were?"

"No, not at all. He was totally shocked when I walked in."

"Then no, but he has gotten himself in a shitty situation."

"He asked me not to tell Nate about us. Just until he can tell him himself. He doesn't want to ruin the party, I guess."

"I mean, that's a good call, but fuck, I do not envy you."

"Mm, you think *I* envy me?"

"Not at all." Mina craned her neck, seeing through the big glass windows. "Well, maybe a little. That man is *fine*."

Illiana looked to where Mina's gaze was trained. There, Emmett was transferring beers from the cases to the cooler on the back deck, muscles flexing as he bent and stood, his strong build evident even beneath the white button-down he wore casually. As if he could sense it, he looked up and his warm brown eyes found her, a flicker of heat passing between them. She blushed and turned back to Mina.

"I get it now." Mina leaned in teasingly. "So, this is the man who went down on you before you even touched his dick?"

"Mina!" Illiana said aghast.

"Just trying to get the facts straight. And the one that introduced you to proper ass—"

"Nope, we're done with this conversation now." Illiana strode from the hallway and into the kitchen.

"There's no shame in it!" Mina called to her retreating back.

The party was in full swing, and Illiana was in *full* anxiety.

Music pumped from the speakers set up around the deck, the beat like the panicked rhythm in her chest. The scents of summer suffused her; fresh cut grass, barbecue, chlorine, flowers, and various foods as well as the lingering haze of marijuana all mingling in the air.

People stood in groups and pairs across the deck, the patio, on the lawn, and in the kitchen. The giant glass doors were propped open so people could come and go as they pleased. Faces constantly passed her, holding drinks and food, but only one stood out to her.

Emmett stood with Nate by the barbecue, the two of them sipping on sweating beers with their other friends. Every once in a while, his gaze locked onto her and every time that heated gaze sent tingles straight between her legs. Memories and fantasies filtering through her mind.

She noticed Emmett's label was picked.

Kids were running across the lawn with squirt guns and bubbles, others were splashing in the pool. Off to the side of the house, the slight sounds of coughing and a distinct scent betraying a group of weed smokers. Mina and Madeline were sipping on sangria, hips gently swaying to the music.

Illiana stood with them, trying to blend in and enjoy the party, but she couldn't help the furtive glances being cut Emmett's way.

The day continued like that, except the groups began gravitating towards each other. Ever so slightly over the course of a couple hours, they shifted, drawn to each other's magnetism, caught in the axis of their orbit. Soon enough their groups became one, and they sat at a glass dining table, all eight seats taken—although, one of Emmett's friends was waiting for his boyfriend to show up. Nate sat at one head of the table, Chase at the other. Directly to Nate's left was Mina, then Graham, and Kieran. On his right was Illiana, then Emmett, and then Madeline. Nate seemed far too pleased that Illiana was next to him, but it was taking everything in her not to touch Emmett's leg beneath the table. She refrained because it was *glass*. Even so, she was viscerally aware of him and the tension between them was palpable—at least to those who knew.

Mina was very tipsy off her sangria, as evidenced by the fact that she was sitting next to Graham, her supposed enemy, and not putting up a fuss. She was rubbing her forehead as if in pain, even knocked her napkin off the table, and when she dove to get it, Graham glanced over mid-conversation, and nonchalantly reached over to cup the corner of the table. She came up under it and instead of hitting her head on the edge, she knocked into Graham's hand instead.

"Ow," she griped. "Why's your hand there?"

"So, you don't split your head open, *Jasmina*. You're welcome, by the way."

"I didn't thank you."

Graham simply smiled and returned to his conversation with the boys.

Illiana's eyes widened, and she glanced at Madeline. The two of them locked gazes and a silent conversation passed between them.

Do you see that? Illiana conveyed. *Jasmina?*
Totally. She's so blind to think he doesn't like her.
Right?

Wait, do you think he like-likes her? Madeline's extra wide eyes lent the question more weight.

Oh. Oh, shit maybe?

Keep watching.

The two of them did, and Illiana came to the startling realization that Graham seemed hyper-aware of everyone at all times. When Nate teetered back in his chair, Graham was ready to hop up and steady him before he righted himself. When Mina dropped her napkin again, he repeated the corner grab. Kieran nearly spilled his drink, and Graham caught it. When Mina fanned herself by tugging at the collar of her T-shirt, his eyes flew to the motion and his eyes heated.

It was like a fucking neon sign.

"Hey, Madeline," Nate said across the table. "Have you had a chance to talk to Emmett yet? I've heard you're into Star Wars stuff—so is he!"

Illiana's blood ran cold.

Madeline's eyes brightened. "No way. Are you an originals fan or prequels? Anything else is sacrilege."

Emmett chuckled. "I'm partial to the prequels."

"Me too!"

Their conversation took off, inserts from Chase and Kieran here and there, but the two of them dominated the talk. Despite Emmett constantly stealing glances at her, jealousy burned through Illiana like a vicious green monster. She ground her teeth and forced herself to swallow down a sip of gin. It burned just as bad as the jealousy.

Insecurity began winding through Illiana.

She didn't know the references they were speaking of, didn't understand the jokes.

Every time they'd tried to watch the damn movies, they ended up fucking instead. That thought made her heat for an entirely different reason. Sure, she had him—between her legs often—but was she enough?

She was spiralling.

She knew it; she could feel it.

She was being irrational. She knew, but she couldn't control it. After Adrian dropped her because the one thing she was to him shattered, he moved onto the next person that could provide a similar alternative. Was this the same? Their talk of romance books and tropes wasn't enough any longer? They flirted through tropes, but those movies had tropes, too.

"They're really hitting it off, don't you think?" Nate whispered to Illiana, leaning in. She could smell the scent of his cologne—something spicy, not like Emmett's scent—and the slight tinge of booze.

"They seem to be," she answered dully.

Illiana stared down at her hands, twisting them beneath the table on her lap. Anyone who was paying attention would see her discomfort—fortuitously enough, no one was.

After a few breaths, she sensed a pair of eyes on her and when she looked at Emmett, she saw he was still locked in conversation. When she glanced across the table, she expected to find Mina's. But it wasn't her, it was Kieran's. He was watching her with a curious air, like he was trying to figure out something about her.

Her gaze quickly flittered away and all her emotions surged up.

"Excuse me," she said quietly. "I need to use the washroom."

She got up and as soon as she did, Mina's eyes shot to her. "I'm coming with you!"

Mina stood up so fast she nearly knocked her chair over—but Graham was there, righting it before it toppled over with her in it. He didn't look irritated in the slightest, though he did look concerned.

Quickly, Mina caught up to her and linked arms with her, both for Illiana's comfort and Mina's need for steadiness.

"Oh man, it always hits you harder when you stand up," Mina griped.

Illiana just made a sound of affirmation while she guided them to the bathroom. Locking the door behind them Illiana turned on the tap and ran cold water, putting her fingers beneath it and patting her throat and cheeks to cool herself. Mina sat on the edge of the bathtub, smoothing the wrinkles in her gray jersey dress.

"He's going to lose interest in me," Illiana rasped.

Mina looked at her pointedly, summoning as much sobriety as possible. "Why do you say that?"

"He—It's just what happens with me."

"Ana. Emmett is not Adrian."

Illiana looked away, emotion thickening her throat. She stared at the salmon walls of the bathroom, forcing her anxiety to quell. She gripped the edge of the white sink, grounding herself.

"You really like him." Mina realized. "Like, want to be with him, not just a hookup with him."

Illiana nodded.

"Oh, damn. Okay. Well, I wouldn't be surprised if he felt the same about you."

"He seemed to be hitting it off with Madeline."

"What I saw was him politely engaging in a topic he enjoys but not being able to take his eyes off of *you*."

Illiana's eyes shot to her.

"I'm not the only one who noticed."

"You're not?"

"Nope," Mina said, popping the P. "So, want to quit this pity party and get back out there and allude to thinly-veiled seduction at your man?"

"You're the worst," Illiana managed through a laugh. "But okay, yes."

CHAPTER SIXTEEN
Emmett

Guilt sat heavy in Emmett's gut. He felt like the worst piece of shit for making Illiana hide their whatever it was between them—relationship?—especially since it so clearly bothered her.

Of course, it was made only worse with Nate pushing Madeline at him.

While he enjoyed her conversation, it didn't hold even half a spark of the interest he had for Illiana. He so heartily desired to take her back to his house and ravish her body, whispering all the ways he wanted her, and how she drove him crazy with longing, how she tortured him just by existing with that sweet persona, that soft joking attitude, that surprisingly dirty mouth, and that incredible body honed to perfection by discipline and dance.

He still could hardly believe that Ana was Illiana. But it made sense. What had Nate said about her charm? You had to meet her to get it? Emmett snorted. Wasn't that the truth?

Madeline and Emmett had long since ended the conversation between them, Madeline having started a scholarly debate with Chase after discovering he was a psychologist and she was currently in her final year before becoming one herself. They were discussing something about brains and thought patterns—it was lost on Emmett.

"Do you see what I mean now?" Nate leaned past Illiana's empty seat. "Why I'm so crazy about her."

Emmett swallowed his guilt. Squandered the thoughts of the way Illiana looked beneath him writhing in pleasure. Fuck, he knew his best friend had been dreaming of her for years, and here Emmett had just swooped in within hours of her arrival on the west coast and took her.

Okay, that wasn't a fair comparison. She wasn't a thing that could be taken. She was her own person, and she more than consented to being with Emmett. It was a shitty thing for him to do to Nate, even though he'd had no idea Illiana was Ana, but honestly, how obvious was it now? He wanted to smack himself for his stupidity.

"She really is something," Emmett finally managed. Then leaned in a bit more conspiratorially. "So, what is actually going on between you two? Like have you gone on a date? Or taken her back to your place?" Emmett's stomach twisted at the thought.

He believed Illiana, but he wanted to gauge how badly Emmett would crush Nate when he revealed the truth. He knew it was going to suck anyway, but having and idea had him convinced it would help.

Nate shook his head. "No, I haven't had the chance, nothing substantial has happened yet. And I told you. I sort of, kind of asked her out but she turned it into friends. But I want to ask her again, straight up. If it's a no, it's a no, but I have a feeling it'll be a yes."

"Why do you think that?" Emmett narrowed his brows.

Nate smiled behind his bottle. "Just some of the ways she's reacted to me saying stuff. Hiding smiles and stuff. She seems…timid. You know? Like she'd be gentle."

Emmett's beer soured in his stomach.

Oh, he certainly knew.

And he certainly knew *gentle* was not what she preferred.

Emmett just nodded and took a swallow of beer to hide his non-answer. The label was nearly picked clean off.

"Nate!" Jade, Nate's older sister called, waddling over to their table, her very pregnant belly on full display through her black stretch dress. "I need a beer pong partner, come on!"

"You're pregnant, you shouldn't be drinking!"

"Hence needing you as a partner!"

"What about Sasha?"

"Who do you think our opponent is?"

"Your husband?"

"He's helping dad. Now come on, you lil' shit."

"What if I don't want to?"

"Then I'm pulling the pregnancy card."

"You're insufferable."

"Yep, but you're going to help, aren't you?"

Nate groaned, took his beer and stood. He turned to Emmett. "Sisters, right?"

Emmett chuckled, then echoed, "Sisters."

As Nate left, Emmett visibly deflated, sinking into his beer. He suddenly became aware of eyes on him and looked up to find Kieran watching with too-perceptive eyes.

"You all good?" Kieran asked.

"Peachy, babe."

Kieran looked unconvinced.

Just then, Illiana and Mina returned, and it took some significant shifting to hide his surge of arousal at seeing her move in that pink dress. Fuck, it was so tight—as if it was made for her. It wasn't long, but it ended just below her knees, her cork sandals adding a little height to her and graceful length to her legs. The dress's straps were so thin he could bite through them. It scooped low against her breasts, showing off that little bumblebee tattoo, and tied in a sweet little bow that he just wanted to tug open. It clung to her flat stomach and hips, curving over her ass and down her thighs, showing off just a little tanned skin from the slit that reached several inches above her knee. The ties of a bathing suit showed beneath it all.

He'd been too consumed with everything earlier to give it much thought, but oh he was giving it thought now.

Illiana returned to her seat next to him, a coquettish glint in her ocean eyes as she tossed back her golden tresses. His eyes never left her, tracing the small pattern on her dress—dots or flowers—it was subtle.

Mina slid into the spot next to Graham—seemingly to her chagrin—and he reacted, suddenly completely aware of her movements. Emmett scrutinized his friend's body language. Was Graham…into Mina? He'd never seen Graham interact with her. But this…no, Emmett must've been reading into things. He had love goggles on for Illiana and he was seeing attraction where it wasn't.

Emmett lifted his beer in toast. "To new friends and a stunning summer!"

"To new friends and more," Illiana echoed, a discreet look sent his way.

"And more!" Nate called out with a pointed look.

Jealousy flashed through Emmett—intrusive, invasive, and insidious. His friend couldn't help his feelings, especially when he didn't realize how tangled and misconstrued they were.

Still, the caveman part of Emmett's brain seemed to give zero fucks.

"To more!" Mina added, sensing an intensity to her cousin.

Everyone clinked bottles and glasses together, and Emmett kept his eyes on Illiana the entire time.

Emmett glanced over and happened to catch Kieran's eye. His friend simply lifted a brow and said nothing as he took a pull from his own bottle.

The hours began to pass and people were grazing on food and drink. The pool was empty, the children having vacated it in favor of a scavenger hunt hosted by Nate's sisters and their respective partners. The happy squeals of said kids was a chorus to the summer tune, the faint sound of neighbors having their own parties, the music pumping from the Ellis Family's speakers.

The heat was heavy and oppressive, and Emmett felt a bead of sweat slide down his temple. It was only just after three, and the day's heat wasn't going to let up anytime soon. Other games were ongoing, groups wandering off to play bocce, washers, or ladder ball.

Illiana fanned herself, perspiration creating a delicate shimmer on her skin. "It's way too hot. Anyone else care for a swim?" she asked.

Emmett's cock hardened at the thought of seeing what she had on under the dress.

Mina stood and immediately rocked back, Graham's hand shooting out to steady her. Mina cast him a deathly glare before returning to her seat. "I'd better not. Honestly, I think I should start on some water."

"Good idea," Graham muttered and went to fetch her a water bottle.

"I'll join," Madeline chirped.

Kieran and Chase chimed in as well.

Illiana's sly eyes turned to him. "Emmett?"

Emmett shot her a look that promised a certain kind of teasing later. "Maybe later." He was not risking everyone seeing his erection in a pair of swim shorts, and he had no disillusions about how many Illiana could give him.

She fake pouted and then finally turned to Nate and Graham just as the latter returned, water in hand. "You two?"

Graham shook his head. "Nah, I'm going to sit with Jasmina and make sure she hydrates."

Emmett looked at Nate and had a sudden realization. Nate hated pools. Not that he couldn't swim—he swam in the lake all the time—but he hated chlorine; the scent of it, the feel of it, the burn on the sinuses. As much as Emmett knew he would have loved to join Illiana, he knew he wouldn't, for fear of ruining his entire day.

"I'm good, but you all go on ahead."

Yep, as he predicted.

Illiana shrugged and then strode over to a wicker lounge chair before tugging her dress up and peeling it off her body, depositing it on the chair. If Emmett was struggling to hide his arousal before, he was in outright war with it now. The pink bikini had a pattern of white hearts across it and it cut high on her hips, showing off those shapely legs and most of that ass that he had—

Jesus Christ.

He was unwell.

Still beside the chair, Illiana reached up with a hair tie from her wrist, and pulled all those blonde locks atop her head. She stepped into the shallow end of the pool and descended in, the glittering surface casting prisms of light across her softly tanned skin.

All he wanted was his hands on her. His mouth. To be inside—

He mentally scolded himself.

Chancing a look at Nate, he found his best friend completely enraptured, and it took Emmett everything in his power not to call him out. Nate was shifting in discomfort, eyes flickering to and away from Illiana.

"I think her eyes are a little higher," Emmett chided Nate carefully.

A slight flush of shame found Nate's cheeks. "Do you see her?"

"I have eyes."

"Fuck, I hope she says yes later."

Emmett didn't have it in him to shatter his friend's hopes and dreams.

Not yet.

But he was going to warn him.

"Just be prepared for anything."

Chase, Kieran, and Madeline all got into the pool, diving and splashing about. Madeline would throw diving rings into the deep end and the two men—boys, really—would race for them. It was nostalgic for Emmett, to see his friends playing as their inner child demanded. It reminded him of summers growing up with his sister—how easy and carefree it was. He would've joined the others—even had swim gear in his SUV—if it weren't for the very prominent problem in his pants.

Illiana waded through the water, casting Emmett flashing looks—a twinkle in her eye, a small smirk, a lip bite—and it was all for him. She never sank beneath the surface of the pool, nor did a single tendril of gold fall from its messy bun atop her head.

Mina made a sound that made Emmett whip his head quickly around. He found her covering her eyes, but what he could still see of her face was in pain. Graham was right there with her, a hand on her back.

"Are you going to be sick?" Graham asked carefully, but firmly.

"No," Mina groaned. "I don't even think I'm drunk anymore. I'm pretty sure this is a migraine. It makes me stupid and uncoordinated—I knew three glasses of sangria wasn't enough to do this."

Graham glanced at the pool house and all the light shining into it. "Are there black out curtains in there?" He nodded his chin in that direction.

Mina shook her head.

"Okay, let's get you inside and into a dark room. You can lay down a while—do you want Tylenol? Or do you have a specific medication?"

"Just Tylenol is fine."

"I'll go get it," Nate intervened, making for the house.

"All right, lets get moving then." Carefully, Graham helped Mina to her feet. "You can keep your eyes covered; I'll guide you."

"Why are you helping me?" she grumbled. "You don't even like me."

Oh boy. Emmett shook his head.

Graham paused but simply continued. "Don't worry about it. The less talking you do, the better you'll feel."

Mina snorted as Graham escorted her through the house.

Emmett watched with genuine surprise. Did…did Graham like Mina?

No, that wasn't possible. He'd only met her a handful of times and for all intents and purposes, they didn't like each other—at all. The stories he'd been told of their animosity only furthered this. This, whatever it was, was an anomaly.

As they disappeared, Illiana began to get out of the pool, a concern frown etched in her brow.

"Is Mina okay?"

"Migraine," Emmett supplied. "Graham is going to help her."

Illiana hesitated. "Maybe I should go instead."

Emmett read between the lines of Illiana's concern. Last she'd seen, her best friend was drunk and now she was being taken to a dark room with a man she didn't know. Emmett felt shame light up his bones. He hadn't even considered how that would look.

Before Emmett could tell her she should, she was already moving into the house.

"Em," a voice called from the pool.

Emmett found Kieran, dark eyes trained on him. Chase and Madeline were playing Marco-Polo or something, but Kieran was hanging on the edge of the pool.

"Yeah?"

"Is there something you want to tell me?"

Lead sat in his stomach.

"Like what?"

"You tell me."

Emmett thinned his lips. "Not right now."

Kieran was silent, almost broody, until he nodded. "All right then."

Guilt wound through Emmett as Kieran swam over to Chase and Madeline, joining them like he realistically should be. Keeping secrets? Who was he?

It's just for today, he reminded himself, *I'll tell everyone after.*

Illiana returned, some concern on her face, but no longer the panic.

"All good?" he asked.

"Yeah, she said she was fine with Graham and told me to come back here and enjoy the party. She said she'd be fine in a few hours." She headed over to her things and wrapped a towel around herself just as Nate returned.

"So, we're out of Tylenol—and literally every other thing that could help Mina—so I'm running to the store. I should be back in a half an hour."

"Should you be driving?" Emmett asked with concern. Drunk driving, no matter who it was, was a no-go for him.

"No, I've had four so I'm not risking it. I'm walking to the corner store." He glanced around. "Does anyone need anything?"

No one did, so Nate left.

"Well," Illiana started. "I'm going to get changed and maybe rinse off a bit."

As Illiana slipped into the pool house, it took everything in Emmett not to chase after her. The thoughts of her all wet and silky in the shower had him losing his mind. It didn't even have to be sexual, he'd enjoy just holding her, cuddled up on his couch, the AC going, the dogs curled at their feet. The idea made his heart ache, especially since he didn't know if she'd be staying. Or how they were going to deal with this whole Nate catastrophe.

The four beers he'd had suddenly hit his bladder and Emmett excused himself before using the facilities. After finishing up in the bathroom he noted at the end of the hallway was a side door, and beyond that side door was a hedge that obscured the view from the deck. It was the same hedge that people had been hiding behind to smoke weed. What Emmett also noted was that it had a completely covered access to the pool house and one of its two entrances.

Emmett paused at the door, deliberating, weighing his plans. He owed Illiana an explanation. He owed her an apology for making her carry on as if nothing was between them—it was cruel. Summer heat or horny thoughts, one or the other got into his brain and he found himself glancing behind, finding no one there, and slipping out that side door.

He followed the flagstone path, voices carrying over the hedge, the music filtering through the air. When he got to the adjoining side door of the pool house, he gently rapped on the door. Through the window he saw Illiana spin on her heel, golden hair whirling. When she saw him, a beaming smile broke across her face. She practically skipped—*skipped*—to the door, and before he could even think about stepping through, she was tugging him in.

The space was cute. Pink and yellow and cheery. A shade was drawn down over the windows and door facing the deck, both for privacy and to block out the sun. Emmett noted, somewhat distantly, that the other door was already locked. He carefully shut the door behind him and flipped the lock. Then, he pulled that shade down too.

Illiana eyed him, freshly washed, smelling of that divine scent of strawberries and cream, ethereal in her soft, dewy makeup. She was wearing that damn pink dress again, only this time, no bathing suit beneath.

"I'm so sorry," he began, "I hate hiding this too."

His hands went to her hips, tugging her against him. She went with him with a gentle sway, their pelvises meeting, their desires barred by the thin layers of clothing between them.

"It's hard," she admitted, her breath raspy.

He refrained from making an '*I know*' innuendo joke, and instead brushed a lock of golden hair behind her ear. "It's not for long. I promise."

"I hope not."

He smirked. "Can I make it up to you?"

"How so?"

"With an apology."

"An apology?" she echoed.

"Mmhmm." He sank down to his knees before her. "Like this."

CHAPTER SEVENTEEN
Illiana

Carefully, Emmett palmed her thighs, watching her reaction as he found that slit in her dress and slowly pushed it up around her hips. His eyes were dark and heady, so much of his pupil swallowing up the amber. When the dress was completely up, her black lace thong was on full display for him, so thin and sheer he could see her smooth, soaked flesh beneath it.

Emmett's lips ghosted from the inside of her knee and up her thigh, his nose skimming against her sensitive skin. When he reached the apex of her thighs, he nuzzled against her first and she saw fucking stars. He kissed her over her underwear and gave a little jolt, a small moan of surprise eking out of her.

"Can I taste you, sweetheart?"

Illiana bit her lip. "Please."

With her consent, Emmett hitched her thigh over his shoulder and then tugged that lace aside, baring her center for him. She knew she was wet for him; she could feel it soaking through.

He gave her one firm lick through her core and her hands instantly went to his hair, pulling him into her. Locks fell from his topknot as she grinded against his face, seeking pleasure. As he pulled her clit into his mouth and sucked, she cried out softly.

"You're going to have to be quiet, sweetheart," Emmett whispered against her pussy. His eyes flickered up to her, smirking, eyes devilish. "But I'm not going to make it easy for you."

"Okay, just keep doing what you're doing," she panted, bringing a hand up to her mouth. She bit down on her fingers as he resumed.

This was so wrong, but God, she didn't want him to stop. This was so unlike her. Never had she done anything sexual in a place that wasn't hers or her partner's—let alone at a large party such as *this*.

His tongue laved up her, swirling around her clit, and then alternated with flicking motions that had her head knocking against the wall behind her. She thrust her hips against him, trying to ride his face as he tongue-fucked her. Emmett reached up and pulled her neckline down, fondling her breast before he found her nipple and rolled it between his thumb and forefinger.

Holy fuck she was going to come apart so fast.

She felt wetness surge out of her, but Emmett didn't stop. His other hand went to his shirt and worked all the buttons free, his chest bare and open. That free hand sneaked up between her legs and with two fingers he slid them inside her core and pumped them, curling against those muscles. She clenched around him, and she felt a flood of wetness. It spilled down his chin and down his chest.

Illiana realized distantly why he'd undone the buttons now.

Her orgasm was building high and tight within her, she felt it cresting up over her. It was seconds later, her breath thin, as she climaxed. She bit down on her fingers as the waves took her over and over, pleasure numbing her mind. She moaned, head hitting the wall, eyes rolling back. Emmett didn't stop, instead, he carried her over the tides of her bliss until her trembling ceased.

When she came back down, Emmett was right there, still. He kissed her recently sated pussy and then grabbed her discarded towel, mopping up her legs, his chest, his face, and the floor. Mortification burned in her cheeks. Righting her panties for her, he swiped stray wetness from the corner of his mouth with his thumb and popped it into his mouth.

It was the hottest thing she'd ever seen.

He rose and took her chin in hand, her fingers twined with his.

"Don't ever be embarrassed about that," he whispered, his lips ghosting across hers. "I just wanted you to know how sorry I am about all of this."

"Apology accepted."

He grinned. "Good. But I've got to go before they realize how long I've been gone. I'll see you back out there."

"What about you?"

"This wasn't for me. Well, it wasn't for me to get off, I should say."

Illiana hesitated. "You're…you're going to wash all my *stuff* off you, right?"

At the door he gave her a gentle smile. "As much as I don't want to, yes."

She bit her lip. "Okay."

"But just so you know, you—everything about you—is my favorite fucking thing in the world."

Illiana's blood heated.

Emmett left through the door he'd entered from and Illiana stood there, reeling.

Holy fuck.

Holy fuck, she was just thoroughly pleasured in her best friend's family's pool house. It was utterly debauched, and the slight kinkiness of it had arousal surging between her thighs again, already. People were just beyond those doors and windows, none the wiser to the fact that Emmett had just given her one of the most intense orgasms of her life.

Illiana strode to the bathroom and wiped any other evidence of her climax from her skin and used the toilet. She noticed that her fingers had deep imprints of her own teeth on them and she hoped they disappeared quickly. As she straightened her dress, she noticed her hair was a little sex-tousled and she battled it into submission. Adding a new layer of lip-gloss to her lips, she heaved a large breath, and then left the pool house.

Emmett was there, lounging on a deck chair, utterly aloof. There was no sign of the pleasure he'd wrought on her—his buttons were done up, sleeves rolled to three quarters, top knot fixed, not a sign of her glistening arousal on him. He caught her eye mid-sentence with Chase, then winked at her before returning to his friend.

Illiana sank into the empty seat next to Madeline and the two of them lapsed into conversation, realizing they had more in common than Illiana had originally thought. Though the entire time she prayed no one could see the lines of sex written all over her.

Hours passed drinking, eating, and playing games as the sun began to set and the chirp of crickets and croaking of frogs filled the air. The sky began to darken with violet and peach tones, Mina's uncle and some of his buddies setting up fireworks at the edge of the lake.

Mina was up around seven with Graham in tow, the dark room and Tylenol Nate brought back seeming to have done the trick. She, however, refrained from drinking anymore as to not tempt the headache's vengeful return.

When the sky fully darkened somewhere between ten and eleven, Walter and Lacey called everyone to attention for the fireworks. Everyone huddled on the grass, either standing or on blankets. The children were bundled against the slight night's chill with their parents, some of them even sporting headphones to help with the sound.

Illiana and Emmett, with his friend group, Mina and Madeline, all hovered at the edge of the crowd. There were at least five dozen people scattered across the Ellis's lawn. Illiana was standing between Mina and Emmett, Madeline and Graham close by. Nate was at the fringes, talking animatedly to Sasha's fiancé while helping with Jade's toddler.

Lacey began passing out sparklers while Walt began lighting the fireworks with one of his friend's assistance. A slight hiss filled the air as she was handed a fizzing sparkler.

The first crack of the fireworks lit the night sky in a burst of gold. Illiana's eyes widened against the beauty of a simple explosion. A hiss started up and then another boom as green scattered across the horizon. Oohs-and-Ahs went up around them, children squealing with glee. Illiana's heart squeezed in her chest, overflowing happiness saturating her blood. Another boom and pink rained around them.

The fireworks continued to go off and she felt a moment of surrealness course through her. This was her life. This was her luck. Nearly a year ago her life had completely imploded around her because of one single event. Her shitty parents dropped her, her ex-boyfriend left her, and her career disintegrated like sand between her fingers. Things had changed drastically. Her dreams had changed. But they were not broken.

She was not broken.

She was here.

With her friends.

With Emmett.

Gingerly, she reached out and found Emmett's fingers already there. They brushed together lightly as three pink starbursts shattered against the night.

The night wrapped up shortly after the fireworks, families dispersing with their young children first. More than one person was throwing up in bushes or sobbing drunkenly. Of their friends, Nate was the most drunk, and even then, he was still perfectly functional. Ubers and taxis were called, designated drivers were organized, and quickly the party halved.

"Anyone up for some drinking games?" Nate asked excitedly.

Illiana shook her head. "I'm pretty tired. Another night, though."

"Yeah, I don't want to risk my migraine coming back, I think we'll turn in."

The two girls said their goodnights and goodbyes, both Nate and Emmett looking disappointed.

In the pool house, Mina sat on the edge of her bed and lightly rubbed her forehead. Illiana, meanwhile, locked the doors and bit her lip, practically bursting with excitement. When Mina glanced up, she clearly noted Illiana's tensely joyous posture.

"Oh, spill. What is it?"

Illiana played with the inside of her cheek with her tongue. "I have a confession."

"Oh God. What did you do?" Mina's eyes widened. "Did you fuck Emmett during the party? When? How? Where?"

Rushing over to her best friend, Illiana bounced onto Mina's bed. "I didn't fuck him. But, well…" She bit her lip. "He wanted to apologize for putting me in this position so he got me off."

"And how?"

Illiana licked her lip in answer.

"Oh, you dirty little—where?"

Her eyes slid to the wall right by the pool house door.

"*Against the wall?*"

"Yeah," she confirmed, putting her thumb to her lip. "He's really good at it too."

"Okay, yeah. I'm going to need details."

So Illiana told her how he followed her to the pool house, apologized, then how he went down on her. She even disclosed her new ability to her best friend—who as a physiotherapist that also practiced pelvic floor physiotherapy, was surprisingly educated about it. Mina's attention was rapt, and it was near the end of regaling her tale that she realized that Mina had just been dumped and cheated on.

"Oh, shit. Mina, I'm so sorry. I didn't even think about David."

"Don't even worry, it's nice to know you're getting some—and getting it good. David sucked at giving head. I had to lie and say I didn't like getting it done to me."

Illiana was aghast. "No, you didn't!"

"I did! At first I tried to tell him how I liked it, but he wouldn't have it. So, I gave up."

The girls erupted into stifled laughter just as Illiana got a text.

She turned her phone over and found Emmett's name there. With the message came a picture. It was his legs extended out before him, a propane fire by his feet, the legs of four others in the image.

Wish you were still out here.

She smiled.

Should I respond sweet or spicy?

He replied immediately:

Give me a hint to both.

Illiana snapped a picture of the wall where he'd gone down on her and sent it.

Hint.

I really shouldn't be hard right now in front of my friends.

It's because you can't resist them, she teased.

Obviously. They've been wearing down my defenses for years and I'm about to fold to their feminine wiles.

I knew I wasn't enough.

Her phone chirped.

You're more than enough.

In that moment she knew she was truly falling for him.

CHAPTER EIGHTEEN
Emmett

He meant to tell Nate about Illiana right away.

He truly did.

But Nate was excruciatingly hungover, puking his guts up from possible alcohol poisoning the morning following the party.

After the girls had gone to bed and Madeline had caught a ride home, it was just the boys up, talking and bonding around the propane fire. Good-natured teasing, passing comments about Illiana—ones that weren't inappropriate, but ones that had him biting his tongue cause none of them knew the truth—and hopes and dreams of the future. They'd gone from their beers to hard liquor and the shots flowed in earnest. Emmett had accepted two and then drew his limit. Nate had not called any such limits. When he realized Nate was going to have a rough night, he encouraged food and water, to which he resisted. However, when the nausea hit, Emmett was able to persuade him and managed to get him to his childhood bedroom with a bowl at the bedside, and Tylenol and water on the nightstand. Emmett crashed on the pillowed window seat, as he had many times in the past when he'd attended one of the Ellis family's many parties.

He'd woken to both a stiff back and Nate's tortured hurling.

Nate was hardly functional all of Sunday and he didn't want to ruin his life anymore with his heart-shattering revelation.

So, Monday it was.

But Monday came around Emmett got an emergency job that he had to leave the shop for—emergency rates were double-time and who could pass that up? He'd hardly been able to text Illiana all of Monday, let alone set up a time to tell Nate that the girl he was hardcore crushing on was the girl that Emmett was with. Or…doing stuff with.

There still wasn't a real title to it despite him wanting one.

Monday night as he was crashing after the long day's work, he was texting Nate to confirm their regular Tuesday guys night. Nate did, but he also added that afterward he wanted to have a beach fire and had already invited Mina and Illiana.

His stomach twisted.

Just then, Illiana texted him.

It was a picture of her, hair in a messy bun, dressed in a pair of daisy-printed pajamas, and a book clutched in her hands. One of Delilah's books. *The* book. The one dedicated to him.

Emmett's stomach sank. Dread twisted through him and soured in his throat.

Just starting this. So far not too many damning clues that you're the author, but I'll find something.

Emmett wanted to crawl into a hole. What had he done?

Even so. She was beautiful and he told her as much.

Thanks, baby, she responded. With a pink heart.

His heart thundered in anticipation, and then a second text came through.

Have you told Nate yet?

He groaned into the gray blankets. Leia got up in confusion and snuffled by his face. He stroked her chocolatey coat and responded.

Not yet, things have been chaotic. I want to, tomorrow.

At the fire?

Before the fire. Or maybe after.

But he had a feeling that wouldn't happen either.

He was beginning to spiral and all he wanted was Illiana.

Do you want to take the dogs for a walk with me?

Her response was immediate. *I'll get dressed and be there soon.*

She got there in record time and was dressed in a crewneck sweater and jean shorts, hair still in a messy bun with tortoiseshell sunglasses perched on her nose. Emmett's breath was taken and he immediately swept her up.

"You're absolutely gorgeous."

She kissed him quickly and firmly. "You're pretty good looking yourself."

He returned the kiss and with the taste of strawberries and cream, so much of his tension faded away. As he inhaled her, the stress became manageable.

How could something as pure as the feelings he held for her be something so damned by his friend?

They pulled apart, and he shook his head from the thoughts as he handed Illiana a leash.

"You take Gimli. He pulls less."

"Done."

Illiana went over to his English bulldog and slipped the collar over his pudgy neck then quickly attached the leash. Gimli started trying to twist himself in circles over the excitement. Leia, too smart for her own good, started prancing and vibrating with anticipation. The second Emmett put on her walking gear she was whining and chuffing, begging for that door to open.

"Slow," he warned Leia as he opened the door.

Leia gave a tug as soon as that summer air struck, but, with a gentle pull, Emmett was back in control. As Emmett and Illiana guided the dogs down the road, they got talking about Rose Point in general.

"So, you own your house, huh?" she said casually, Gimli trotting happily beside her.

"I do," he confirmed. "We moved to Rose Point when I was eighteen and I knew this was going to be home. Getting the house is a mix of happenstance and hard work. My grandfather was a survivor of a residential school—I told you this, right?" She nodded, so he continued. "As reparations, the government gave some money to those harmed, but he was in bad health, so rather than spend it himself, he divided it between his grandchildren. It, paired with my income from my business, was enough. Otherwise, I don't think I'd be in this position—at least at the time it happened."

Illiana was quiet as they walked together, the streets quiet, the summer breeze, lifting their hair.

"I'm sorry your family had to go through all of that."

He nodded. "Yeah, but this is a pretty heavy subject, so let's pivot to something happier."

"Agreed."

"Want to share your favorite performance? You don't have to share specific details, especially why you're not dancing anymore, but…"

"No," she said softly, eyes contemplative. "I…I want to talk about it. Not all of it but…" she drew in a breath. "I loved being part of Swan Lake, even when I wasn't the lead. The Nutcracker was also one of my favorites."

He watched her slip into a dreamy expression, eyes far off. A small smile graced her lips and it made his heart squeeze. He wondered if she was reliving those days—dancing across the stage, the crowd, the spotlight, the dream. A distant part of him imagined a fantasy of him there, watching her, supporting her, kissing her after the show. Emmett had never been to a ballet, but for her, he'd go all the time.

She was changing his world. It sounded corny as all hell, but it was true.

"I would have loved to see it."

"Maybe I'll show you some of the recordings one day."

"I'd be honored."

They slipped into new conversation, but as they reached the edge of the commercial area that was close to a trail, Illiana skittered to a stop. Directly on the corner was a shop, a sign in the window proclaiming FOR SALE. It had large plate glass windows and limewashed brick. Said windows were boarded up, but inside was completely open and stripped, ready for anything.

"What?" he asked.

"What's the story with that building?"

"It was a boutique, but a main waterline burst and ruined all the merchandise and the entire thing had to be gutted. It was part way through before they realized their insurance didn't cover it so they cut their losses. It's been sitting there ever since."

"Oh, that's so sad."

"It was. The family even left Rose Point after—they were new to town at that time—and I guess they took it as a sign that they weren't meant to stay."

"When did this happen?"

"February, I think. We had a cold snap and a lot of waterlines froze and burst. Nate's brother-in-law owns one of the restoration companies in town, and they did a lot of overtime that week."

Illiana nodded half-heartedly, but it was like she was seeing something else. Her eyes were far off as he scrutinized her.

"You're thinking very hard."

She shook her head. "Sorry, yeah. I…I'll tell you later."

They continued the rest of the walk with his dogs, stirring up their familiar banter. Near a field they stopped and threw a ball for the dogs, both of them darting after it—Leia snatching it before Gimili's short little legs could catch up. When the dogs were lagging, they called it to an end and returned to his house, and Emmett realized that with Illiana he felt more at ease about the whole situation—about them. How could something that felt so right be *wrong?* But it was when Illiana left that the heavy cloud of guilt descended upon him and all that effortlessness and dreaminess vanished.

Real life and consequences awaited.

He was right. There had been no time to talk to Nate before the fire.

Emmett had been swamped with work all day Tuesday, not having a chance to respond to any personal texts and calls beyond quick picture updates to Illiana when she teased him via text. Though she told him his answering wasn't necessary if he was busy—but if he were honest with himself, he liked doing it.

The cherry on top was that beer at Blue's was cancelled Tuesday night because *everyone* suddenly had something come up and decided to forgo the bar and just do the fire. Nate's excuse—though valid—was simply that he didn't feel like drinking after having just suffered the mother of all hangovers. Chase and Patrick were waiting for someone from Marketplace to pick something up; Kieran had been helping a fellow teacher with some summer school curriculum, and Graham had to work late.

It felt like the universe was having a laugh at Emmett's expense.

As soon as he'd gotten home from work, he'd showered, taken the dogs for a quick walk, and then threw some leftover spaghetti in the microwave. As it warmed, he filled the dog's food and water, made sure both the AC units were working and keeping the house cool, then put on some dog sensory videos to entertain Leia and Gimli while he was gone. Once the pasta was ready, he scarfed it down, still very hot, and shot off a text to Nate.

Hey, can you make it to the fire a bit earlier?

Emmett finished his spaghetti in record time and had the dish rinsed then in the dishwasher before Nate replied.

Sorry, man. I'm actually running behind. Did you want me to pick anything up?

Fuck.

No, it's okay. I'll see you there.

Sounds good!

Emmett tapped his brow several times in self despair.

"You stupid, stupid fuck," he said to himself.

He knew this was going to blow up in his face, and he was trying his best to mitigate the blast radius as much as he could, but the more time that passed, the more he knew this whole thing was going to go nuclear.

Sighing deeply, he pocketed his phone, grabbed his wallet, keys, travel cup, and a bag of chips. He said goodbye to his dogs, armed his cameras, and went out the door. As he locked up behind himself, Illiana messaged him.

Mina and I are catching a ride with Nate, so I don't think telling him before is going to happen unless you want me to do it.

Please don't.

I figured as much. After?

In his SUV he leaned his head against the steering wheel, reluctance heavy on his shoulders. He responded:

After.

Feeling a surge of confidence, he messaged again.

Illiana?

A third message.

What are we?

The response was instant.

I'd like to talk about that after.

Heart emoji.

He pulled out of his driveway with a smile you couldn't beat off his face.

By the time Emmett arrived at the beach, Nate and the girls were just trekking down to it. Everyone had camping chairs that they carried down with their assorted bags.

The sun was still high in the sky, sunshine bearing down with its oppressive heat, promising a heatwave of record temperatures coming. The waves of the ocean crashed gently against the surf, kelp and seaweed lining the rocky edges where the tide typically found the sand. Around a small fire, a large bucket of ocean water beside it, was Chase and his boyfriend Patrick, Kieran, Graham, and Madeline.

And Jace.

Son of a fucking bitch.

Emmett groaned internally and made it down, discovering the only free spot was between Kieran and Madeline. Illiana meanwhile was seated with Mina on one side and Nate on the other. She made an apologetic expression but he waved it off. He didn't have to sit next to her to know she was—for lack of a better word—his.

He pulled out his phone and texted her.

At least across from you I can see your reaction in real time when I tell you that you're gorgeous.

Illiana looked at her phone and a small smile crossed her face, a slight blush following.

And that you taste delicious.

That blush turned into a full of red inferno. Her eyes flashed up to his, a mix of teasing and warning.

Maybe not. Unless you want him to look over and take note of this.
Realization struck him. *You're right.*

Emmett pocketed his phone and took a drink from his travel cup.

"Please tell me there isn't any alcohol in there," Nate said, looking green. "And if there is, just lie to me."

Emmett laughed. "It's just water."

It really was, but Nate didn't look convinced.

"I'm still bummed I couldn't make it," Jace inserted, and Emmett had to stop himself from rolling his eyes. "Especially since the infamous Illiana was there."

Illiana hid her face behind her drink, and no one else deigned to acknowledge him. It was clear that no one wanted him around, but he had a terrible habit of coming uninvited.

"I'm swearing off hard liquor for the foreseeable future," Nate said. "Unless something big happens."

"Is my birthday a big enough thing?" Graham asked, chuckling. "Or have you forgotten?"

"You're definitely big enough for me, babe," Nate fake-flirted.

"And I'd never forget. It's July 29th, asshole."

The same terms of endearment for *babe* went for *asshole.*

"Anyone here birthday twins?" Mina asked.

Everyone went around calling out their birthdays. No one was, not even day twins. The only thing in common was they had two Leo Zodiac signs—Chase and Graham—when Madeline pointed them out.

"So, which signs are most compatible?" Nate asked Madeline curiously. "I'm the scorpion—Scorpio, right?"

Madeline deliberated for a moment. "I think Pisces is their perfect match."

Emmett tensed.

Illiana was a Pisces.

As Madeline had just announced to everyone.

Nate was giving Illiana a glowing look. Emmett tried to squander his jealousy.

"Yeah," Madeline continued. "I think Pisces and other water signs. Earth signs too."

"What kind of sign is Aries?" Emmett asked, fiddling with his cup.

"Aries is a fire sign," Madeline supplied and then a thought struck her. "And funny enough, on the topic of Pisces—they're their worst compatibility."

You have got to be fucking kidding me.

Illiana thinned her lips, casting a dark look at Madeline even though she couldn't see.

"But honestly, compatibility doesn't necessarily equate to an ideal relationship. Signs that don't make the perfect pair are not the end of a relationship, it just means that more communication will be necessary. And as much as I love zodiacs, it's not a flawless thing. Everyone can't fit into these perfect boxes, especially when you factor in other things that shape a person—life experiences and such—but it's fun to me."

Madeline's fun was not so fun for Emmett.

"Let's keep going with the *getting to know each other* thing!" Mina said, clearly sensing Illiana and Emmett's tension. "Why don't we play two-truths-and-a-lie?" Affirmation sounded around. "Okay, I'll go first."

Mina visibly pondered, tapping her light brown finger against her chin. Her green eyes looked skyward before she came to some conclusions.

"Okay. One; my first concert was Nickelback. Two; I am terrified of thunderstorms. Three; there are only five outlets in my apartment."

"That last one is oddly specific," Nate said critically.

"It is, isn't it?" Mina taunted.

The group went around deliberating, but Illiana stayed silent, probably because she knew the answer already. When they agreed that number three was the lie, both Illiana and Mina smirked.

"Nope, that's a truth. The lie is thunderstorms—I actually love them. I'll sit out on my balcony and listen to them." Mina turned to Kieran. "Your turn."

The next couple rounds were easier for the group as all the guys knew each other so well—though Emmett was shocked that he didn't know Graham once had a threesome—but when it came Illiana's turn, they were back to the difficult guessing.

"One; I once binge watched all the extended editions of *The Lord of the Rings* in a single day." Emmett already knew the lie the second she spoke. "Two; I love strawberry scented things. Three; I've taken pole dancing lessons."

Illiana had to have taken pole dancing lessons. He knew she'd be good at it. That dancer's grace, the strength. He wondered if she'd worked out a routine that blended both her ballerina skills and pole. Could she dance Swan Lake to a new beat? He wanted to find out. It was utterly fascinating—*she* was fascinating.

Nate slightly leaned toward Illiana and gave a delicate sniff. "Well, I know two is true, so it's one or three."

"That's cheating!" Illiana said aghast, waving him off with a laugh.

Nate smiled, joy beaming out of him. Illiana seemed to realize her faux pas immediately and her eyes darkened with shame. Emmett noticed it darken even more—presumably realizing she'd brought up a sensual activity around Nate.

Everyone began deliberating, but Emmett kept his mouth shut. He figured knowing the answer was cheating, so he kept quiet, opening his bag of chips and fishing a few out. Nate looked at him quizzically.

"You're not going to guess?" his friend accused him and Emmett processed how he'd just fucked up. It seemed like he was snubbing Illiana. *Dammit.*

Emmett cleared his throat and glanced at Illiana. Her lips were thinned when he caught her gaze. He debated on lying, but he already had one foot in his mouth, he didn't need to stuff the other one in it too.

"I think number one is the lie."

"You're assuming because she did ballet that she also took pole lessons?" Nate inquired.

Jesus fuck. Time for a small fib. "She told me she'd never seen *Star Wars* or *The Lord of the Rings*. At the party," he quickly amended.

Nate's prickliness dissipated and he settled into the chair at Illiana's side. "Ah, I'm guessing that's why you didn't say anything. 'Cause you knew."

Emmett nodded. "Didn't want to spoil the fun."

"Fair enough, fair enough, babe."

"Emmett is right," Illiana sighed. "I haven't seen them yet. I've been trying to, though."

Emmett tried desperately not to react, and he could have sworn he felt calculating and suspicious eyes on him, but he refused to meet them for fear of confirmation. He shovelled another handful of chips into his mouth, the bag crinkling noisily as he wordlessly offered them to the others. The bag was passed around as Emmett wiped his hands free of crumbs.

"So, you do pole dancing?" Jace asked, leaning forward, his foppish blond hair on his brow.

Emmett's hackles immediately went up and he wasn't the only one to evidently react. All the others shifted, the air growing palpable with tension. He curled his fingers in his fists, knuckles whitening. He kept his eyes locked on Jace as a muscle feathered in his jaw. He was just waiting for Jace to say the word *stripper*, and he knew if he did, he'd deck him. Not because being an exotic dancer was a bad thing, but because of how Jace associated the word with something dirty.

"I took a couple classes," Illiana corrected, sensing the turn of energy. "It was more for upper body work and some co-ordination."

"Well, I mean you do have a gorgeous body," Jace said, looking her up and down. "A bit skinny, though."

"*Jace,*" Emmett bit out viciously at the same time as Chase reprimanded, saying:

"That's not appropriate."

Patrick's brown eyes were wide, but he said nothing, knowing he could complicate things as being involved with the family already. It was a delicate, messy balance, but there would be a line—Emmett knew—and Jace was fast approaching it.

"What?" Jace said defensively. "It's just the truth! She's hot—she knows it!"

Illiana looked like she wanted to crawl in a hole. Her eyes darkened as she visibly slipped into herself, curling in and disappearing. It had Emmett's anger surging up, thickening his throat.

"Stop talking," Emmett hissed. "Right now."

"Don't talk about her like that," Nate said sharply, adding to the chastisement of Jace.

"It's not like I called her fat. All I said was she's sk—"

"You should leave," Emmett commanded. "Now."

He'd had enough of Jace. He was ignorant and a pig. No matter what size or shape her body was, Jace had no right to comment on it. He knew Illiana dealt with disordered eating—he'd observed her enough with food— though he didn't know the specifics, and *this* kind of comment was the *exact* thing that could derail her. He felt extra sick to his stomach wondering what Jace would've said about Delilah—and felt terrible for his ex at the idea. It made the dislike for Jace transform into pure loathing.

"I think you need to cool down," Patrick said tentatively, head tilting to his partner, brown waves falling over his brow. "We can talk some things out later."

Jace pointedly ignored his soon to be brother-in-law. Emmett seethed.

"Jace," Chase said, softly. "I think you've put your foot in your mouth. Maybe it's best if you—"

"Oh my God, you guys are a bunch of sensitive little snowflakes. I'm fucking out of here!"

With that, Jace stormed off, dragging his chair with him. They all sat in silence, Emmett trying to meet Illiana's eyes, but she averted them. She took a sip of water and worked her jaw against tears. All he wanted to do was hold her.

But he didn't.

He couldn't.

Because they had a secret that would ruin the night even more.

They all stayed where they were until the sound of Jace's car starting met their ears and the crunch of gravel between his squealing tires left the lot.

They all seemed to let out a collective exhale. Silence filled the air, nothing aside from the crash of waves on surf, the squall of gulls, the crackle of the fire.

"Well," Nate said, breaking the silence, inclining his chin at Emmett. "Your turn."

Emmett felt like he was treading on dangerous territory and elected for the safe options. "I hate brussel sprouts; I've never gone scuba diving; I once forgot my sister's birthday and she forced me to be her servant for a week."

"I remember that one," Graham inserted. "We were away at Riley's bachelor party. We were, what? Nineteen?"

"Nineteen," Emmett confirmed.

"Boo," Nate said. "Substitute the last one. Something fun. Drinking misadventures, wild stuff with an ex—I'm sure you have stories about D—"

"Maybe let's *not* with the exes," Kieran interrupted. "We don't need to talk shit. Not after Jace's comments."

"I wasn't going to; she was perfectly nice—"

"She was," Emmett confirmed. "But I made my truths and lie, so it's narrowed down to two."

Illiana shifted and Emmett glanced over. Illiana was uncrossing and recrossing her legs. She licked her lips and smirked, then mouthed a single word with a raised brow.

Wild?

Emmett burned from the teasing, his blood rushing. Oh, he was walking so many narrow lines. Inadvertently keeping secrets and purposely keeping from others until the time was right. How had he gotten things so messy? He had always prided himself on being honest. This was the *furthest* thing from honest.

They deduced the lie was about scuba diving—he had in fact gone when he'd taken a trip to Mexico with his brother and sister. After that round finished, they filtered into conversations rather than prompting for another game. More questions were asked about Illiana, Mina, and Madeline, as they were the newest to the group. Though everyone seemed to be conscious of not crossing certain lines. The guys lapsed into nostalgia and memories, jokes and teasing, bullshit and whatever. The tension in the air that was so tight finally released, and he just enjoyed the soft warmth from the fire while they could—a fire ban would surely be in effect any day now—and the steady pulse of the waves against the shore. The briny air mingled softly with the smoke, hints of pine from the surrounding trees adding to the essence.

"So, Illiana," Nate began, tapping his hand on his knee. A nervous tic Emmett recognized. "Are you planning to stay for the whole summer?"

"I...I haven't gotten that far yet. I hope so, but only as long as Mina and your parents are still fine to have me—which, I may add, I am so appreciative of."

"They love having you around. It's like you're part of the family."

Illiana cringed slightly, but she hid it with a smile. Emmett's mouth tightened at the comment.

Family—he knew what kind of family Nate was talking about. The kind Nate wanted her to join. He was frustrated with his anger because Nate didn't know. He was hiding this huge thing from his best friend. Illiana hadn't said anything either—which was no fault of her own, she didn't know.

"All right, Romeo," Mina chastised Nate. "Laying it on thick, aren't you? You haven't even asked if she's seeing anyone."

Beneath Nate's light brown complexion, he flushed with embarrassment.

"I thought—I mean, I guessed…I'm sorry, are you seeing someone?"

Illiana looked like a deer in the headlights, and Emmett could see Mina visibly cursing herself for opening up this can of worms. She visibly blanched and stuffed her face with some chips while glancing apologetically at Illiana. Nervous perspiration beaded on Emmett's brow—he didn't want it all to come out *now*. Not *here*. Not like *this*. Emmett was praying to the universe that Illiana lied or stretched the truth. But at the same time, he half wanted her to rip off the band-aid and just get it out there so he didn't have to.

God, what a coward he was.

"I, um…sort of. It's casual, there's no title on it."

The light dimmed from Nate's eyes and his expression slipped. Nate was like a deflated balloon. The wind fell from his sails. He sank back into his chair, taking a sip from his Coca-Cola, and forced a smile—he knew it was forced because Emmett had known him long enough. His friend was hurting and he was at fault.

"Well, I hope he treats you well."

"He does."

The night seemed to fall apart after that, everyone picking up on the morose vibes so easily damaged from what Jace had already shredded. Madeline tried to inject some positivity into the group, but it was half-hearted. Nate wasn't pouting or making a scene; he was just more reserved. He still smiled and laughed and joked, but there was a blunt edge to it—the clear betrayal of his lost hope. Chase and Patrick toned down any lovey-dovey-ness while Graham and Kieran tried to carry on conversations with Illiana and Mina, pulling Emmett and Nate into them. But when prickling tension arose between Mina and Graham, things seemed to change. Immediately after, things dissolved and the fire was put out.

As everyone trudged up the beach, Illiana kept casting apologetic looks to Emmett behind Nate's back. The girls were bringing up the rear, and it was clear the three of them knew exactly what was up. Emmett wondered if Madeline was let in on the secret.

Fuck.

The *Secret?*

Who was he?

No, this had to end. Nate needed to know.

Emmett loaded his things into his SUV, dusting off the sand from his shoes, clapping them together as he sat on the open trunk. He watched Illiana climb into the back of Nate's truck, a slight solemnity in her eyes beneath the streetlight. Fuck, he just wanted to comfort her from Jace's barbed words and making her be the one to rip the band aid off with Nate—even though the hurt was far from over for his best friend, all thanks to him—he prayed that they didn't set her back. The sky had darkened to a lush violet, streaks of orange still lingering overhead. The girl he was falling for slipped into the vehicle and disappeared from view behind the tint.

"You were weird tonight."

Emmett jumped with Nate's approach. He'd been so focused that he hadn't been aware of his surroundings. Did Nate notice?

"I was?"

"Yeah, around Illiana. You like…didn't want to talk to her at all but jumped to her defense."

"Nate…about that."

"Is it because you knew she was seeing someone?"

"I—yeah, kind of. I didn't know how to tell you, the timing was just bad, and—"

"So, you let me look like an idiot all this time? Pining after her? Encouraging me to ask her out?"

"I didn't know until after. At the party."

"You could have told me as soon as you knew."

"I—I didn't know how." Emmett pivoted slightly. Time to come clean. "Look, I need to tell you—"

"No." Nate put a hand up. "I'm sorry I just…I'm not ready to hear anything. I'm not in the right headspace." Nate looked up, his hazel eyes holding a shimmer. *Awe, shit.* "I'm hurt you didn't tell me. She's allowed to do whatever she wants—she doesn't owe me anything. But you…I had hoped you would let me know about something like this."

"That's what I'm trying—"

"Em. I told you not right now. I just need a little time to process." He sighed and started walking away. "I'll talk to you tomorrow. Love you, bro."

Emmett sank down. "Love you, too," he mumbled.

This was not how he expected this going. He was trying to tell Nate, but it was like the universe was refusing him. He didn't want to shout it, but damn, it was getting to that point.

He watched Nate get into his truck and pull away. Emmett was still standing there in the near dark, the last to leave. Heaving a sigh, he scrubbed his hands through his hair, fixing his topknot. When he got into his SUV and started it, a phone call immediately came through. He accepted the call handsfree as he shoulder-checked before pulling out.

"Hey, Kieran," Emmett said into the dark interior. "What's up?"

"I'm not going to pussyfoot around it," Kieran said sharply. "Are you alone?"

Emmett's heart sank. "I am."

"Are you seeing Illiana? Because it sure as fuck seems like it."

Emmett exhaled harshly as he pulled onto the main road. He pinched the bridge of his nose and nodded, but then he remembered that Kieran couldn't see him.

"Yeah. I am."

"What the fuck, man?" Kieran sighed. "I'd hoped I was wrong, but I have fucking eyes."

"I didn't know. I didn't know she was the same person. *Ana* was the girl I met at the bar—you remember?" Kieran confirmed, so Emmett continued. "*Ana* was Ill*iana*. None of us put it together because Nate's been mispronouncing her name for ten years. I know it's obvious now, but it wasn't in the moment. I only figured it out when I saw her at the Canada Day party."

Kieran blew out a breath. "Look, I'm not getting involved, so I won't tell him—but you should. You really should. He deserves to know and if you wait too long, I *will* say something. I think Graham is figuring it out too. Chase hasn't said anything."

"I know. I keep meaning to. But I didn't want to ruin the party, and then he was hungover Sunday, and I didn't want to make his day worse. Then yesterday I was swamped with work and he didn't answer my calls—and I was not going to tell him this over text—and then I literally *just* tried to tell him and he wouldn't let me."

"It's shit luck, but you're all adults and you have to take responsibility for this. Illiana is her own person and doesn't belong to anyone—you can't call dibs, or first, or whatever the fuck. So, just...keep that in mind when this comes out. And don't be shocked if Nate struggles for a bit. He's a good guy, but this is going to be a blow, and he might act…regretfully."

"I know," Emmett whispered, languishing.

"It'll be okay, babe, just give it time."

"I will."

The call ended and Emmett drove the rest of the way home in silence, alone with his thoughts and his guilt. This secret would continue to fester inside him. The connection between him and Illiana couldn't suffer for this. He needed all the hidden out, and that included not telling the full truth about Delilah, too.

CHAPTER NINETEEN
Illiana

Illiana had a date with Emmett at his house, and it was the anniversary of her accident. Of her life imploding so completely.

She'd asked him if she could spend the night with him, first because she missed him, but secondly, because she felt lost and floaty. She wanted to open up to him. She'd already started with telling him about some of her performances, and she felt safe with him.

She wanted to expand on it.

To tell him everything, to connect with him, and to tell him that she was pretty certain she wanted to be with him. As more than a fling. She didn't come here with the intention of finding a boyfriend, but she'd found more than she'd bargained for.

She found her place.

Her home.

With him.

She knew he felt it, too, and her heart swelled.

Home.

It felt right.

When she'd gotten home from the fire last night, she'd showered off the scent of woodsmoke and then Illiana and Mina talked about the absolute fucking mess the evening had turned into.

"I'm so sorry, Ana," Mina was apologizing, her tone anguished. "Jace is a fucking prick, and I didn't expect Nate to flat out ask like that."

"It's okay," she assured while braiding her golden locks into two plaits. She had begun pulling into herself as the hours crept toward midnight, the first anniversary drawing her into the depths of darkness, spurned on by Jace's comments about her body.

It had taken so much will-power to force herself to eat something when she got back, vile words echoing in her mind, telling her she was worthless and never good enough. Emmett had texted her, apologizing profusely for everything and assuring that she was okay. He'd even gone so far as to beg her to forget anything Jace said and that no matter what she looked like, he thought she was a goddess. It helped.

Mina had also texted Madeline—with Illiana's permission—to fill her in on the messy Illiana/Emmett/Nate situation and the redhead immediately came back with explicit apologies. She even texted them herself when Mina gave her Illiana's number. It was all sorted out, but she could tell Madeline felt guilty.

While she was braiding, Mina cleared her throat.

"Tomorrow is the anniversary," Mina said softly.

"It is." Illiana's voice was dull.

"Do…do you want to do anything? Can I help?"

Illiana flexed her jaw. "If I'm being completely honest, I think I just want to be with Emmett."

"You really like him, don't you?"

"I think it's more than that."

"Oh…damn."

"I know."

They had lapsed into silence, keeping the quiet even when they had gone to bed. Illiana had texted Emmett again, and that's how she was now in his kitchen in a tank top and a pair of sweat shorts.

The AC was humming, and Emmett was cooking Pad Thai for them while she petted the dogs with her foot, both of them surrounding her. She watched Emmett's back flex through his white T-shirt as he moved about, reaching for spices and ingredients. He was in a pair of gray sweatpants and they hid zero secrets.

"I wanted to talk to you about a few things," Illiana started, looking down on the dogs. "Before this becomes *more*."

Emmett turned, setting the wooden spoon he was cooking with on the rest. He turned down the heat and then leaned against the counter.

"What about?"

"My past. What today is for me."

Emmett was listening intently. His face was so open and earnest that it made her heart clench.

She drew in a deep breath. "Today is the one-year anniversary of the car accident that shattered my foot and ruined my ballerina days." Illiana sucked in her cheeks as she wrapped her arms around herself. "I was driving home after practice and some kid was on his phone—not paying attention—and turned left into me when I was going straight. I was in a little car—a fucking Honda Civic—and he was in a jacked-up truck. It didn't stand a chance, and when he hit me, it was so bad. The engine ended up in the passenger's seat and my foot was crushed when I tried to hit the brakes."

Illiana looked away, tears welling up in her eyes. She bit her lip.

"When they got me out, I heard the word 'amputation' and everything started getting hazy. I was in so much pain—my wrist was sprained; I hit my head on something; my ribs were bruised, and I had seatbelt and airbag burns. When I got to the hospital, they gave me something for the pain and told me that they could save my foot, but that the mobility would be severely impacted. I didn't quite understand what that meant in the moment, but all I knew was that if I got to keep my foot, I could keep my life." She scoffed. "Two days later, they did the surgery and when I woke up, they told me they had to fuse more than they expected and that my range of motion was even less than they'd hoped."

Illiana's fingers tightened on her arms and Emmett took the food off the heat and crossed to her. He wrapped her in his arms, gazing down at her. She knew her eyes were glassy with tears because he was blurry above her.

"My parents completely abandoned me then. After they found out their prodigy was no more, they virtually disowned me. The only contact I really have with them is my pity rent that they pay only because they probably can't excuse being more of a set of assholes when they drove me to a career that damaged my body so much *and* gave me an eating disorder."

Emmett flinched and brushed her hair back from her brow. He didn't say anything, still listening.

"I'm getting better. I've learned I can eat more food in moderation. I've gained eight pounds since last year and it's been an uphill battle in accepting it." She'd gained two since being on the west coast. "And then of course, after hearing I'd no longer be a ballerina, Adrian dumped me. Left me for my understudy, Violet, and packed up all his things from our apartment. He took the cat, and everything that marked us as a couple was neatly packed into a box and left on the kitchen counter.

"I've refused to accept it for a year—fighting in therapy and physio with Mina—but it's time to accept it. I'll never be a ballerina again. I'll never dance on the stage ever again." She breathed out and looked up at Emmett. "I am not broken. My dreams are not broken—they've just changed."

"What changes have you made to your dreams?" he whispered ardently.

She blinked away tears. "Being a prima ballerina would have been a detriment to me one day starting a family. But now, it's something I can actually consider—and I'm learning I want it."

He didn't say anything so she drew in a breath and continued.

"I don't know if it will happen—if it *can* happen—being severely underweight has really fucked with my cycles, but it's been normal for the past two months, so I have hope." She smiled shakily. "Have I scared you off, yet?"

Emmett tightened his arms around Illiana and suddenly lifted her, boosting her onto the counter. He stood in the cradle of her thighs, her arms draped over his shoulders. The stone was cool beneath her thighs and she shivered between the cold and how Emmett caressed her face with the back of his hand.

"The complete opposite, actually. I think I've fallen for you more."

A gasp lodged in Illiana's throat and her eyes widened as she took in his face. The planes and angles, the high cheekbones, the brown of his eyes and the amber starburst, his proud mouth, his strong brow. All the features of the man, she too, was falling for. Fast, hard, heavy, and desperate.

"You've fallen for me?"

"Hopelessly," he whispered, leaning in, his lips ghosting across her mouth. "Thank you for trusting me with all this. For being vulnerable with me."

"Of course."

"Do you want to meet my family tomorrow?"

Her heart surged. "I'd love to."

"Good. But tonight is for us."

Illiana could have cried. Emotion surged up within her, a blade straight to her heart, pouring utter devotion into her soul. She tugged Emmett closer to her, a single tear leaking down her cheek as she pressed her mouth firmly to his. Their tongues tangled together; his mouth slanted over hers. He tilted her chin up to give him greater access and swept in—claiming her, her surrendering.

She wanted to fall into him, and he into her. She wanted to be with him—wholly and completely. She wanted him to take her heart, for she had already given it. She wanted him to offer his because she needed him. He was this incredible human being who wanted *her*.

Her—who had been discarded once her celebrity use vanished.

Her—who had been left when the lifestyle and status had to change.

Her—whose career evaporated overnight.

Her—who left the city she'd known all her life and found her home.

Illiana whimpered as Emmett's hand fisted in her long golden locks, his other slipped from around her waist, fingers trailing between her legs. The dogs vacated from the kitchen, sensing the mood shift and pouted by the window as Emmett let out a soft groan. Her hands both fused in his black waves, tugging at his top knot. Their breaths were desperate, devouring. Their touches, possessive and claiming. She broke for breath and his mouth found her throat.

"I'm falling for you, too," she rasped.

He paused and then met her eyes. He grinned, and it was so sexy and so endearing. "Well, thank fuck for that."

Their mouths met again, the kiss deepening as the emotion flooded between them.

The dogs' feet suddenly scrabbled on the hardwood and the sound of glass bottles shattering on the floor pierced their romance.

"*What the fuck?*"

Illiana and Emmett broke apart just to turn and find Nate standing in a sea of broken glass and spilled beer in the entryway.

His face was fucking devastated. Nate's mouth dropped open, eyes widened to show whites all around. He was frozen, staring in shock and horror.

Emmett and Illiana were frozen as well, hands still on each other, mouth's kiss-bruised, hair tousled, arousals very much apparent—even more so for Emmett who was wearing *gray sweatpants*, of all clothing items.

"What the *actual* fuck."

CHAPTER TWENTY
Emmett

Emmett's friends had always been welcome to come over whenever they wanted. They'd each had personal codes, specifically keyed to each of them, but now Emmett was sorely regretting that generosity. Because now, here he stood, in gray sweatpants, boner on full display, with his hand between the legs of the girl his best friend thought he loved—the girl *he* might even love.

I am so *fucked.*

"I can explain," Emmett rasped, disentangling from Illiana and trying to hide his embarrassingly hard dick.

"Oh, can you now?" Nate spat, fury radiating from him. "What the *fuck*, Emmett?"

"I didn't know."

"Didn't know *what?*"

"I didn't know she was Illi*ana*," Emmett began to explain, specifically mispronouncing her name as Nate had done for the last ten years. The tiny slip of tongue that had gotten them all into this mess in the first place. "I met her as *Ana*—started seeing her as Ana."

"Fucking her as Ana, too?"

Illiana jolted, and Nate's fire instantly banked. He looked remorseful immediately.

Anger roared in Emmett's veins, the need to defend Illiana borderline-territorial. All traces of his erection faded, and he took a step forward, ushering Illiana behind him. She softly slipped from the counter and straightened her clothes as Emmett stood, seething in front of her.

"Watch yourself. Don't you dare try to drag her for this," Emmett hissed. "This was my fault."

"No, you're right on that." Nate's guilty eyes flickered to Illiana. "I'm sorry, it's not your fault—I shouldn't have said that. It was wrong. I'm not mad at you—a little disappointed, but that's not on you, I get it." His face swung to Emmett. "But *you*. I'm pissed as hell at *you*."

"I tried telling you—"

"You could have told me just to shut up for a second and listen!"

"You told me you weren't in the right headspace! What was I supposed to do? *Text it to you*?"

"You could have yelled it in my face! Maybe made time! Instead, you decided to just let me look like a fucking idiot." His nostrils flared in anger. "Does everyone know?"

Emmett hesitated, his heart hammered with a rhythm rival to a drum. "Not everyone."

"Who." Nate said it so flatly—so lethally. It wasn't a question; it was a demand.

Emmett had never seen Nate this furious. Had never seen this cold anger before. It sent fear skittering down his spine, his nerves sparking. He didn't do fights—especially with his friends—but something was broken in Nate right now—betrayal singing in his eyes.

"Kieran figured it out last night. He said Graham suspected something. I don't know about Chase and Patrick. Mina and Madeline have known since the party, I think."

"I imagine Mina has known longer." He spoke directly to Illiana. "Right?"

She shrank a little but nodded. She hadn't reacted to who all knew because he'd informed her earlier—much to her mortification. "She knew I was seeing someone here—she didn't know it was him until the party. Madeline didn't know until after the fire."

"None of us realized until the party," Emmett added calmly. "And we didn't want to ruin the day. I asked her to let me be the one to tell you. Everyone that knows, I asked to wait until I had told you myself, please don't be mad at them."

Nate looked like he'd been struck. Pain and tears glimmered briefly in his green eyes before wrath burned it out. "So, everyone kept me in the fucking dark."

"Nate…it's not like that."

"Isn't it?" he spat. "You know how I feel—" he broke off and flickered to Illiana, "*felt* about her."

"I know," Emmett said, hands up in submission. "I'm sorry Nate. This isn't how I wanted to tell you."

"I came over here to fucking apologize for my behaviour last night." Nate snorted. "Surprise for me, I guess!"

"Nate, I'm so sorry I didn't tell you."

Nate's lip curled up over his teeth. "You aren't forgiven. This was a shitty secret to keep, Em." He stared at the floor, a muscle in his jaw feathering. "I'm not ready to accept an apology—just give me some time." Nate started backing out, navigating the sour beer and broken glass. "Sorry about the mess." Free of the shards, he looked up at Illiana. "I'm sorry for putting you in this position."

And with that, Nate swept out of the house before either of them could get another word in.

In the wake of the storm that was Nate, Emmett and Illiana stood stunned still in the kitchen, Pad Thai forgotten. Both of Emmett's dogs were perched on the couch, watching Nate leave. Emmett realized distantly that they'd left the kitchen in favor of the window not because things between him and Illiana were heating up, but rather as a warning to Nate's approach.

Fuck.

Illiana met his gaze, blue eyes subdued. It was like there was a dark rain cloud hovering between them now. She opened her mouth once, twice.

"Do you want to go after him?" she asked gingerly.

"Yes, but I don't think I should. He's too angry."

"Should I leave?" Her lip trembled.

Emmett's voice was concrete. "Please don't."

She nodded. "You finish dinner. I'll clean up the mess."

"I can do it; you can take over here."

"I would end up ruining it," she deflected. "Are supplies under the sink?"

"Yeah, left side."

The next half hour was spent with Emmett silent at the stove, finishing off their dinner; Illiana on her hands and knees picking up every bit of glass and putting it in an old ice cream bucket Emmett usually kept for nuts, bolts, and screws. Once the visible pieces were disposed of, the rest was wiped, vacuumed, mopped, and finished with a natural wood cleaner. Illiana washed her hands and Emmett set out plates for them.

"Take as much as you want," Emmett told her, smoothing a hand over her head. He kissed her temple. "I'm so sorry sweetheart."

Illiana shrugged. "It's okay—I'm a little embarrassed to be caught like that, but…" she sighed. "It is what it is."

"I know today was hard enough for you as it is."

She nodded, eyes watery.

"Do you want to call Mina?"

She shook her head. "I'll tell her tomorrow."

They took their food and ate in relative silence, a somber mood lingering between them. It smelled of spices, lingering beer, and cleaner in the house, and it had his stomach twisting. The guilt was thick and despite how much they cared about each other and were attracted to each other, the culpability was too heavy to ignore. Emmett noticed Illiana took a generous plateful, and he was proud of her for taking that step, though he didn't acknowledge it—he'd read something about never commenting on the amount of food someone recovering from an eating disorder took, even if it was positive.

Emmett received several texts from his friends in varying degrees of support.

You really fucked up, huh? From Kieran.

You need to talk? Nate just told us about Illiana and you. He didn't say too much, but I can't see you trying to undermine him. Graham.

You know, I usually don't offer this to my friends because it's a conflict of interest, but let me know if you need to talk—professionally. Chase, of course.

He ignored all of them for the time being. He was too focused on helping Illiana through her emotions and whatever was still between them.

"I just want you to know," she started while they were curled on the couch together, the first movie starting. "I never promised him anything or did anything with him, but I still feel bad."

"I know, sweetheart. I trust you."

The damper lightened some and they were able to converse and flirt again as he pulled her more snugly against him, but this time when they put on *Star Wars*, they actually finished it.

When Emmett woke the next morning, Illiana was wrapped in his arms. In his bed. He was in bliss. But then yesterday's events came crashing down, and he sank into himself. He stared at the ceiling, stroking Illiana's golden tresses, her face contentedly nuzzling against his chest. Her shoulder was perfectly slotted under his arm, their legs twisted together.

He reached over for his phone, hoping for a message from Nate.

Zero luck.

He exhaled then started typing out a message.

I'm so sorry. Text me when you're ready to talk.

Hours later and he'd still heard nothing.

CHAPTER TWENTY-ONE
Illiana

When Illiana got home to the pool house, it was obnoxiously early.

She came into the space like a whirlwind, slamming the door behind her. Mina jumped out of bed, frazzled. Her gray T-shirt hung off her shoulder, her legs on full display, and her hair—in a protective style—was the only tame thing around her.

"What the hell, Ana?" her best friend groaned, voice heavy with sleep.

"Nate knows," she announced in a rush, flopping onto the white bed, facedown. "Mina. Oh fuck, it was so bad." She turned her miserable face to her best friend. "He walked in on us."

Mina was instantly alert and straightening up. "He walked in on you two *fucking?*"

"No! We weren't that far. Yet. But I was on his counter and his hand was between my legs and we were kissing—oh hell, Mina it was terrible. He walked in and then all we heard was the sound of glass shattering and then they were arguing," she explained, covering her face with her hands. "It was so bad."

"Okay, no. Back up, tell me everything."

So, Illiana did. She recounted all the night's events, how Nate had shown up and found them, the words thrown like barbs, the unaccepted apology, all of it. Mina whistled when Illiana was done.

"Yeah. It really sat on us like a wet blanket last night."

"I can imagine," Mina scoffed, moving about the room and getting dressed.

"Also, I have dinner with his moms and sister tonight."

"You what?" Mina asked, surprised.

"He asked me to meet them."

"That's big."

"I know." Illiana covered her face. "I hope they like me."

"Ana…" Mina began, biting her lip. "It sounds like you want to be with him."

Illiana suddenly felt pulled in two different directions. Mina and Toronto, and then Emmett and Rose Point. She knew Toronto; it's where she'd been her entire life. It's where she'd met her best friend. But now *here*. Here was where she'd met Emmett. The guy she'd never had a closer connection with. The guy who made *here* feel like home.

Back there was Adrian and her parents and bad memories.

Here was the possibility of marriage and kids and a future.

But she was used to people leaving—expected it. Maybe it would be better do maintain a relationship across the country. Hard as it may be.

"I think I do."

Mina's eyes welled. "I'm happy for you."

"I don't know how we'd make long-distance work though."

"You could move here."

"I can't. I can't leave you. Besides, nothing is in stone—we're not officially together," Illiana comforted, going over to her and rubbing her arms. "It's a thought though. But I'm not uprooting my life on a whim."

"We already talked about this on the way here. I half-expected it."

Illiana looked at her quizzically, reading between the lines. "Mina…are you saying this because you want to move back here?"

Mina's chest deflated with relief. Those brimming tears spilled. "Yes. I miss it here. I miss my family. But I didn't want to leave, because…"

"Because of me."

Mina looked away.

"Oh, Mina…"

Tears trickled down her best friend's brown cheeks. "I couldn't do that to you, not after everyone abandoned you already. You were so alone. So low. It would have been cruel. So, I stayed. For you. Because I love you."

Illiana teared up as well. "I love you too."

They embraced and Illiana felt her heart surge and crack as Mina wrapped her arms around her, squeezing her tight as if she was the only thing keeping her from falling apart.

"This wasn't meant to be a guilt trip," Mina mumbled into her shoulder.

"It wasn't taken as one," she returned.

They broke apart and they both wiped tears from their cheeks.

"Do you want to spend the day together until you go to dinner?" Mina asked.

"That sounds perfect."

Illiana and Mina spent the day together around the Ellis house, reading by the pool, watching movies, making lunch. It was nice, effortless, and free. It was what summer always was supposed to be—that dream they sold you all those years growing up. Not mentioning the oppressive heat waves and mosquitoes and wild-fires. No, for the day it was that golden, dreamy thing, so effervescent and intangible with the scent of sunshine and sunscreen, chlorine and wine, the distant smoke of barbecue and mowed lawns. She'd come here, most importantly, to spend time with her best friend and this is what she was doing.

Too soon, the day wrapped up and it was time to get ready. She was, she had to admit, as equally excited as she was nervous for the night. She enjoyed her day and she was hoping the evening would shape up to be just as good.

Illiana decided to wear a floaty pink dress with a pattern of sequined red strawberries on it, the sleeves sweet and puffed. It might have been overdone, but she wanted to impress Emmett's family. She applied a thin coat of red lipstick but left the rest of her makeup as the dewy, natural look she gravitated to. Her hair was mostly down, parts of it pulled up at the back, wisps brushing her jaw.

She felt pretty.

When Emmett arrived to pick her up, his eyes widened with pleasure.

"You look beautiful," he said, tugging her close. He brushed a chaste kiss across her lips. "And these strawberries? You look good enough to eat, sweetheart."

"Ooh, back to the clichés?"

"I never gave them up."

She grinned and pressed her lips more firmly against his and then wiped the lipstick smear from his mouth with her thumb.

"I hope it left a mark," he said lowly.

"It did."

"Good, because I intend to leave my mark on you later." His fingers trailed down her throat. "Maybe here." They swept lower, down her back, tracing her spine until his hand cupped her hip, straying to her backside. "Or here."

Blood rushed through her. The idea of Emmett's lips dragging down her body, pressing kisses, his teeth nipping her ribs, her hip, her ass. Oh, she wanted it.

"And I think we'll find this lipstick in other places later," she said hotly, eyes straying meaningfully southward.

"You know, we don't actually have to go to dinner."

Illiana laughed. "No, let's go." She stroked his nose playfully. "Just know what's waiting for you later."

He took her overnight bag and stuffed it in the back.

They drove to Emmett's moms' place, fingers intertwined over the center console. At one point Emmett had brought her hand up to his mouth and gently kissed each of her knuckles, eyes never leaving the road. It made Illiana's heart swell. A few minutes—because everything was a short drive in Rose Point— they were pulling up to a modest two story house with red cedar shingles, gray stone, and white shutters. There was a wraparound porch, a trellis with roses climbing up the façade of the house, and a plum tree in the center of the yard. The front door was painted a rich burgundy, a wreath of greenery and baby's breath beheld a small heart-shaped knocker at its center.

Emmett helped Illiana out and together they walked up the paved drive, hands interlocked.

"Do I look okay?" Illiana asked, smoothing her hair with her free hand.

"You look like a goddess."

Illiana positively beamed. "You're just trying to score points for later."

"On the contrary, I just think you are. A gorgeous, glowing, golden goddess."

"You're giving me a lot of G-words here."

"Why don't I give you an O-word later?"

She gasped delightedly. "Oh, that was smooth."

"It was, wasn't it? I'm pretty proud of it."

She tugged him closer, giggling as they made their way to the front door. He didn't bother knocking, he just opened the door and called in.

"Hi, we're here!"

He tugged her through the house to the living room, done up in deep shades of merlot, rust, mahogany, and pumpkin. The couch was softly worn leather, an orange and canary knitted blanket hung over the back of it, throw pillows of brown and wine stripes stuffed into the sides. The wood furniture was all red cedar; the coffee table held a perfectly preserved live edge. Family photos lined the walls, pictures of Emmett and another girl with two women, summers and Halloweens, Christmases and school pictures. One complete wall was taken up by built-in bookcases, filled with battered books.

The quick shuffle of feet sounded inside, and Illiana was greeted to the sight of one of Emmett's mothers. She was short with gentle curves, long brown hair and glittering green eyes. She stood before Illiana and leaned on the doorframe of the kitchen, amused and pleased just as another figure rounded the corner.

"Is this boy good to you, Ana?"

Emmett huffed. "Ma," he said with a plea and warning in his voice. "Be nice to me."

"I'm always nice," she said in mock affront.

The second woman came into view—taller, with raven dark hair and the same amber-brown eyes as Emmett. She waved softly.

"Hi, hon. I'm Emmett's mom, Ashley." She cast a proud look at her son. "He told us about you, but not how beautiful you are."

"Oh! Thank you, Emmett's told me a lot about you, too."

"All good, I hope."

"Knowing you, it's the worst," his green-eyed mother teased.

Ashley playfully swatted her.

"Oh, and Riley couldn't make it, he's taking the girls camping," Ashely added quickly.

He shook his head. "Ma, this is Illiana. Illiana, this is Danika."

Danika wrapped Illiana in an embrace, warmth suffusing her. "It's so nice to meet you."

"You as well."

They broke apart and then Danika's clever green eyes flickered to Emmett, assessing. "Illiana?"

"Yes," Emmett confirmed, waiting for the fallout.

"As in…Nate's Illiana?"

The silence struck the room, and it was like a pin drop could be heard. Illiana cringed, twisting her fingers with nerves behind her back. Emmett puffed his chest in rebuke.

"That's a case of mistaken…intentions. Mistaken identity. He, uh, thought she was interested in him and she wasn't, and I met her by her nickname. It's been…messy. He just found out."

Understanding and concern grew on both women's faces. Danika put her fingertips to her lips.

A feminine snort from behind both women could be heard in response.

Illiana craned her neck and found herself face to face with a stunning woman with a fall of shining black hair and thickly-lashed night dark eyes. Her skin was a rich russet gold from a mixture of the sun and her Indigenous heritage. She was dressed in a pair of flouncy shorts and a black tank top, beaded earrings hanging from her lobes.

Illiana recognized her from the photos. This was Emmett's sister.

"This is going to make for an awkward dinner now, isn't it?" she said leaning against the wall, knuckles to her mouth.

"What do you mean?" Illiana asked with concern.

"Nate just pulled in the driveway."

CHAPTER TWENTY-TWO
Emmett

Emmett's heart fell through his stomach, and he glanced at Illiana to see the glimmer of panic in her eyes.

"He's still coming?" he asked in shock.

Danika shrugged. "Did you ever uninvite him?"

"No."

"Well, that's that then."

Just then the door opened—Nate also had permission to walk into the Adams-Reese residence when invited, just as he was allowed to at Emmett's even uninvited. His mothers had both given Emmett and Sloane their father's last name to honor their heritage and to give them the link of a sibling name. No one had ever expected for his moms to marry.

"Hi, sorry I'm late, I—" Nate froze when he caught sight of Illiana. "Shit. I didn't realize this was—I should go."

"No!" Ashley protested. "Please stay. We made plenty of food."

Nate scrubbed a hand over the back of his head, stressed. His eyes strayed to Emmett's, and they both held still. "I shouldn't."

"Oh, get over it," Sloane called. "It's a little awkward, but you two have been best friends for years. Besides, it's not like you were both sleeping with her." Her eyes went to Illiana's. "You weren't, were you? No judgment if you were—you do you—I just don't want to be called an idiot if I'm wrong."

Illiana shook her head. Emmett's heart flipped uneasily.

"Sloane!" Danika and Ashely gasped in unison.

"See!" Sloane announced. "Simple. No sharing. Let's eat, I'm starving."

And with that Sloane spun around and sat down at the dining room table.

Emmett had to give it to her—she was effective. Sloane was a clear no-bullshit kind of person, discarding with sugar-coating. It was admirable.

"You good?" Emmett asked Nate, a thin thread of tension hovering between them.

Nate hesitated for a moment before nodding. "Yeah, let's eat." He hefted the tub of cookies and cream ice cream. "I brought this, and there's no sense in letting it go to waste."

Nate brushed past Emmett to the kitchen—likely to put said ice cream in the freezer there.

Illiana and Emmett shared a look. "Say the word and we go."

"No," she whispered. "It's fine. He's your best friend. He won't make a scene. Will he?"

Emmett slowly shook his head. "It's not like him."

"Good, let's go."

When they took their seats, Danika shifted the conspicuously spare chair to the corner of the room and Emmett realized it was because Nate was supposed to bring his date—Illiana. He internally cringed as he straightened in his chair. Ashley took up one head of the table while Nate took the other. To Ashley's left was Illiana and then Emmett beside her. To Nate's right was Sloane and then Danika next to her. In the center of the table was a vase of pink peonies—peonies which had come from Emmett's backyard. The table was filled with barbecued chicken, roasted potatoes, and three different kinds of salad—Greek, green, and fruit. Everyone silently filled their plates, reaching and passing items.

Nate and Emmett did so with a palpable tension, Sloane taking items with them, unamused.

"What are you—in high school?" Sloane prompted, skewering a bite of pepper on her fork. "Talk." When they didn't, she rolled her eyes. She turned to Illiana. "So, how did you and my brother meet?"

Emmett's eyes whipped to Illiana as she hesitated, chewing her garden salad. She swallowed and clearly made sure no lettuce was stuck in her teeth. "At Blue's. I was there waiting for my best friend to get off the phone so we could head back home, and Emmett came up to me and we got talking about books."

"Any excuse he has to talk about books, he will," Sloane said. "How'd it come up?"

"I had a book with me."

She looked at Illiana, quizzical and impressed. "You just might be his soulmate after all. Bringing a book to a bar?" She looked at Emmett. "Dream girl, much?"

"Very much," Emmett said gently.

Nate, at the end of the table tensed slightly but tucked into his meal, not saying a word. Emmett felt guilt slip through him, thick like syrup. Sloane patted Nate consolingly. Surprised eyes flickered to her, to her hand.

"Sorry the universe dealt you shit cards, Nate," she said, then leaned in conspiratorially. Nate jolted, his gold-green eyes widening. "If it's any consolation—"

"Don't even finish that sentence," Emmett warned his sister.

Sloane smiled mischievously, showing off slightly sharpened canines.

"Don't do that smile," Emmett chastised.

"What smile?" Sloane asked innocently, her smile broadening.

"That one. The creepy one."

"This is how I always smile."

Emmett rolled his eyes. "She used to do that creepy-ass smile and just hang out in my door frame in the middle of the night as kids. She knew it gave me nightmares."

Illiana stifled a laugh.

Sloane batted her eyelashes. "Now who's a dream girl?"

"Oh my God, you're the worst."

"No, the worst is telling Illiana how you used to—"

"No, don't you dare."

"—make your stuffed toys act out the scenes in those bodice rippers so you could understand what was going on in them and begged me not to tell Ma and Mom when I caught you."

This time not even Nate could stifle his laughter, choking on his food as Illiana burst out with a very unladylike sound and Emmett's face flamed. Even Ashley and Danika giggled, the former whispering to her wife.

"As if we didn't know."

Danika tried to shush her.

"Emmett, no you didn't," Illiana teased, clutching his shoulder.

His beet red face answered for her.

"You'll regret that," Emmett said. "When you finally bring someone home, I'm bringing up all the embarrassing shit you used to do."

Sloane opened her arms wide in invitation. "Try me—I have no shame."

"What about how you used to pretend Legolas was your boyfriend?"

Sloane didn't even flinch, sitting like a rock, cocking a brow. "Is that your worst? Orlando Bloom is fine as hell."

Nate was laughing though.

Emmett grumbled but surrendered when it was clear he was fighting a losing battle.

Sloane had the magical ability to seemingly draw out the tension between the men and toss it out. He realized that Sloane's sibling nagging and pestering was a ruse—a device at Emmett's expense to lighten the mood. It was clear Illiana had discovered this too, and he was eternally grateful for his sister and conveyed it through his eyes, mouthing a *thank you*. Sloane smirked and held the back of her hand beneath her chin, as if propping it up.

For the most part, the rest of the dinner passed and it was—luckily—very uneventful. Nate didn't say anything uncouth; Sloane continued her incessant commentary—which he was extremely grateful for—and Emmett continued being very much himself—the older brother, the son, the friend, the guy who was falling, or had fallen in love with Illiana Hastings.

When dinner wrapped up and the ice cream Nate had brought over was served, he waited only the few requisite minutes longer, probably out of politeness alone, and then turned to Illiana.

"Are you going over to his house tonight or are you coming back for game night? My sisters will be there too."

Illiana visibly deliberated and turned to Emmett. Emmett shifted, and it was awkward because the three of them very much knew what exactly was supposed to happen after dinner—and it involved Emmett and Illiana alone and under the covers. Nate's face reddened when he realized and ducked down.

"Right, I should've realized."

Emmett opened his mouth, closed it, then tried again. "If you're okay with it…we could both come over for game night tonight?"

Nate hesitated; eyes nervous—hurt still playing through those hazel irises. "Yeah, I actually think that would be nice. It'll be good to start getting back to…normal."

Emmett's mouth pulled into a pained smile, as if unbelieving of his luck. That he got the girl and got his friend. Illiana beamed, her own smile on full display.

"Do we get to play Cards Against Humanity again?"

Emmett cocked a brow. "You say it as if you haven't played it much."

"I haven't," she said, turning to Nate with a smile. "It was a lot of fun."

"We can probably get that one going when everyone else is too drunk. Mom wanted us to try out Werewolf first."

"We'll be there later. Does eight sound good?"

"Eight is good."

They bid Nate goodbye and watched him pull out in his white truck before the two of them headed back inside, seeing Emmett's moms and sister standing there—expressions on their faces like triplets ready to give a *what for.*

"That boy is devastated," Danika said, a mix of solemnity and chastisement in her tone. "I feel for everyone here, but seeing that…"

Sloane elbowed Danika. "Illiana doesn't owe him anything. Sure, it sucks, but did anything happen? Did he make his intentions clear? Did he tell her exactly how he felt? If all that criteria isn't met, then that's on him. He made his bed and now he has to lay in it."

Emmett was watching his sister admiringly. "Thanks for that, Sloane."

She scoffed. "Don't get too excited. You don't get off free. You really should have told him. You lack communication skills, or your fear of fallout so you put it off. Either way, I'm guessing the way he found out wasn't the most ideal of circumstances from the way he's acting."

Illiana and Emmett shared a pained look.

"Oh hell, he walked in on you two, didn't he?"

Danika and Ashley both covered their ears, yelling *La-La-La-La-La* as they went. They disappeared into the kitchen, and soon as they did, Sloane doubled down.

"So, how bad was it? Naked-on-the-couch bad?"

"I'm your brother."

"And? I need to know how traumatized your best friend is." Sloane paused. "And speaking of friends, did all the others know?"

Emmett sent his eyes skyward. "Kinda."

Illiana cleared her throat. "On the counter, clothes on."

Sloane whistled lowly. "That's a classy one, brother of mine."

"It gets worse. He dropped his beer and glass went everywhere."

Sloane cocked a brow. "You two did a fucking number on him, huh?"

"A little," Illiana admitted. "I feel really bad about it."

Sloane waved it away. "I like you. You're able to own up to your mistakes. That's huge." Sloane side-eyed Emmett. "Not that he has brought many girls around, but I like you the best."

"...thank you?"

"You're welcome."

Illiana couldn't help it—she laughed.

CHAPTER TWENTY-THREE
Illiana

Eventually the conversation pivoted away from Nate and they were able to chat for a little before everyone had to clear out. They all—aside from Illiana—had work in the morning, and if they wanted to make game night, they had to leave now. Good-byes were bid and promises to return were sworn. Illiana and Emmett took the few minutes drive to the Ellis house and then pulled in behind Nate's truck. When they found their way into the house, Lacey, Walt, Mina, Jade, Sasha, their men, and Nate were all there.

"Illiana!" Lacey greeted warmly. "And Emmett?"

Mina choked on her cider. "Oh, shit. We're doing this, huh?" She looked at Nate for support. He looked away, so she shrugged. "Okay, yeah so Emmett and Illiana have been seeing each other. They stumbled across each other right when she first got here."

"Really?" Lacey grinned. "This is wonderful!"

The Ellis family was thrilled by this turn of events, evidently. Lacey gave her a big hug and both Sasha and Jade gave her an encouraging hand signal; mouthing *"nice"* behind everyone's back. Walt was also happy but showed it in a more subdued manner, especially since his gaze flickered to Nate and Illiana deduced that Nate had confided in his father some of his feelings. Illiana didn't watch per se, but she was attentive and she noted the silent conversation flow between father and son. The sadness, the acceptance, the curiosity, the shrug. Walt ended it with a nod and returned to his drink—a mojito—and spread out a bunch of cards and circular tokens.

"Emmett, Illiana, can I get you two drinks?" Lacey asked.

They both accepted sparkling waters as Walt divided up the players of the game.

"Okay, well if everyone is here, want to explain the rules?" Walt asked his wife.

Lacey beamed eagerly and then laid her hands flat on the island counter and explained.

The rules, for the most part, seemed only complex when it came to the roles, but they were assured that once a round or two was played, they'd catch the hang of it. An iPad was set up nearby, the game queued up with a timer, and then it was time to begin.

"I can't believe every time you got Werewolf, you survived," Emmett griped to Illiana playfully. "I mean, the poker face on you!"

Illiana preened. "All in the talent of knowing the stage, baby."

The two of them were walking out in the dark to Emmett's SUV, fingers twined. He helped her in and straightened her skirt to make sure it didn't get pinched in the door. When he got in his side and started the vehicle, he continued.

"I mean, honestly—the deception! You never once claimed Villager if you weren't one."

"I figured if I took on an active role, I'd have more success being believed."

"Risky but effective."

Illiana playfully flipped her hair. "My new motto."

Emmett chortled and then took her hand over the shifter as they cruised down the lazily winding road to his house. Shortly thereafter, they pulled in the driveway and caught the two pup noses against the window. As they walked in, they were playfully assaulted by the dogs and they gave them attentions and affection, taking them out into the backyard for their business. Illiana eyed his peonies in the backyard—she could still scarcely believe he had her favorite flowers growing here—and lingered in the kitchen.

"We never got to finish what we started in here," Illiana whispered, finger trailing up Emmett's forearm, following the ink lines and then a vein—God, his arms looked good.

Emmett cocked a brow. "Are you asking for something, sweetheart?"

Illiana felt the lust darken her eyes. "I want you to put me on that counter and have your way with me."

"You'd like me to defile my kitchen?" he asked, sultry, tugging her against him with his free arm.

"Please?"

He kissed her firmly. "I'll reward you for those manners."

And then he backed her against the edge.

The counter bit into her lower back, the prospect of it promising so much pleasure that she whined for it. Emmett grabbed her by the waist and hoisted her onto it.

"Was this where we were before we were so rudely interrupted?"

"Almost," she said, kissing along his jaw. "I think your hand was someplace else."

"It was, wasn't it?"

His fingers trailed against her knee, tucking beneath the crook there. "Here?"

"Higher," she said, kissing lower.

He went slightly higher, brushing the sensitive skin of her inner thigh. "Here?"

"Higher," she moaned.

"Higher?" His fingers were at the edge of her panties.

"So close."

"So, higher?"

"Yes."

Emmett wasted no time, and between one moment and the next, he'd pushed aside her panties and a finger was entering her. She bucked and moaned embarrassingly loud, clenching around him. She was wet—so wet already.

"High enough?"

Illiana couldn't manage words as she bit down on the juncture on Emmett's neck and shoulder, rocking against his playing hand. That heady scent of amber woods filled her lungs—it was like a drug and she was already addicted to it. His thumb slipped against her and found her clit, rubbing firm circles there. Her fingers dug into the tops of his shoulders and she was frantic, moving, constantly moving, seeking friction.

She yanked off his shirt and worshipped his body. The muscles, the softness overtop it. His abs weren't defined, but they were there. He was the kind of hot where he clearly worked out, but he also enjoyed food. She found it extremely sexy.

Emmett continued with those talented fingers, working her up, twisting her up, winding her up. She could feel pressure build in her and then he curled his fingers. She clenched and gasped.

"If you keep doing that, I'm going to ruin this dress and soak your counter."

Emmett listened without being told anything more. He worked the dress and undergarments off her so she sat there in nothing, and then he parted her thighs and returned to his ministrations.

But he didn't just do that.

With his other hand, he wrapped his arm around her waist and hoisted her off the counter before walking to the hallway, pressing her against the wall.

Oh.

OH.

She'd never been fucked against a wall before.

The idea had her drenching Emmett's hand.

"Oh, that's my good girl," he whispered against her throat.

"*Emmett.*"

"That's right. Say my name. Say the only fucking name that's going to make you come."

"*Emmett,*" she repeated.

"Thank you. Now soak me, sweetheart."

He rubbed that spot inside and she squirted, the pressure and pleasure rushing through her. It was so slippery between her legs. So wet and sticky—and she loved it. She thrashed against him, her enjoyment utter bliss against him.

"Do you have a condom?" she rasped as her climax built low in her belly.

Emmett smiled deviously and with his hips, he pinned her against the wall, his hand still between her legs and reached with his free one to a hallway table drawer.

There's no way he had a—

He opened the drawer and pulled out a condom from there.

"Do you just have those around the house?" she managed as he continued pleasuring her. Fuck, how was he so talented?

"Just there, for on my way out the door."

"Convenient," she said, knocking her head against the wall.

He captured her mouth with his, tongue sweeping in her mouth, stroking with the same motions that his fingers were making in her pussy.

"If you want me, there will never be anyone else," he said against her lips.

Her eyes—which had closed without her own volition—flew open. "What?"

"If you want this to be real—to be more than a fling—just say it."

Whether it was the devotion in his eyes or the effect of his words, she came. The orgasm struck her like lightning, lighting her up like fucking fireworks as he pumped his fingers in and out, that thumb never ceasing its sensual rhythm. She knocked her head against the wall again and again, biting her lip, crying out.

"Inside me," she rasped as the waves of her climax began to wave. "Now. I need your cock."

Emmett wasn't about to be told twice. He shoved his pants down and rolled the condom on. In one smooth stroke he was seated inside her completely. She clenched around him as he began to thrust in and out, filling her so completely with his thick length. Her arms were around his shoulders, tangled in his hair as his hands went to her hips as he guided himself in and out of her, literally using her to fuck himself—and fuck if it wasn't the hottest thing.

Her legs were wrapped around his waist, heel at the small of his back as she used him for leverage and rolled herself to match his plunges to press against her clit. It was so good—too good—and she felt another orgasm working through her. His mouth went down to her chest, laving kisses there and then he was pulling her nipple into his mouth, and she shattered.

It was fireworks. Flowers. Bliss. Mind-numbing bliss as she came on his cock.

When Emmett came, falling after her, he thrusted his hips against her in slow, deep motions. He pulsed and spilled and then slumped against her, still pinning her to the wall. His mouth was at her throat, kissing down the line of it with gentle sucks.

"I adore you," he murmured against her skin.

Her heart rate kicked up. It wasn't the word. It wasn't those words. But it was alarmingly close.

She tucked her face against the side of his and breathed it back.

CHAPTER TWENTY-FOUR
Emmett

The next morning when Emmett dropped Illiana off at the Ellis house, Nate was just getting in his vehicle. He started when he noticed his best friend and immediately felt shitty for it. They were on the road to recovery in their friendship—sure, it was a little strained and bruised at the moment, but it would recover.

"You okay?" Illiana asked from the passenger's seat. Her pink overnight bag was in her lap, that sweet strawberry dress he'd nearly ruined tucked safely inside.

Emmett glanced over and saw her beautifully toned legs, tanned from the sun and exposed in her bike shorts. He traced the line of them before he nodded. "Yeah."

He helped her get out and walked her to the steps, just as Nate was getting out of his vehicle too. He was in a T-shirt tucked into dress pants, semi-formal for casual Fridays. Nate nodded at them both, politely not commenting on the thinly veiled Walk of Shame.

"Morning," Emmett greeted his best friend. "Heading to work?"

"Yeah, I spent the night here after game night."

"Right," Emmett answered, nodding his head. "Are we still on for beers tonight?"

There was the slightest, most imperceptible hesitation in Nate's frame. But then he shook free of it and smiled. "Yeah, same time, same place as always?"

"Always."

This time Nate's smile was real, and Emmett beamed in response.

He was comfortable talking about his feelings—as Nate was; actually, all the guys were—but these feelings felt all twisted and snarled up and he was so glad they were finding unwinding and straightening out. His heart swelled with the hope of things going back to normal—that he hadn't utterly fucked everything up.

Emmett glanced at Illiana. "Do you mind if I talk to Nate for a second?"

"Of course," she said with no hesitation.

They held a breath for a second, eyes flickering to Nate. Nate, not being stupid, turned away. Emmett quickly drew Illiana in and kissed her firmly, allowing his tongue only to trace the seam of her lips before he broke away.

"I'll talk to you later," he said lowly.

"I look forward to it."

And then she was skipping up the steps and slipping into the house.

And then Emmett and Nate were alone outside.

Fingers of cold still hung on from the night, the heat not having taken full grasp of the day yet. The scent of sun-warmed grass on the breeze, the slight blue-gold of morning, the sound of distant cars—it was all cemented in Emmett's mind as he looked at his friend.

He couldn't remember the last time they'd been on the outs. The last time they'd fought. Nothing compared to this and he was out of his element. These were new waters, and he was learning to tread in them.

"I just wanted to say, I'm really glad you stayed for dinner yesterday," Emmett said.

Nate sucked in his cheeks. "Yeah, me too. It was a little awkward, but Sloane was pretty good at calling out the bullshit."

"She was, wasn't she?" They both laughed, and then Emmett's mood sobered. "I just want to apologize—again. I'll keep saying I'm sorry until you're ready to hear it."

"I know." Nate nodded and drew in a breath. He exhaled it. "And I think now's the time. I know you didn't mean anything malicious by it. It was just really shitty luck. I keep thinking how we just missed it, and it's stupid—comical even—looking back on it."

"It is. But really, I'm so sorry. I know how you fe—"

"Let's not think about how I felt or feel about your girl-friend."

Emmett's stomach twisted in a mixture of anticipation and nerves. "We uh…there's no title on it."

Nate looked at him assessing. "I think you and I both know that title is coming, or it's ending."

"What do you mean?"

"Babe, you told me how you felt about her when you thought she was Ana. I know you like her even more now. It's okay." Nate shrugged. "But if she doesn't want that commitment, I know you can't do casual if you're in that deep."

"That deep?"

"Love."

Emmett startled and went still. "I…I—"

"It's okay." He clapped Emmett on the shoulder. "But I've got to get to work." Nate stuck his hands in his pockets. Then concern lit his face. "Aw, hell. I forgot my wallet." He began walking back to the house. "I'll see you tonight."

Emmett waved as Nate took the stairs two at a time, stretching his long legs. Without another word, Emmett got back in his SUV and headed off to work.

The day rushed, Fridays and Mondays always ridiculously busy due to trying to get everything in before the weekend and then having to get in after the weekend's events—whatever they may be. Emmett and his employees were on a tight schedule, so tight that Emmett didn't even take a break. It wasn't until after work he finally looked at his phone and when he did, he saw texts from Nate and Illiana that had his stomach dropping through his feet and sinking into the ground.

He swore Nate's name out to the universe and frantically tried to call Illiana.

CHAPTER TWENTY-FIVE
Illiana

Illiana was dressed up with a stack of books in her arms and Mina beside her, waiting excitedly.

When Emmett had dropped her off that morning, she'd gone to the pool house but found both the beds made. Putting away her duffel bag, she grabbed the book she'd been reading, tucked it under her arm, and ventured to the main house. There, she'd found Mina at the kitchen island, eating a bowl of yogurt, granola, and raspberries.

"Good morning, sunshine," Mina said teasingly. "How was your night?" Her eyebrows did a little wiggle as she shimmied.

Illiana rolled her eyes as she laughed. She took a sip from the iced matcha Emmett had gotten her that morning and sunk down on one of the stools next to her best friend, putting both drink and book on the marble.

"I'd never had it against a wall before."

Mina's spoon froze in the air. "Fuck, me neither." She leaned in. "Was it good?"

"So good."

Mina gave a silent scream while Illiana urged her to hush. Just then, Nate walked in the door.

"Just me!" he called. "I forgot my wallet."

The wallet in question was sitting on the island in front of them. Nate sauntered in and swiped it up. As he did, his eyes flickered down to the book before her and they widened. Illiana caught the expression immediately.

"Do you know the author, too? Emmett said she was his friend."

"Uh…yeah, I've met her." There was a halting progress in the way he spoke.

"You have?" She was positively glowing.

"Yeah, just casually. She's nice."

"I was teasing Emmett about her, saying that I was going to put together all the clues that he was actually her, but—" she pulled up Delilah's Instagram, "I had no luck, even checking her socials and—oh my God."

"What?" Nate said quickly—too quickly.

"She's doing a pop-up signing tonight at Sugar & Spice Books—the shop Emmett showed me!" Her eyes flashed to Mina, Nate forgotten. "Will you go with me, please?"

Mina seemed immediately thrilled. "Of course! That sounds like so much fun!"

Nate was frozen before them.

"What?" Illiana queried.

"I…nothing. You two should have fun. I've got to go before I'm late for work."

And with that Nate skated out of the house, phone in hand, leaving Illiana and Mina in anticipation for their event. Before she forgot, she texted Emmett her evening's plans.

Illiana and Mina were now lingering at the front of the bookstore, front of the line. There was a pink and white striped tote bag slung on her shoulder, matching the same shade of pink as her cotton blouse with wooden buttons, paired with jean shorts and white tennis shoes. Mina, beside her was in a taupe cropped top and olive-green slouchy pants, with white high tops, a canvas bag hanging from her elbow.

When they were let in, Illiana recognized everything—the shelves, the butterflies, the cushions—only now there was a table set up near the back, evening golden-hour light filtering through the glass. Sitting behind the table laden with books was a stunning red-headed woman, her curves voluptuous and lush, eyes of sparkling blue. Her features were clever and fox-like, tilted in a slightly mischievous way. Her mouth was wide, meant for smirking, her lashes charcoal sweeps across her cheekbones. Illiana took a hit to her self-esteem just by looking at her.

Well, one thing was for certain, Delilah Rose certainly wasn't Emmett.

When Illiana approached Delilah's table with Mina in tow, she was practically bursting at the seams. She was jittery with anticipation. The bookstore worker beside Delilah was whispering something in her ear and she listened intently. When she pulled away, Delilah laughed.

"Yeah, that sounds good." And then she turned her attention to Illiana and Mina. "Hi! Thanks for coming out!" She caught sight of the books in Illiana's arms. "Can I sign those for you?"

"Please!" Illiana said, handing them over. She bit her lip as Delilah opened one up.

"Who is this to?"

"Illiana," she told her. "With two Ls."

"Oh, such a pretty name!" Delilah's hand swooped against the paper with a graceful flourish, her lavender Sharpie staining the page.

"Thank you." Illiana shifted. "I actually found out about your books from your friend, Emmett."

Delilah smiled cheekily. "Emmett King?"

"Yeah, that's him."

"Did he recommend this book specifically?" she asked playfully, indicating the one Illiana was in the middle of reading—the furthest from Delilah's signing line. "Because if so, what a guy to tell you to read the one dedicated to him."

Illiana's smile fell. For some reason her heart began beating an odd rhythm. A sick feeling was unfurling in her throat.

"What dedication?"

Before Delilah could answer, Illiana picked up the book in question and flipped to the dedication page.

For Emmett, because the wall scene would not be what it is without your assistance.

Illiana's blood went cold as she stared at the page, gape-mouthed. Her dumbstruck expression lifted to Delilah's as Mina craned her neck to look at the page. She let out a low gasp and a barely audible, "Oh fuck."

Delilah looked at Illiana not understanding. Until she did. Then Delilah's face fell.

Delilah covered her mouth. "Oh. Oh shit. You're seeing him." Illiana nodded mutely, and Delilah continued. "He's my ex. We're not still together."

"He never mentioned that," Illiana said numbly.

Hurt coursed through Illiana. Why hadn't Emmett told her? Why had he recommended his ex-girlfriend's books? Was he still hung up on her? Pain, completely unexpected, swept through her. She felt tears threatening to burn her eyes like they burned in her throat.

"Oh, baby doll," Delilah whispered apologetically. "I'm so sorry. It—it ended well. It was mutual and amicable. A while ago. He wanted—oh, dammit, he should really tell you himself."

Illiana looked away, trying to hide the surge of emotion. Delilah started again. "Illiana."

Her face swung to the author—Emmett's ex—before her. "He's a good guy. He really is. Talk to him about it. I'm sure it was just an oversight. Are you two new?"

Illiana nodded. "Yeah. It's not even official yet."

"But you've already fallen for him, huh?"

Illiana's eyes widened on Delilah's. Delilah smiled softly, so at odds with her feisty features and the golden glow of her tanned skin. What surprised Illiana the most was that Delilah wasn't blushing at all—not with anxiety or embarrassment, she was utterly self-assured in herself.

"Baby doll, I've been where you are—trust me, I get it."

Illiana's stomach soured at that, but not in such a visceral way like it had minutes before.

"Talk to him," she repeated. "But before you go, do you still want me to sign the books?"

Illiana laughed. "Please do."

Delilah did and tucked in some bookish goodies too—art prints and bookmarks—and returned them. "Let me know how it goes—if you're comfortable with it."

For some reason, Illiana felt she was. Despite the odds against her, despite the expectations, despite the prerequisite Other Woman Trope, she liked Delilah Rose.

"I will," she promised.

"Good luck."

Illiana and Mina left together, Illiana still half shell-shocked as she got in their rental. In the passenger seat, Illiana checked out what Delilah had given her, and in doing so, she saw the note written against the page with her signature.

To Illiana,

The next one is for you, baby doll. So sorry for the unplanned ex reveal.

All my love,

Delilah

Illiana let out a bark of a laugh, and then that bark turned near hysterical.

"What the actual *fuck*, Mina."

"That was very unexpected."

"You're telling *me*!"

Mina's fingers drummed on the steering wheel as she cruised back to Rose Point. A few moments of silence passed.

"Am I taking you back to the house, or Emmett's?"

"I don't even know, I—"

The sound of Illiana's ringing phone cut her off.

It was Emmett.

Illiana sighed and pressed accept.

"Illiana!" he said in clear relief. "I'm so glad you picked up before—look, I need to tell you some—"

"I've already met Delilah," she interrupted.

There was a breath of silence on the other end before Emmett cursed. "And did she—"

"She told me she's your ex."

Another curse. "I can explain."

"I sure hope you will."

"Can you come to my place? I'll tell you everything."

Illiana glanced at Mina who could hear every word due to the volume in the car's small interior. Mina nodded when she glanced over.

"I'll be there in twenty minutes."

CHAPTER TWENTY-SIX
Emmett

Emmett was pacing when the rental car carrying Illiana pulled up. Immediately, he broke from his wearing a hole in the carpet and leaped for the door. He swung it open, just as Illiana was getting out of the car. She waved to Mina as she closed it and then came up the path. Mina was already pulling away.

He greeted her immediately, but he wasn't sure if he was supposed to touch her—if he was allowed to—so he stood stiffly.

"Come in, please."

"Thanks," she said, subdued, and he cursed himself for his stupidity and evasiveness.

He should have just told her. He should have said something like, "Hey actually, this friend is my ex, hope that's not an issue!" Just like he'd avoided telling Nate about him and Illiana, he neglected to tell Illiana about him and Delilah.

He prayed there was still a *him and Illiana* to salvage.

Illiana walked into his house, familiar with it already and it made his heart clench. She sank down onto the couch, setting the tote bag on the floor. He'd closed his dogs up in his room for the time being so that they wouldn't overwhelm her. He didn't know what he was setting himself up for, and he wanted the environment to be as calm as possible. Before she'd showed up, he'd been stress cleaning. And before that he was texting the guys to tell them he couldn't make it out and that Nate would explain.

He couldn't help the insidious thoughts that tried to convince him that Nate set this up deliberately. That under the guise of an olive branch, this was a deceitful trick to pull him and Illiana apart in revenge. But Emmett had to banish those thoughts—his friend wasn't that cruel, and he chastised himself for the thought. Intrusive as it was.

"So, Delilah is evidently not you."

"No. She certainly isn't."

She huffed a breath out. "I'm a little disappointed actually. I had my red thread ready and everything."

He managed a choked laugh. "Sorry to be the bearer of bad news." Then he shifted. "Illiana, I'm really sorry I didn't tell you about Delilah. It didn't cross my mind initially and when Nate made me realize, I knew I'd fucked up. I thought about when and how I'd tell you, but it was embarrassing and there was never a right time. And then everything with Nate just happened and we're getting through that, and I just didn't think it was right to add more to it."

Illiana nodded and let out a slow breath. "Do you still have feelings for her?"

"No," he said firmly. "No, my feelings for her are completely in the past."

"Then why'd you tell me about her?"

"Honestly? Because I got caught up in talking to you about books, and it just didn't occur to me that it was a stupid idea—don't look at me like that, I know it's dumb now. And she really is just a good author."

"It had nothing to do with the dedication?"

He groaned. "I was really hoping that wouldn't come up."

"Oh, it did."

"I'm so sorry, sweetheart." He took her hands in his. His, scarred and nicked; hers, perfectly smooth and soft. "We were so new and we were so caught up in the banter—in that moment I really was just thinking of her as a friend. It was the first time I talked about her and felt nothing—because of you."

She held her breath for a moment, then squeezed his hand. "It's okay. But no more secrets."

"No more secrets. I'll tell you everything."

And so, he took a deep breath and did. He told her how he and Delilah had been together for nearly a year and after her meeting his niece and nephew from his older brother, it came to light that they wanted vastly different things. Specifically, that he wanted kids one day, and she adamantly didn't. She'd even gone as far as having a tubal ligation. Immediately, the relationship crumbled and they went their separate ways.

They didn't fight; they didn't yell or try to convince the other of their life choice; they accepted it and moved on.

It hurt, but it wasn't messy.

After he wrapped up his side of him and Delilah, he felt lighter, like a weight had been lifted off his shoulders. He hadn't realized how much he was holding back by not telling her about Delilah. But it was finally out, and he vowed never to pull that bullshit again.

"Is there any chance you want to consider this being more?" Emmett asked tentatively. "That maybe all this could decide if you think it's worth it. Maybe it'll help you realize whether you want to stay or go back." Illiana opened her mouth to answer, but he continued. "You don't have to decide right now, maybe we'll just trial it for the summer and at the end when you're supposed to go back you can choose."

A slow smile spread across her perfect pink lips. "Okay."

"Okay?" he asked, disbelief bright in his voice. "We're doing this?"

"We're doing this," she repeated. Her fingers skimmed over his arm. "For now…until the summer—or longer—we're together. I…I don't want to confirm if I'll stay until I'm sure, but by September you'll have a real answer."

"So, you're my girlfriend?"

She threw her head back on a fucking beautiful, tinkling laugh. "Yes, I'm your girlfriend."

Emotion surged through him and he tackled her into the couch cushions.

"I have a girlfriend!" he shouted into the empty living room. His dogs upstairs barked, and Illiana was laughing and it was all so fucking perfect.

"Emmett!" she said playfully, flattening her hands against his chest.

"Yes, my girlfriend?"

She rolled her eyes. "What are we, in high school?"

"Definitely not, I don't date below twenty-three."

"Oh, well this is an awkward time to tell you I'm twenty."

All the blood drained from his face before she let out a cackling laugh. A witchy, cackling laugh that was so at odds with his golden goddess.

"I'm just kidding! I'm twenty-seven."

"Thank fuck," he said with a groan, pressing his brow to her collarbone. "I was questioning many life choices." He sighed and wrapped his arms around her. "I'm so glad we didn't get the third act breakup trope."

Illiana snorted. "Who's to say that isn't coming in the fall?"

He could feel her smiling against his chest so he brushed off the fear. "We already got close enough to the miscommunication trope—please don't."

"But it's a staple!" she protested, lifting her head.

"I thought we were subverting staple tropes."

"Maybe we can follow a couple."

"Well, I'd like to stick to more favorable ones."

"Like?"

"The make-up sex trope."

"I don't know if that's a thing."

"Let's make it one," he whispered, hands spreading, cupping the gentle swell of her ass, her perfect cheeks fitting in his hands. He began massaging her, rubbing down the backs of her thighs.

She groaned lowly, her fingers curling in his shirt.

"Want to start being creative?" he asked, hoping he sounded seductive.

She mumbled a soft-enjoying yes and suddenly their clothes vanished.

This time when they joined, it was intimate. It was lovemaking. It was soft strokes, slow undulating thrusts. It was brushing fingers through hair and gentle caresses across skin. It was the scent of strawberries and cream, and amber and woods. It was the glitter of perspiration and the music of moaning. Of wet thighs and ruined couches.

He fucking loved all of it.

His.

She was all his.

And hers.

He was all hers.

And he'd fallen head over heels for her.

He was utterly and completely in love with Illiana Hastings.

CHAPTER TWENTY-SEVEN
Illiana

Late Saturday morning Illiana was hanging out by the pool with Mina. Nate and his sisters with their partners and their children were over for a family day. In addition to them were some of the extended family that Illiana had met the evening of the first time she'd gone out with Emmett. The girls were sipping on mimosas when Nate took up the chair next to Mina.

"Hey, I heard about Delilah's event last night…" he hesitated, scrubbing a hand over the back of his head, and his short-cropped hair. "Is everything okay with you and Em?"

Illiana pursed her lips and nodded. "Yeah, it's all good. He explained it. We're uh…we're official now."

"You're *what?*" Mina squawked, sitting upright.

Nate's brows rose, but he smiled after a breath. "I'm happy for you both—really." He cleared his throat. "I'm really sorry for not saying anything yesterday, I just…didn't think it was my place to say who she was. It would've felt like…vengeful. Like really fucking petty."

Illiana pondered that for a second. "Yeah, that actually makes perfect sense."

Nate exhaled. "Good. Good."

"I'm sorry, are we still glossing over the fact that you two are *together*?"

Illiana shrugged shyly. "We decided that at least for the summer we'd have the title."

"So, you're his girlfriend."

She smiled and wiggled playfully. "Maybe…" She bit her lip. "Yeah. I am."

Mina squealed happily for her and Illiana blushed. Nate, though with a lingering edge of sadness, genuinely seemed happy for them.

"Congrats. Emmett's a really good guy," he said.

"He really is." Illiana looked directly at Nate's face. "And I'm genuinely sorry about everything."

He waved it off. "Don't worry about it. Water under the bridge."

"Uncle Nate!" a child screamed. "I'm going to get you!"

And then suddenly Nate was assaulted with a blast from a water gun. The spray sprinkled on Illiana and Mina, both the girls letting out oaths of surprise. Wasting no time, Nate chased after his nephew. The air filled with the squeal of a child's joy as Nate playfully taunted.

Just then, Illiana's phone went off. She looked at the screen and was surprised to find her landlord's name on the screen. She swiped to answer the call.

"Hey Leonard, what's—"

"Ms. Hastings, your rent is now two months late."

Illiana's heart sank. "What?"

"Your rent hasn't been paid for the months of June or July."

Illiana mentally calculated. They were a week into July, but the rental agreement required the current month be paid beforehand. "I assure you, that can't be right. It's an automatic deposit."

"Yes, for the past several years it was. Until May when it changed."

"Changed?" Illiana asked dubiously. "I didn't authorize a change."

"Someone else with the allowance did, then. Look, this is a courtesy since your name isn't on the lease."

Illiana straightened, this wasn't right. "There must be a glitch. A money transfer error."

"Not what it's looking like on this side, and if it's not paid by Tuesday, we'll be evicting you."

"What?"

"I'm sorry, but that's the way it is."

Illiana's ire flared. She wasn't the most educated about tenant rights, so she wasn't sure if he really could evict her for this or not. "Can you at least tell me if there's any paperwork stating who changed this and when?"

Leonard gave a grievous sigh as if she was asking the most demanding of favors. She could hear the tapping of keys through the speaker as her blood roared in her ears.

This wasn't happening. This couldn't be happening.

"It appears to be a Meredith Hastings."

Illiana's stomach bottomed out. "That's my mother."

"Well, it sounds like you need to pay your mother a call." He cleared his throat. "I'll be on standby waiting on an update. I understand this is the weekend, but these are extenuating circumstances."

"Yes, of course. I understand. Thank you."

They disconnected the call and she sat there shocked still. This couldn't be legal. She knew landlords could be disgusting, but this seemed above the bar bad. Rage coursed through her veins and she got to her feet and stomped over to the pool house. Mina got to her feet and took a few steps after her.

"Ana, is everything okay?"

"No. Just give me a minute."

Illiana shut the door firmly behind her and furiously dialed her mother.

Meredith Hastings had the audacity to answer on the third ring.

"Hello, darling."

"Mom," Illiana started through her teeth. "Why is Leonard telling me the rent isn't paid?"

Her mother's voice was airy, audacious, and utterly nerve-fraying. "Why, I don't know. I transferred allowances to Adrian."

Illiana was floored. "Why the fuck would you do that?"

"Language! Don't use that disgusting word with me, daughter."

Illiana ground her teeth, nostrils flaring as she parsed her words carefully. "Why would you sign anything over to Adrian?"

"Because he asked."

"We broke up!" she shouted into the phone. "More than a year ago!"

"That's news to me."

"Bull fucking shit!"

"Illiana Jane Hastings, don't you dare speak to me like that. I am your mother, and you will respect me."

Illiana gave a sharp bark of laughter. "Now that's news to *me*."

"Adrian is good for you," Meredith continued. She could practically see her mother brushing away Illiana's concerns with a wave of her hand. "You'll come back around to him. He's perfect."

"He dumped me while I was in the hospital and left me for someone else!"

"Yes, well he wants you back."

Illiana was positively floored. "He *what?*"

Illiana could already hear her mother's smugness bleeding through the line and she hadn't said a single word yet. In fury, she paced the floor, clenching and unclenching her fist. She tried to breathe and calm herself.

"Yes, he asked for the apartment back for you. He should be there now, actually. I gave him the keys."

"What the actual fuck?"

"How—"

"No, you are not interrupting me on this. What the hell do you mean you gave my ex my fucking apartment?" Illiana tugged at her hair. "What kind of mother are you?"

"I will not be disrespected—"

"Then start deserving it!" Illiana had finally had enough. She'd snapped. "You are quite possibly the worst parent in the goddamn world."

"I am ending this conversation before you say anything else regretful." Meredith sniffed in disdain. "I expect to see you back soon from your vacation in the slums."

"I'm on the west coast, on an island."

"It makes little difference to me. Goodbye."

Meredith hung up.

Illiana stared at the phone in shock and she allowed herself three breaths before she launched into action.

She called Adrian, but he didn't answer. This was a nightmare. She tried again. But rather than accept the call, he very clearly denied it.

"Son of a bitch," she hissed to herself.

Undiluted rage coursed through her. She ordered a ride and then grabbed her duffel bag and shoved everything she could into it—clothes, toiletries, all of it. She zipped the bulging bag closed and dashed out the door with it over her shoulder.

Mina shot up immediately and looked at Illiana with concern.

"Where are you going?"

"My mom hasn't been paying my rent for the past two months and has signed over the apartment to Adrian."

"*She what?*"

Illiana rushed past her and Mina dashed to keep up.

"So, you're just going back?"

"I've got to sort out this mess. He's there now. All my stuff is there—important documents, my books, everything. I don't want Adrian and his slimy hands near anything of mine."

"What about here? About us?" Mina grabbed Illiana's arm and she whirled. "What about Emmett?"

"I'll text him and explain."

"Are you coming back?"

"When I can."

"And when do you think that'll be?"

"As soon as possible."

Illiana ran for the door, her driver already there, and she hopped in. She watched Mina fade away and through the anxiety and rage, regret began to flood through her. She shoved it away. She pulled out her phone and got booking a plane ticket for a direct flight from Victoria to Toronto. It was going to be expensive, dipping into her savings, but she had to. Flight secured for that afternoon, Illiana texted Emmett.

Hey Emmett, I'm so sorry. I have to leave.

She sent a follow-up text.

I'll explain later, but I'm going back to Toronto. It's a mess. I don't know when I'll be back yet.

She hesitated before sending a third.

I'll miss you, but I hope I'll be back soon, and I'll have a real answer for you.

She slipped the phone beneath her leg as she rooted through her pink duffel, searching for her ID and other documents. She got it all ready and then she knocked her head back against the rest and shut her eyes.

Hatred for her parents blinded her. It flooded her veins, made her see red, had her seething. Meredith Hastings was one of the most despicable people on the planet, and Phillip Hastings was just an enabler. And for the two of them to allow her useless ex back into their life for the sake of image? Fuck, if steam could billow from ears, it would be fuming from hers.

She zipped her bag closed and sat ramrod straight in her seat while the driver navigated the many streets of Victoria until he reached the airport. She was fuming, but she was remaining calm. When they arrived, Illiana got out and slung her bag over her shoulder and headed in—internally promising this wouldn't be the last time she came here.

Illiana checked in, checked her bag and took a seat. It was at that very moment, an hour before her flight was supposed to leave that she realized her phone died. But not before she caught a glimpse of her texts to realize Emmett hadn't responded to her yet and her *'I'll miss you'* text hadn't gone through. Nor had her follow-up.

She searched through her bag only to discover she'd forgotten her charger.

She cursed herself out as she sat, wallowing in misery and anger with a dead phone.

She didn't want to leave Emmett. She missed him already. She missed the island and Rose Point. She missed Mina's family and Madeline. She missed Leia and Gimli. She missed the dynamic of Emmett's friend group. The ocean, the lakes, the trees. Nothing in Toronto held a draw for her anymore. She knew at that moment that she was going back just to collect her things and cut her losses.

The announcement came overhead for her flight. She stood and slung the bag over her shoulder and began walking to the gate.

As she did, she heard a voice call her name.

CHAPTER TWENTY-EIGHT
Emmett

Hey Emmett, I'm so sorry I have to leave.

Emmett couldn't read further past the text over the sound of his heart breaking. The silence was deafening around him, yet blood roared in his ears and the sound of lawn mowers growled in the distance. It didn't matter because nothingness was surging up in him and numbing all.

Below Illiana's text was a message from Nate.

Illiana left for the airport, it sucks, so let me know if you want to get a beer or something. I'm here.

All he could do was stare down at his phone. Shock flickered through him mixed with disbelief. He didn't understand. What did he do? What had prompted her swift exit? Did he scare her off with his declaration? Did she get overwhelmed with their summer arrangement? Did he miss something? Were they too intense? Did she not forgive him for the Delilah mishap?

The texts were more than an hour old, Emmett having missed their arrival due to helping his moms fix their back deck. So, when he'd stopped to get some water, he was greeted by their sight.

He tried calling her, and it went straight to voicemail. Immediately, he checked all the flights leaving from Victoria. He swore colorfully when he saw the departure time.

"Everything okay?" Sloane asked from behind him.

"Illiana left," he said flatly.

"What?"

"I've got to go."

He spared not a word more as he dashed into the house to get his keys and wallet, jumping into his SUV. He sped for the airport, racing against the clock. He was about to pull the ultimate of cliché tropes. He was rushing for the airport, praying she wasn't gone already.

What he felt with Illiana, what was between them, he knew it was love. They'd followed other tropes, so he'd make sure he'd catch her before that flight. He had to tell her how he felt. He had to assure her he'd do whatever for her—whatever to make it right.

In the movies they always made it to the airport. They always had the reunion right at the last minute. After rushing through the gates and past security. They always made it in time.

He made the airport in record time, peeling into the lot, serendipitously finding an empty stall and throwing himself out—as if it were fate. He raced for the entrance, asking where the Toronto departures were. He was pointed in the right direction. He hoped he'd find her in an area where he didn't have to pay for a ticket—he'd do it if he had to, but he hoped against hope he wouldn't have to dish out hundreds for a ticket he wasn't going to use.

Sweat beaded on his brow, a mixture of the heat and his exertion, adrenaline running through his blood like a drug. He wasn't going to fuck this up. His heart pounded.

An announcement came over the speakers, but he wasn't listening to it. Because he watched a blonde woman stand and shoulder her duffel bag. He called out.

"Illiana!"

The woman turned and Emmett's heart sank as he realized it wasn't Illiana. She was several years older and had brown eyes. Never mind that the features were entirely wrong as well. It wasn't his girlfriend and devastation strummed through him.

"*Last call boarding for Montreal, Quebec,*" the overhead speakers announced.

Emmett froze.

Montreal?

Quebec?

He looked up and sure enough, that's what the sign announced. He'd taken a wrong turn.

Emmett turned on his heel and went for the Toronto gate.

But when he got there the gate was empty and the flight had already departed.

Illiana was gone.

Emmett and Nate were at Blue's, Emmett picking at his label. Nate sat there with him, being an unparalleled support system, despite the fact that for all intents and purposes it was likely in his best friend's mind that he'd stolen the girl he wanted to be with. But Nate was such a good friend and he'd gotten past it.

Emmett was lucky to have him.

He just didn't feel lucky in general at the moment.

Music crooned from the jukebox yet Emmett couldn't enjoy it. Conversations were happy around him, the bar not currently hosting any day drunks, the hour too early for pre-dinner drinks. That didn't stop Emmett. The scent of fried food, beer, and air conditioning was thick in the air. Dated Christmas lights adding a joviality that Emmett didn't feel. Everything felt a little dimmer.

Illiana still hadn't responded to him.

Nate had just sat down, their regular server setting his regular beer down. They ordered loaded nachos to share and for Emmett to drown his misery in.

"I don't understand why she left," Emmett said forlornly to the table top.

Nate paused, pulling the beer from his mouth. "What do you mean? She didn't tell you?"

"No," Emmett shook his head. "I wish I knew what I fucked up."

"Em. You didn't fuck anything up. Her landlord called and said he was evicting her."

Emmett's head shot up. "What?"

"Yeah, she got a call that her rent hadn't been paid in the last two months or something. So, she called her mom—who sounds like a mega bitch by the way—and she told her she signed over the apartment to Illiana's ex because he wanted to get back with her."

"She what?" Fury flamed in his chest.

"A piece of work, that one. Illiana was pissed. I've never seen her like that. I could hear her yelling on the phone in the pool house."

"She's been separated from her ex for a year." Emmett rubbed his chest.

"Apparently he wants her back, and he was given a key to her place—so she's panicking."

Rightly so. "That can't be legal."

"Oh, I'm sure it's not. But she wasn't going to risk him tampering with any of her shit. That's why she left so quickly."

Emmett deflated, some of his grief ebbing away. "So…it wasn't me?"

Nate clapped him on the shoulder and gave him a sympathetic look. "It wasn't you, babe. I promise."

"I'm so sorry," Emmett whispered, looking down. "This can't be easy for you."

"I'm nearly over it. It helps that you're not just fucking around with her and actually love her."

Emmett's eyes shot to his friend.

"Don't try to deny it." Nate rolled his eyes. "Have you not figured it out? It's obvious. Unless I'm wrong and you're a really good actor and a really shitty friend."

"No. No, I love her."

"I know." Nate smiled. "So, when she gets back—tell her."

"You think she's coming back?"

"I know she is."

"How are you so sure?"

"Because she told Mina."

Emmett's heart swelled.

Nate took a swig of his beer and snorted.

"What?" Emmett asked.

"I was right."

"About?"

"That you can't forget her."

Emmett flashed back to when Nate was talking about Illiana, dreamy-eyed in his shop as he said that he just wanted to exist around her and wanted her to notice him. He was right.

"Nate, how did I fall in love with her?"

His friend shrugged. "You tell me. You met her here and charmed her with books."

Emmett palmed his head. He checked his phone again—nothing.

CHAPTER TWENTY-NINE
Illiana

Illiana had been back in Toronto all of five minutes, and she hated it. She'd taken two deep breaths of air that felt wrong—more polluted than Rose Point—before she was jumping into an Uber and demanding it take her to her address. Her phone was still dead, and she was still furious. She'd walked into a heatwave and she was about to enter a shitstorm.

Before she'd boarded her flight, she thought someone had called her, but when she'd turned, she'd found a dad chasing after his young daughter, repeating the plea of Anna.

Not her.

Not Emmett.

The car maneuvered the streets until it deposited her before her building. She stormed into it, hair tied up in a messy tail, pink bag still over her shoulder, dead phone in hand. She was in a tank top and shorts, nothing impressive as she punched the elevator button—fuck the stairs, and fuck Adrian. Fuck her mother and her landlord, and her useless father, and everyone and everything that was keeping her from being with Emmett right now.

The elevator doors dinged, and she leaped inside, urgently pressing her floor number and the close door button. She fished out her keys from her bag and held them between her fingers, wanting to punch Adrian with them. When the lift stopped, she made her way to her apartment, anger fueling every step.

When she stuck her key in the lock, it turned—Adrian evidently hadn't changed it yet, fortuitously enough. As she stepped in, she was greeted to—or cursed to—the sight of her ex-boyfriend leaning on the kitchen island, a box of his junk beside him.

Adrian straightened in surprise, his blue eyes growing wide with astonishment. That astonishment quickly faded into joy, and he crossed over to her, all the grace of the ballerino that had once charmed her. Now it sickened her. She put a hand up to halt him in his tracks.

"What the hell are you doing here, Adrian?" she demanded, cold fury in her voice.

He seemed to be surprised. "I wanted to see you."

"By breaking into my apartment?"

"I wouldn't call it breaking in—I had a key."

"How did you manage to get it from my mom?"

"Your mom just gave it to me without asking." He seemed puzzled. "I told her I was rethinking things with Violet, and she encouraged me to get back with you, especially since the academy wants to offer you a teaching position at—"

"Stop," Illiana commanded. "What are you talking about?"

He softened and moved closer, extending a hand out. It was pale and unblemished. So completely at odds with Emmett's strong hands that she so desperately missed.

"I wanted to tell you in person, babe."

"Don't call me that," she spat.

She didn't care that the academy was asking her to take on a teaching position, but she wondered why Adrian knew before she did. Regardless, it was going to be a no, so there was no use lingering on it.

"I thought you'd want to get back together."

Illiana barked an ugly laugh. "In what world did you think I wanted you back after you left me for my understudy?"

Adrian shifted, fidgeting with his tousled brown hair. "Well, you know since you didn't have much going anymore, I thought me coming back would be a good thing."

Illiana stared at him in disbelief. That ugly laugh came back. "Are you fucking kidding me? You insult me and in the same breath try to be my savior?"

"I didn't insult you."

"I have nothing going for me anymore?" She cocked a brow.

"Well, you don't."

Wrath intruded upon her senses. "I'll have you know that I have a whole fucking lot going for me, including a boyfriend who I am very much in love with."

Adrian looked like he'd been shot. "You have a boyfriend?"

"Yes, and I am very happy with him. In fact, so fucking happy that I'm leaving this goddamn city to be with him."

It was the first time she'd admitted it to herself. Aloud or otherwise. But it was true. She loved Emmett with all her heart. Somehow, he'd healed that damaged, lonely part of her that would have spiraled on the anniversary without him. He'd gotten under her skin, into her heart. He lived inside her, in her thoughts, in her soul. They were the perfect orbit—the perfect compliment. He understood her. He understood her comfort in books and the comfort of tropes. He understood trauma because he'd lived it himself.

She loved him, and she needed him to know.

Adrian was before her, gaping very unattractively.

"What? You can't be serious. I just left Violet for you and—"

"Was that before or after you found out she'd been cheating on you?"

That juicy tidbit of information had made its way into her circles a few weeks ago through some of the dancers she still distantly associated with.

"After, but that—"

"Oh my God, Adrian. You're pathetic." Illiana rolled her eyes. "Look, I'm leaving. You can have this apartment, I don't care."

Illiana strode past him and went to her room and dug in the closet for her backup suitcase. She threw it on the bed, flipped it open and started emptying her meagre closet into it, most of it still at the Ellis's pool house. Following after was the documents from her filing cabinet including her birth certificate and other pertinent tax information as well as her spare phone charger. She grabbed an empty cardboard box and filled it with her remaining items, which consisted mostly of books. When she came across ballet slippers, she paused—there were several pairs untouched and unused. She put those in as well because she had new dreams for them, starting in her new life. Aside from that, she left it all. Everything else was replaceable. She wasn't all that attached to her furniture, and the cleaning supplies and remaining food was needless to take with her.

Kicking the wheels of the suitcase into gear, Illiana stacked the cardboard box of books and slippers on top and crossed to Adrian. She unhooked the key from its ring and slapped it on the counter.

"All yours. I hope I never see you again, Adrian."

And with that she swept out the door with all that she cared from Toronto with her—content to leave everything else behind.

Illiana had ordered a new Uber after charging her phone in the apartment complex's lobby and in it she was booking a new flight back to Victoria. After that was done, she'd called her landlord and filled him in. She promised to transfer the necessary funds from her savings for the remainder of her tenancy up until to-day—as her mother would not be paying it any longer herself. Once that was wrapped up, she texted her mother once.

I will have no contact with you ever again.

And then she blocked Meredith Hastings from her phone and her life.

She didn't care if Adrian or Meredith was telling the truth. None of it mattered. Neither of them mattered.

In her Uber, she cancelled all her service providers, and she hoped that it took Adrian a while to reacquire them. She stopped at the post office and mailed her cardboard box across the country, taking the hit to her bank account as she did so—the cost of postage was no small thing. Back at the airport she had to wait for her flight so as she did, she charged her phone from the dismal 10% the lobby had provided her.

She wanted to text and call Emmett, but she figured eve-rything she wanted to say would be better done face to face. So, she waited, anticipation thrumming in her blood as she did. Even-tually, it was time for her to board her flight and she did so, antsy and staring out the window.

The flight went without a hitch, take off and landing smooth, no turbulence, no rowdy passengers. She had no one sleeping on her, no one kicking her seat. It was as if the universe was telling her this was exactly what she was supposed to be doing. Where she was supposed to be. She had the fortuitous luck to catch an Uber straight from the airport, having waited out front for whomever needed a ride post flight. Illiana gave directions to Emmett's house and sat back.

The Uber pulled up to Emmett's place and Illiana's heart thrummed. She grabbed her suitcase and duffel and dragged them up the drive. Once she ascended the steps she hauled in a deep breath and then knocked.

Seconds later Emmett was opening the door.

Shock and amazement flooded across his features. Disbelief colored his eyes before it all faded and adoration took its place. Adoration—and dare she admit it? Love?

"Surprise?" she said softly.

CHAPTER THIRTY
Emmett

"I know it's impulsive, but I gave up everything in Toronto."

"Illiana…" Emmett whispered. He couldn't believe it. He couldn't believe after the day he'd had that she was here. Back. Standing on his front step.

"I choose you, Emmett," she breathed.

Emmett's heart swelled in his chest, emotion surging through his blood.

"Are you sure?" he asked.

"I'm more than sure. The second I touched down in Toronto all I wanted to do was get back here. To Rose Point. To you. This is my home. You are my home." She looked side to side, looking off into the night, an edge of nervousness in her posture. "Can I come in?"

Emmett didn't have words to answer. He simply swept her off her feet and pulled her in. Illiana seemed to have the sense to hang onto her luggage as all of it was hauled inside. She let go of it all at the door, and he shut it behind her, pressing her against it.

"I can't believe you're here."

He brushed hair behind her ear. She still smelled like strawberries and cream, of warmth and sunshine, of Illiana. The scent intoxicated him, got stuck in his lungs until it was the only thing he could breathe in. Emmett twisted a golden coil around his finger, tugging it, pulling her close.

"I did the stupidest thing today," he whispered to her. "I chased after you—ran through the airport."

"You did not," she gasped.

"I did. The ultimate of rom-com tropes. I have to admit…it's much cooler in the movies."

Illiana laughed and pressed herself against him and suddenly that laugh did very different things to their bodies than the jovial joking he was summoning.

The heat between them ratcheted up, burning with a low ember, begging to grow to flame. He felt he was going to burst, desire sweeping through him in a burning wake. But it was more than lust. It was love. It was ease and adventure, wanton yearning and endless comfort.

"I didn't want to spend another minute away from you," she breathed.

"Are you sure you want to give up everything back there?"

"There's nothing holding me there. No hope. No future. No dreams. No *you*."

"You really want me?"

"I do," she whispered.

"I'm pretty sure that's your line next year."

"Proposing already, are you?"

"Not yet." He grinned. "Have you forgotten our September timeline?"

"This isn't a trial anymore. This is the real thing. I've decided. I want you."

"You want me?" he teased. "How much?"

Illiana's eyes softened, that blue turning powdery soft. Like flowers and silk. Her mouth parted into that perfect pink heart. All of her sparkly and bright despite the travel. She was beautiful and she was his and she was in his arms.

"So much," she managed. "But more importantly…I love you. I came here for fun, for a fling, and instead I fell in love with you. You weren't supposed to happen, but you did, and I'll spend every day grateful that our paths crossed that night."

Emmett's heart had never felt so full. He pressed his mouth to hers, firmly, tilting her face up to his. He swept his tongue across her lips, tasting the slight frost of mint on her mouth. Pulling back, he leaned his forehead against hers.

This was everything he dreamed it would be. *Illiana* was everything he'd dreamed. This was all he'd wanted. Their dreams matching—the house, the marriage, the 2.5 kids, the dog, the fence, and all. She wanted it and wanted him. And he'd never wanted anyone more. He was utterly enamored by her and her teasing, the way tropes had led them to love. The way romance books had paved their way and shaped their perception.

They knew how this was supposed to go.

They knew how this was supposed to end.

He could imagine them growing old together, under blankets and in rocking chairs—hopefully still banging each other's brains out as often as they challenged and accepted cliches.

"I love you, too."

"You do?" She positively glowed.

His glowing, golden goddess.

"I love you beyond words, Illiana. I wasn't looking for anyone. I wasn't looking for anything. But I found you anyway, and you stole my heart the first moment you spoke. After you all my plans changed."

Illiana's eyes watered with emotion, but he continued.

"I know we said this was just supposed to be the summer, but you and I both knew that was a lie. We could never be so short. This is it. This is the end for me. You and I are what they make movies out of. Only we get to live the happily ever after when the credits roll. We'll never have to wonder if they stay together, because we know." He kissed her. "And we do."

"More vows already?"

"Oh, sweetheart, our story isn't over yet, no need to rush."

"I think rushing is what we do best."

"I can think of a few other things we do better."

"Oh? Care to elaborate?"

"I'd rather show you."

With that, he picked Illiana up, wrapped her legs around his waist, and carried her upstairs.

He was going to worship his goddess.

CHAPTER THIRTY-ONE

Illiana

Emmett dropped her onto the bed and then he dropped down onto her. His weight settled in the cradle of her thighs, his big hands cupping her hips as he lifted her against him and rolled against her pelvis. The undulating motion had the hard ridge of his cock pressing against her wet sex and she arched back, mouth opening. He took her mouth with his, pressing passion into her soul. His tongue traced the shape of her mouth, learning and memorizing her. Illiana's tongue met his and danced, lips sliding against his, realizing she was tasting mint and liquor.

"How much have you had to drink tonight?" she gasped as his mouth slid down her throat.

"Two drinks and a shot. Don't worry, I'm perfectly sober."

Her hands that had been in his hair to free the locks skated down his back, finding the hem of his shirt to push it up.

He allowed her as her hands coasted over his abs, the softness over the hard muscles. She loved it. She loved *him*.

Emmett's shirt disappeared and her hands went to his chest as his lips kept trailing down her jaw.

"What does this tattoo mean?" she asked as she traced the lines of the symbol over his chest.

"Love," he whispered as his lips ghosted across her bumblebee tattoo. "And this tattoo?"

"In a roundabout way, love as well. A love story that saved me from going to a dark place."

He kissed that little bumblebee over her breast. "It's perfect."

Emmett tugged her shirt down until he exposed the satiny cup of her white bra, the stark contrast making her skin look darker—golden. He pulled the cup down and found her nipple. It was hard with arousal, and he flicked his tongue against it before bringing it into his mouth. The wet heat of it made her pussy clench. His teeth scraped against it, and her hands went to his backside, digging in. He thrust against her in response.

Illiana moaned as he began wringing pleasure from her in earnest, his erection stimulating her clit perfectly, his mouth driving her to insanity. The hands that were gripping her hips tucked into the waistband of her shorts and pulled them down and off. He helped kick her ankles out and then his hands swept the bare expanse of her legs. The swept higher, over the band of her underwear to the edge of her top. He managed to get it around her ribs before she arched frustratedly and removed it, tearing her bra with it.

"Impatient, are we?" he teased.

"I am."

"But what if I wanted to make you wait?"

She whimpered. "I need you—oh God!"

His fingers had sneaked down and with delightful skill, he'd found her clit and rubbed it.

She writhed under him, and she was wet—so wet—for him already. She was begging without words, her entire soul wanton yearning embodied. She wanted him in her, to feel his fingers to plunge inside her and curl, to find that spot.

As if reading her mind, Emmett pulled her opposite nipple into his mouth and teased her entrance, a finger stroking down her slit. He entered her slowly and then, exactly as she'd hoped, he curled that finger, hooking into her. Her head slammed back against the pillows and then his thumb took over on her clit. She turned frantic, hips rocking against him, fingers scrabbling at his pants as she pushed them down. Her nails carved tracks into the bare swell of his ass, anxiously trying to get closer, deeper—just more. More, more, more.

"I need more," she begged.

"More what?" Emmett taunted against her breast. "Another finger?" he asked, inserting a second one. She let out a throaty moan and he chortled in response before continuing. "Or do you want my mouth here?" He emphasised 'here' with a press of her clit. She jolted and mewled and fuck, she felt that pressure build. "Or is it my cock you want?"

"All of it," she rasped.

"Greedy, greedy goddess."

"Goddess?"

"Mmhmm," he said, licking the underside of her breast before nipping it. "My golden goddess."

Arousal surged between her legs, that pressure pushing at the restraints of her will. He pumped those two fingers and wetness flooded around his hand. She gasped as the wave struck her, building to her orgasm.

Emmett slipped from her breast and traveled down her body, mouth tracing every line on the way down, tasting her and devouring her. He finally dispensed with her underwear, and then, with his fingers still inside her, he kissed her clit. He kissed it and licked it. And then he applied the most glorious suction as his fingers worked in tandem hitting that fucking spot that made her see stars.

Illiana came and wetness surged as she did. She cried out, moaning Emmett's name as the waves drowned her in pleasure, pushing her down beneath the riptide. She was utterly at his mercy as the overflow didn't stop. Pleasure and pleasure mounted bright and blinding.

When her orgasm dissipated, Emmett did not stop, eager to wring another climax from her body. She realized when he returned that suction again.

"Emmett, I don't know if I can," she rasped. She was so sensitive.

Her thighs jolted as he sucked. "Let me try," he breathed against her pussy.

Somehow, through his incredible sexual prowess, he coaxed another orgasm from her body.

When it finally faded, she panted, sweat shimmering on her skin. He pulled back and she shimmied to the edge. She hung her head from the side of the bed, her body exposed for his viewing pleasure. "Come over here and fuck my mouth."

Wicked desire gleamed in Emmett's eyes. At some point she couldn't recall, his pants and underwear had disappeared. He came to the side of the bed and he did as asked—slipping his cock into her mouth. Illiana swirled her tongue against the head of him, licking up the pearl of precum at the tip before sucking. She took him, swallowing deep as her hands went to his balls and gently fondled them between her fingers. He rocked against her ministrations and his hands touched down on her body, tracing her ribs, her belly. She parted her thighs wide so he'd have a perfect view of what he did to her and it made his movements falter.

Emmett thrust into her mouth, going deep—but she took him, priding herself on her impressive lack of a gag reflex. He kept moving, her tongue laving against him. He was moaning above her and she was loving it.

Suddenly, he pulled from her and she heard the sound of a drawer opening and the crinkle of a condom.

"I need to fuck you now."

"Then what are you waiting for?"

Emmett rolled the condom on and suddenly he was on top of her. Her parted thighs were still open wide, and he slid between them. In one stroke, his cock entered her and he was seated fully. She moaned and arched her back. He was stretching her so deep, so tight—it was heavenly. He moved with wonderful rolling motions, the upward stroke hitting her clit.

Pulling her hips up, she was helpless as her ass was lifted and gripped in his hands. He pounded into her and every pump had her drawing closer to a third orgasm. Tears were streaking from her eyes, the pleasure so much, so good. The room was filled with the sounds of their rasping breaths, the slickness of their skin, the heady smell of him—of amber and woods.

Suddenly, he flipped her over so she was on her hands and knees and yet he still kept going. He swept wetness from her pussy and brought it to her ass, pressing against the tight hole as she clenched. Her hands curled into the sheets, dragging them to her, pressing herself into them as he continued massaging. That pressure was perfect, the titillation without entrance doing over-whelmingly erotic things to her body. He was fucking her, but he was playing her like a fucking violin—he knew what to do to make her sing.

She loved it. She loved him.

"Emmett," she moaned—keened. "I'm going to come, oh fuck, I'm going to come."

"Do it, sweetheart. I want to feel this pussy squeeze my cock."

The orgasm hit the peak before it took her. She squirted a second before she came, wetness flooding between her legs, squeezing everything so fucking tight she couldn't breathe. It was so good she was going to burst. She came, and it was everything.

Fireworks and heaven erupted within her and she moaned, muscles trembling. She writhed through the wall of bliss that crushed her.

The powerful third orgasm was enough to take Emmett and he was moaning her name, his release hot inside her. She felt the pulse even through the condom and he carried them through the final vestiges of their lovemaking.

Finally, it all dissipated and she collapsed. Emmett pulled out of her and fell next to her. She was breathing heavily and he stroked her hair back from her face.

"You're really here? And you're really staying?" he asked.

"I am," she responded, pushing dark locks from his brow.

"Fuck, I love you."

She curled into him. "And I fucking love you."

A moment of silence passed before she said, "I seem to remember something about you tying me up."

His surprised laugh filled the room and then hers joined.

CHAPTER THIRTY-TWO
Emmett

"So, since you're staying here…do you know what you're going to do?"

He was trying not to be presumptuous, but there was hope in his voice.

"My ex actually confirmed an idea." He shifted and harrumphed when she mentioned another man, jealousy rearing its ugly head, so she soothed him with stroking fingers before she continued. "I want to open up a ballet studio here for kids—to teach them. That's what I was thinking about when I saw that building. They were going to offer it to me back in Toronto, but why would I do it there when I could do it here? At home."

"Speaking of home…" His fingers trailed down her bare back. "Have you thought about living arrangements?"

She let out a low laugh. "I figured you were going to ask that, but yes, I've considered a few."

"And...?"

He didn't want to get his hopes up but the idea of Illiana living here, in his house, had his dreams glowing. He didn't care if she decorated the entire thing in baby doll pink. But he wanted her own personal touch on it, evidence that she was here and she was his. He could picture it bright as day and he wanted it.

"I think, as long as Mina's family is okay with it, I'll continue formally staying with them for the rest of the summer as originally planned, but..." she trailed off and then lifted her gaze to his. "Maybe come September, we could discuss a more permanent situation."

"A new September agreement?" he teased.

"If it works for you."

"And would this possible new living situation involve you moving in here?"

She bit her lip. "Um...what would you say to that?"

He grinned. "Absolutely."

She smiled back. "Then it's settled, come September we have a new agreement."

Suddenly, Illiana leaned forward and kissed him, pressing her palm to his cheek, curving over his jaw and he couldn't fathom being any happier in his life than he was in that very moment.

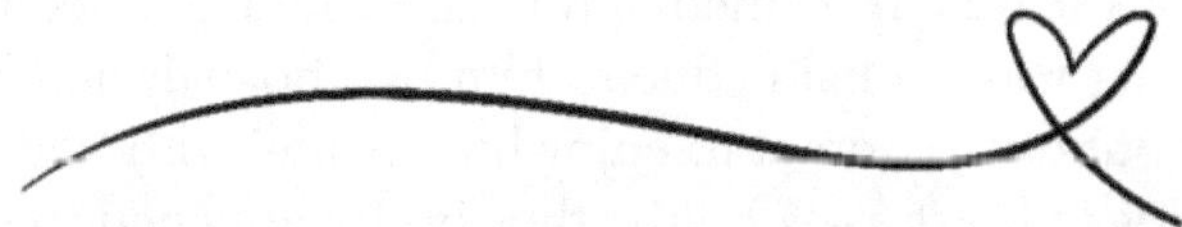

The next day the two of them went to the lake house, Illiana having slept in due to having travelled the entirety of the previous day. To say everyone was surprised was an understatement. The two of them were holding hands, talking to Mina and Nate, Walt and Lacey, explaining the situation.

"So, you're here to stay?" Mina asked, hope and delight shining in her green eyes.

"I am," Illiana confirmed.

"Good. Then I have something to say as well." Mina turned to her family. "I'm moving back to the island as soon as I find a job."

Lacey erupted into tears and wrapped Mina up in the warmest embrace Emmett had ever witnessed. Walt beamed, patting his niece on the shoulder and kissing the top of the head over his wife's still continuing hug. Even Nate let out a cheer.

Emmett went over to Nate and wrapped an arm around his shoulder.

"We good?"

Nate smiled. "We're more than good." Then he leaned closer. "But treat her well or you're going to have hell to pay."

"Noted." Emmett grinned.

To celebrate the girls staying, the Ellis family decided to throw an impromptu barbecue and invited a few close friends and family. Not everyone could make it, but Madeline arrived almost immediately, delighted by the news. Sasha and Jade couldn't make it, but Sloane and his mothers did. Ashley and Danika had met Lacey and Walt on a few occasions, but had never been particularly close—he hoped that was about to change.

As in Sloane's typical style, she was razzing the hell out of all his friends, Nate, Graham, Kieran, and Chase treating her like the hellion she was. It seemed only Chase could half-keep up with her, but that was probably due to him psychoanalyzing her. Patrick kept out of it, content to enjoy his cocktail with Walt, talking about ships in bottles—a hobby they both happened to possess.

Night was falling and Emmett sidled up to Illiana as she stood at the deck railing, phone in hand.

"What are you up to, sweetheart?"

She turned her phone to his view and he was shocked to see direct messages on Instagram open and Delilah's name at the top, bubbles of conversation already in the past. He read them over.

ILLIANA: *Hi Delilah, you were right. He is a good guy, and we talked. All is well and he had nothing but good things to say about you while we patched things up. We're officially together now.*
DELILAH: *Yes! Oh, I'm so happy to hear that baby doll. You are truly a lucky one, I wish you all the best. Thank you for letting me know it worked out.*
ILLIANA: *Of course, thank you for everything.*
DELILAH: *Don't thank me, I did nothing but speed up a conversation that was surely coming.*
ILLIANA: *You're probably right, but I'm still holding you to your note.*
DELILAH: *Haha, I'm standing by it. Save me a wedding invitation?*
ILLIANA: *If we get there, I'm sure we can manage that.*
DELILAH: *You will. Have a goodnight, baby doll.*
ILLIANA: *Good night to you too.*

"Becoming friends with my ex now, are you?"

"Maybe," she teased. "I like her."

"She is genuinely a nice person. But you…" he said, plucking her phone from her hand and tucking it in her back pocket before wrapping his arms around her. "Are the best person."

"Best person in general? Or best person for you?"

He leaned his forehead against hers. "Both."

They smiled at each other just as Walt, by the lake, lit off a few spare fireworks.

"Do you think we played into the insta love trope?" she asked.

He laughed. "I think the timing of falling in love is subjective."

"So, you're saying it's up to the individual."

"Possibly. I'm only concerned about how you feel."

"Then there's no concern here," she whispered, tugging him closer.

Pink shattered against the sky as gold boomed against the dark, raining sparkles around them.

"To think, all this started because you brought a book to a bar."

Illiana threw her head back and laughed as she pulled him in for a kiss.

EPILOGUE

Snow was falling, leaving a thick, white powder on the deck railing of Illiana and Emmett's house. It was incredibly dark outside, minutes before the countdown to the New Year in the midst of the first party they were hosting together as a couple in their home.

The word *party* may have been a bit of a stretch, considering it was a little less than a dozen people, but the music was loud, the drinks were freely poured, and happiness was abundant. Said party was in full swing.

The gold and pink Christmas decorations were still up, only there were now golden streamers and stars hanging from the ceiling. Everyone was donning party hats of black and silver and gold, ringing in another flip of the calendar.

Illiana could see her reflection and the glittering black dress she wore in the polished glass and everyone behind her.

In the six months she'd been in Rose Point she had come a long way. Finally, she'd put on a little more weight, giving her slightly more curves that Emmett was absolutely obsessed with. He was, however, always quick to reassure her that he loved her body any way it was, but he was seemingly happier to see her healthy and not counting every calorie or restricting everything she put in her mouth.

She wasn't healed, but she was close.

The ballet studio was slated to open in two weeks and while she was nervous, she was also excited. She had a full class registered—all thanks to Sasha and Jade and all their mom connections, as Sasha was now five months pregnant with her first. Not to mention Jade's husband and his restoration company— and then the employees' wives. And then the whole town, really.

Their children were eager to be taught by a real-life ballerina.

Illiana already met a couple of the children, and one of them had actually asked her if she was a princess. She'd never received a more glowing compliment than in that moment, and she knew she'd found her calling. Not for one second did she regret turning down the offer in Toronto and everything Toronto had to offer.

Illiana hadn't spoken to her parents since that fateful day in July, not even an acknowledgment at Christmastime. She did get a half-hearted Merry Christmas from Adrian whom she returned the sentiment to and then promptly blocked—which she had thought she'd already done, but evidently it was an oversight.

Through the grapevine, her cousin Leo caught wind of it all and told her all the bullshit her parents had been feeding the family about her. She was doubly pissed she didn't cut them out sooner, but was happy to hear from Leo and him wanting to be there for her. He'd also revealed he wanted to stop traveling and finally put down roots.

Illiana didn't hesitate to tell him about the beauty of Rose Point.

She could see Mina and Sloane, dressed in emerald and bronze, challenging Nate and Graham to beer pong, her best friend and her self-proclaimed nemesis practically at each other's throats. Ever since Mina moved back in October, Illiana noticed the tension between them and she agreed that perhaps Mina had been right after all and they really didn't like each other. She'd yet to talk to Emmett about it, but she would soon.

Chase, Patrick, and Kieran were hovering around the food spread across the island, the latter's eyes flittering over to Madeline and Delilah who were engrossed in conversation over the author's latest book. Leia and Gimli were happily begging for scraps at the men's feet, the two of them both festooned with New Year's regalia.

Delilah had stayed true to her word and had dedicated the next book to Illiana. She still laughed when she read it.

For Baby Doll, you know exactly why. You're welcome, and I'm sorry. Enjoy the smut.

Emmett had also laughed at the dedication.

Illiana saw Emmett approach from the reflection in the glass. His hand slid across her back and curved around her hips, splaying across her stomach. She leaned back into him, champagne in hand, and tilted her head to the side, the free cascade of her blonde hair slipping from her shoulder and offering him access. Wrapping his other arm around her, he kissed a light path up her throat, ending on the hinge of her jaw. Illiana smiled behind her flute, taking a sip and marking it with red lipstick.

He looked *so* good in black dress pants and an ebony satin dress shirt. His thick, dark waves were also left loose in a way that she admitted did wild things to her libido. She devoured him with her eyes, promising filthy things later.

"Care to step outside with me?" he murmured against her skin.

Illiana's eyes flickered to the clock. "The countdown is starting soon."

"That's okay. We can kiss in the privacy of the outdoors with these totally not-revealing windows at our back."

She leaned into him on a laugh, breathing in the scent of his amber woods and champagne.

"All right."

Illiana stepped into a pair of slippers to protect her bare feet from the snow, and set her glass down on a side table as the two of them slipped out the door. The chill was biting cold and Illiana was suddenly wishing she had sleeves on her dress. It was very short and skimpy, the straps mere threads on her shoulders. Emmett stepped out behind her and wrapped her up.

"Well, I really wasn't thinking of the cold when I dreamed up romance," he muttered.

"It's okay," she said with a laugh. "It's stifling in there so a moment out here will be fine."

She blew out a breath and clouds escaped her lips, drifting into the night. Emmett walked them further onto the deck, near the part that wasn't protected by the roof. He cupped her face and stared down at her ardently as she heard the first sounds of the countdown from inside.

"Illiana, I made you promises in the past and some of them have been hell to hold onto. But none more than this one, especially since I didn't want to break my word."

He took her hands in his and squeezed once, still holding her gaze. She was surprised by the slight tremor in his voice—and she realized, in his hands.

Illiana drew her brows together in concern. "Emmett, what are you—oh my God."

Emmett's hands slipped from her grasp and then, in one smooth motion, he dropped down onto one knee and produced a velvet box from his pocket.

Ten…

Nine…

Eight…

The chant began inside.

"I once told you that we weren't going to get a Christmas ornament engagement. That at the earliest, I'd propose next year."

Seven…

Six…

Five…

"Well, it's just about next year, Illiana. And I have just one question for you."

Tears welled in her eyes as she cupped a hand over her mouth.

Raucous sounds of delight and cheering and chanting continued in the house.

Four…

Three…

Two…

"Illiana Jane Hastings…" Emmett's eyes were pure warmth. Pure love. Absolute devotion and adoration. "I love you beyond every trope in the book."

One…

"*HAPPY NEW YEAR!*" A chorus erupted inside.

The New Year struck and a question finally left Emmett's lips.

"Will you marry me?"

Illiana's heart soared in her chest as he opened the box, and there sat a perfect oval diamond set in a floral halo, a band of rose gold holding it all together. Emmett was slightly shaking, his brown eyes so full of hope. Emotion choked her and behind her hand, she nodded.

"Yes. Yes, of course I'll marry you."

Emmett released the breath he'd been holding and plucked the ring out of its box and slid it effortlessly onto her finger. She stared at it; sparkling, perfectly matching the color she'd just recently had her nails painted.

Illiana threw her arms around his neck and kissed him as his hand went to her waist and to tangle in the golden fall of her hair. Her lips slanted across his, opening to grant him access as he slipped his tongue inside. They tasted of strawberries and champagne. Her hand went to his face, cupping his cheek.

Her *fiancé*. She was kissing her *fiancé*. The man who would soon be her *husband*.

She laughed against his mouth. "I love you."

"I love you too."

Cheers roared in their direction as everyone in the house realized what just happened, noting the sparkling ring on her left hand, even through the dim outside. Emmett turned his face in their direction and her lips ghosted across his cheek.

"We should *really* give them something to cheer about," he said tauntingly as he lifted her and spun her around. She squealed in happiness just as Graham opened the door and peeked his head out. "*She said yes! We're going to get married!*"

Party favors were blown in return and drunken congratulations were shouted out the door. Illiana looked to the people gathered inside and to the man who had his arms wrapped around her and she considered herself the luckiest person in the world.

"Come on," she said, laughingly. "Let's go celebrate with everyone."

"Only if we can celebrate privately later," he murmured into her ear. "Maybe test out that gift I got you."

Illiana mentally flashed to the silken rope he'd gifted to her and blushed rose red, the alcohol adding to the flush.

"I promise."

"Good, but just so you know; I take back what I first said."

"Oh?"

"I am definitely more interesting than whatever guy you were going to read in that book."

Illiana laughed, recalling the first time they'd ever spoke. Back when they hadn't introduced themselves and they played a game of mistaken identity while they flirted and bantered. Back when she thought a fling was all she was going to get out of him. She'd learned. And now she was going to marry him. And hopefully one day have a family with him.

But for now, it was just them.

And they were enough.

She took his hand and they stepped into the house.

Together.

AUTHOR'S NOTE

While I am not Indigenous, my husband is, and many of the experiences lived by Emmett's family regarding residential schools are similar to those he and others around us endured. I understand not everyone who survived a residential school underwent the same treatments or turned to substances or the other things stated within Emmett's family history, but I thought it was important to highlight the lasting effects of generational trauma and how it trickles down.

One of the last residential schools in Canada closed down in 1997 in Alert Bay—just hours away from the fictional town of Rose Point—the year after I was born. The very last was 1998 in Nunavut.

Regarding Illiana's car accident and the long-term impacts, that drew elements from a very real car crash I was in as a child.

ACKNOWLEDGEMENTS

My fifth published book and writing this never ceases to amaze me. Thank you to everyone around me who has celebrated and eagerly anticipated this book. I'm a romantasy girly, but sometimes I need a good contemporary—and I'm certainly excited to write more about Emmett and Illiana's friend group.

But onto the thanks.

As always, thank you times ten million to my absolutely incredible husband—who sometimes I swear really was written by a woman—for supporting me, encouraging me, and loving me. And thank you for making my dreams come true with this cover. Speaking of the cover. Thank you to Sam at Ink and Laurel for this absolute perfection of a cover. She absolutely nailed the design and this cover is everything I had ever dreamed it would be. My gosh, a huge thank you to Indigo Melanson for the GORGEOUS artwork of Emmett and Illiana—I'm forever drooling over them. I can't wait to see what you come up with next.

Thank you to Katy Michele for editing and supplying the commentary that absolutely gave me life. I am so glad you enjoyed it and for catching all of my atrocious commas. Your feedback was invaluable. I appreciate you.

(SIDE NOTE: If you thought your backups were secure, this is your sign to double-check because I was very wrong when I thought mine were and I lost 12K words.)

Vivienne and Rosalie, my precious baby daughters, you both are my best dreams. I love you so much, thank you for existing.

Thank you to my family, friends, and everyone I've met online for supporting my writing dreams. Thank you to every person who shared my cover reveals and snippets, the artwork and comments, I appreciate you.

To my street team, thank you for taking a chance on a baby indie author like me—I hope you stick around for whatever else I have in store!

My safe space book/writing groups—you know who you are—thank you for maintaining excitement when I share every update on artwork, cover work, and everything else. I know it's a lot, but thank you for being there for me.

(Added in 2025) Ashley, @the.other.sistr, thank you SO much for bringing the boys houses to life! You are insanely talented and I cannot wait to collab on our next piece!

And finally, as always, thank you Dear Reader for picking up my books. I am eternally grateful for you. If you enjoyed—or even if you didn't—I'd be so appreciative if you left a review on Amazon or Goodreads! Reviews are so important to get books seen and create opportunities for authors.

ABOUT THE AUTHOR

Kayla McGrath has been writing since the age of thirteen out of spite, having read a book with a love triangle that didn't go her way. After that, it became a passion. If she's not writing, then she's reading, or drinking endless cups of chai. Kayla lives on Vancouver Island with her husband, two daughters, and two boxers.

She is the author of the Cold as Iron trilogy, the Infernal Curses series, the upcoming A Deathless Empire series, and the interconnected standalones of the Love and Other Tropes novels. Love & Other Tropes is her fifth book.

You can find her mostly on Instagram/Threads (@kaylamcgrathbooks), TikTok (@kaylamcgrath_), and sometimes on Twitter/X (@KaylaMcGrath_).

OTHER BOOKS BY KAYLA MCGRATH

THE COLD AS IRON TRILOGY
This Broken Memory
These Ruined Dreams
Our Shattered Fates

INFERNAL CURSES
The Nightmare Curse
The Hallow Curse (Summer 2025)

A DEATHLESS EMPIRE
A Deathless Empire (08/06/24)

"It all began, once upon a nightmare curse..."

Book one in the Infernal Curses series, available in paperback, e-book, and on Kindle Unlimited.

"He isn't who he says he is, but more importantly, she's not who she thought she was."

Book one in the Cold as Iron trilogy, available in paperback, e-book, and on Kindle Unlimited.

9 781738 226542